Chinwe

by

Keith Hoare

Chinwe

By

Keith Hoare

***

Published by: Ragged Cover Publishing
ISBN - 978-1908090-66-9

Chapter 1

Ryan Selby lay there in the dark, his eyes wide open, ears straining. Above the gentle flapping of the tent in the wind, he was certain he heard voices. Not loud, but whispering. Just thirteen years old and something of a computer nerd, he'd been reluctant to go with his brother of seventeen on what he called 'an adventure into the wilderness'. Although to be fair, a trek from Seahouses on the north-east coast of the UK to a place with a view of Holy Island, where they could pitch a tent, was not exactly the wilderness. But his brother Jonathan had purchased the tent from eBay and wanted to try it out.

Believing he had dreamed the sound of voices, Ryan began to drift off to sleep. That was until he heard the voices again. He sat bolt upright, at the same time digging his brother in the ribs.

"Jonathan, wake up. There's people outside," he urged, poking him once more.

His brother turned around in his sleeping bag and opened his eyes, then sat up listening for a short time, but heard nothing. "You're dreaming, Ryan, go to sleep, it's just the wind catching the tent."

He thought for a moment. "Maybe you're right, sorry."

They both settled back down. Jonathan's thoughts drifted back to the reason he'd purchased the tent. His intention was to spend the summer trekking in the Cairngorms with his girlfriend Sarah. In fact, she would have come with him this time if it hadn't been for exams and her parents putting their foot down, insisting she had to study hard and achieve the grades. Because Sarah couldn't come, Jonathan's mother suggested he take Ryan. At first Ryan had refused, he didn't do camping, but she was adamant he go, secretly hoping it would give Ryan interests beyond constantly playing games on his computer and not even wanting to kick a football around in the garden, like lads do.

It was at that moment that they both heard a man's voice. "The bastard's got to be somewhere, find her," he demanded curtly, obviously annoyed with someone.

"I'm not dreaming that," Ryan commented.

"You're not," Jonathan answered, at the same time unzipping his sleeping bag and climbing out. Rummaging around in the dark, he found his jeans and pulled them on.

"Where are you going?" Ryan asked, switching his torch on to see his brother fastening his shoes. "It's nothing to do with us."

"I never thought it was, but with people wandering around outside the tent, I want to know who they are, it could even be the police. Stay here."

Ryan gasped. "You're not leaving me here on my own - they could be axemen?"

"Oh yeah, you play too many video games. This is the real world and people don't wander around carrying axes. Anyway, I'll only be outside, so if they are axemen, I'll stop them from chopping you up into little pieces," he mocked. Then, without another word, and grabbing his own torch, Jonathan unzipped the tent flap and went outside.

Ryan, determined not to be caught in his sleeping bag by anyone, be it the police or a supposed axeman, got out of his own sleeping bag, pulling his jeans and shoes on, before sitting back down and waiting for Jonathan to return.

The tent was pitched on some banking above a footpath that led down to a beach from a car park. To protect it from an easterly wind, it was in a nook set among a number of small bushes, so unless you came off the path it couldn't be seen. They hadn't chosen the position to hide the tent from people passing along the path, but because it offered a spectacular and uninterrupted sea view, as Jonathan enjoyed watching the birds dive into the sea to catch fish.

Jonathan moved closer to the top of the banking, giving him the best view of the path and beach. He could see three torches bobbing about further down the path. On the beach below, illuminated by the moonlight, was what looked like a small dinghy at the water's edge. Two more people were down on the beach, both smoking.

'What the hell, they must be smugglers bringing drugs ashore,' he said to himself. 'If that's the case, who are they looking for?'

Going back into the tent, Ryan looked at him. "Well, who is it, the police?"

"Not the police, Ryan, but they could be drug smugglers."

"No way, this is awesome. We should call the police, we'll be heroes, maybe even get a reward," Ryan answered enthusiastically.

"I'm not sure you get rewards for reporting a crime, but you're right, the police should know about it. Where's my phone?"

"Use mine," Ryan said, passing it to him.

Jonathan grabbed it from him and unlocked the screen. "There's no signal, didn't you use it earlier to call mum?"

"Give it to me, I'll sort it, I think it has a bad connection inside, you have to give it a bash. Dad said I can't have a new one till my birthday."

He began to shake and hit the phone on the sleeping bag,

but it refused to work properly.

"Forget it," Jonathan told him, "where's mine, at least that works? Keep that torch covered, besides pointing down, we don't want them to know we're here."

Both lads began to feel around the tent, looking for the other phone.

"If you weren't so messy with your clothes it'd be easier to find," Ryan commented. "Maybe I should ring it?"

Both on their hands and knees, Jonathan stopped and sat up. "Maybe you should get yourself a brain? How can you ring it, if your phone's duff?"

Ryan stopped looking for a moment and sat up himself. "Good point," he said, at the same time pushing his brother playfully with one hand, sending him off balance.

As he fell, and using his arm to prevent himself from going down completely, there was a loud crack from under his elbow. Both lads froze, each fearing the worst. Jonathan pulled out his mobile from under a T-shirt that was lying between his elbow and the ground. The glass front was completely shattered.

"You stupid idiot, that will cost me a fortune to get repaired."

"Me, an idiot? Who hides his phone under a shirt, either of us could have stood on it?"

Jonathan looked at the phone, pressing a side button to see if by some miracle it still worked. Nothing happened. "What do we do now, calling the police is out?" Jonathan asked, voicing his thoughts aloud.

Ryan shrugged. "There's nothing we can do, we may as well forget our moment of fame. It'll take ages to find somewhere to contact the police, and by the time we do, they will be long gone."

They sat quietly, trying to decide what else they could do, then Jonathan had an idea. "Will your phone take pictures, even if it won't connect?"

"It will, why?"

"We should at least take some pictures, then we'll have proof someone was here."

They both scrambled out of the tent and began to make their way along the edge of the bank, looking for a position that gave them a better view of the beach. Finally finding a suitable spot, they lay face down, peeping over, with Ryan taking photos as well as a movie.

"They don't seem to be in any rush, you'd think they'd just drop off the drugs and get away as fast as possible?" Ryan commented.

"You would. Anyway we've got our photos, I'm going back to the tent to get some sleep. It's boring now," Jonathan replied, at the same time pulling away from the edge, before standing.

Ryan took one last shot and followed, even he was getting fed up with nothing happening.

They had just arrived back at the tent, Ryan unzipping the entrance cover, when both of them heard the sound of bracken cracking underfoot from someone or something very close by.

Jonathan went cold, his body began to shake, as he realised that the men must have seen them and come up to see who was there. He spun round bravely to face whoever it was, although inwardly he was terrified. These men, if they were drug dealers, would not take kindly to being watched.

However, he wasn't looking at a man, but a small figure, taller than Ryan and completely in shadow, with the moon behind them. “Please, sir... will you help me?” came a very low but stuttering girl’s voice, the speech sounding more African than English.

“It’s a girl,” Ryan said, coming up close to Jonathan and talking softly. “Do you think she’s anything to do with the boat and maybe the one they’re looking for?”

“That’s pretty obvious in both respects, the point is what can we do?” Then he looked towards the girl standing there. “What sort of help? Do you want me to take you back to the beach, or are you trying to escape them for some reason?”

“I was taken on my way home from school. I’ve been on a boat for weeks and brought here. I kept hearing bad things from others on the boat about what they do with girls and ran away as soon as I could. I don’t even know where I am. Please don’t send me back to them, I beg you.”

“They’re human traffickers, not drug dealers, Jonathan. This is really heavy man, you read on the internet just how dangerous these people are, we could get ourselves killed.”

Whether because of their reluctance to show any compassion, offer to help, or Ryan’s negative comment, Jonathan wasn’t sure, but the girl gave a sigh. “I don’t want to be any trouble, but please don’t tell them you saw me,” she said - then turned and began to walk away.

However, whatever Ryan said, Jonathan knew they couldn’t let the girl go. She was obviously very scared and thousands of miles from her home. Alone, she would have little chance of avoiding the traffickers.

“Wait, I never said we’d not help, in fact I think we can. There’s a police station in Berwick. It’s a good ten or twelve miles, but keeping to the footpaths and heading towards the A1, we’ll not be seen."

She stopped and turned to face them again. Still not certain the other lad would agree.

"What, leave our tent and everything?" Ryan asked.

"Yes, Ryan, the girl needs help and I'm going to give it. So grab something to warm to wear and let's get out of here. We can always come back with the police and get everything later." Then he turned to the girl. All she was wearing was a dark blue loose-fitting dress and sandals. She looked very cold. Going into the tent, he came out with the only other jumper he had with him, and handed it to her. "Put this on, it'll be a little big, but at least you'll be warmer."

"Thank you, sir, I am very cold," she answered, pulling the jumper over her head.

As he'd told her, it was oversized, but had the advantage that its length covered her bottom.

"You're welcome, but I'm not a sir, my name's Jonathan and this is my brother Ryan. What do we call you?"

"Chinwe."

Ryan handed her his baseball cap. "You can have my cap as well, Chinwe," he said with a grin.

Chinwe didn't really need it, but with him offering, she didn't want to refuse and put it on. "I've never had a cap before, in our village such a cap would make everyone jealous. Thank you, Ryan."

Soon they were on their way in single file, with Jonathan leading. He had considered closer places like Belford, or even returning to Seahouses, but neither had a police station and this girl needed police help if the men standing around the boat really were traffickers.

"Where do you come from, Chinwe?" he asked as they walked.

"Our family came from Nigeria, but when I was younger, Boko Haram - the Jihadist terrorist organisation - were on the rise. Mum told me children were no longer safe, so we left Nigeria."

"I've heard of Boka Haram at school. Didn't they take a load of girls?" Jonathan asked.

"Recently yes, but by then we'd already left ago along with thousands of others, ending up in a refugee camp in Cameroon. But there was a lot of violence and gangs in the camps had control of food, even water. What aid was handed out, they'd take half from you in exchange for so-called protection and sell it back at much higher prices. We left the camp, taking the long trek through Cameroon to the Central African Republic. Dad was told there was work in the diamond mines and we'd be safe there, so we joined a guide who had convinced a number from the refugee camp, for payment that is. In fact it took everything we had, only to find there was no work, poverty was high as well as a lot of crime."

"God, isn't anywhere safe in Africa?"

"Of course, but live from hand to mouth and people do things they wouldn't normally do to survive. But if you're a refugee people don't want you and you're moved on. It's understandable - they can hardly feed themselves without thousands of others coming."

"So that's where you were taken from? Ryan asked.

"No, South Sudan."

Jonathan came to a halt and looked at her. "But that's even farer fron Nigeria, isn't it."

"It is. Then we like many who had to move from Nigeria, ended up further from home than most, but there were some with us we knew, and the contacts and lorry drivers we met led us there. Again Sudan is a dangerous country to live in, but we were in a village away from a lot of the trouble, and while you'd get armed gangs raiding for food, it wasn't that bad."

"How old are you, Chinwe?" Jonathan wanted to know.

"My mother says I'm fifteen years old, but there are no papers to show when I was born."

"That sounds awful, to live like that. But you speak English very well, are there schools?"

"We do go to school, but they are very crowded and teachers don't stay long. Then, most of the teachers don't teach English. I was lucky, my older sister was a good learner and she'd spend many hours with me and my other brothers and sisters teaching us not only to read but speak and understand English. She told us it will be important for us in the future."

"Well you've really picked it up, and like I said, speak it well."

"Thank you. What country is this?"

"You're in England."

She suddenly stopped.

"Why have you stopped?" Ryan asked, very nearly walking into her.

"If this is England, you will know Karen Harris?"

Jonathan turned. "Everyone knows Karen Harris, she's dead famous. Why - do you know her?"

"No, but in our village she is talked about all the time. A woman who helps children taken and brings them home. Can we go and see her, not the police?"

"Oh, right, now I understand. But you see, Chinwe, while it's well known that Karen Harris does rescue victims of trafficking, people like us can't just ring her up."

"Why? We are all told to ask for her by name if we are taken by the gangs who sell children to the traffickers, and manage to escape."

"You need to explain, Jonathan," Ryan suggested.

"It's like this, Chinwe. According to the papers, Karen Harris is a colonel in the military and I don't think she even lives in England, I thought she lived in France. Then, how we would find her mobile number, I've no idea, and if we did, I don't know whether she'd even talk to us - that's if either of our mobiles worked, and they don't. Maybe the police can call her, or at least get in touch with the charity she runs to help girls like you, we'll have to ask."

She said nothing and they carried on walking. Eventually she spoke. "You are wrong, in Africa we trust Karen Harris, she has brought many girls home herself. She is a Christian woman and would never turn away a child."

Jonathan sighed inwardly. He knew he could never sway Chinwe's absolute belief that Karen would personally help her, after all, that was what Karen was famous for. But in his view the reality for Chinwe would be very different. The police would hand her over to social services. They may pass her on to the charity Lost But Never Forgotten, but he wasn't sure even that would happen.

Chapter 2

Fabian Nowak had been in the UK for nearly three years, along with his business partner Eryk Kowalski. Both in their early thirties, they'd come to the UK to make easy money. They were into drugs, besides supplying girls to pimps, who'd work them as prostitutes in Glasgow, Manchester and London. At first they used contacts in Poland to get the girls, but such was the demand they sourced other suppliers, in particular in a number of African states. These girls were younger, and in demand.

Tonight, they had arrived at the coastal car park and parked up alongside the vans of two of their hired drivers, before walking down the path to the beach. As arranged, a ship moored offshore had launched one of its lifeboats, sending it to the beach with ten trafficked girls.

The girls heading to Manchester and Glasgow had now left. The problem was one of the four girls heading to London, named Chinwe, had escaped. She had to be found at all costs. It wasn't just because of her potential earning value, but more to keep the route secret - not only for girls destined for the brothels, but immigrants from the subcontinent, who were avoiding the usual entry areas of the ferry terminals or the South Coast.

Spreading out their search, they came across the tent belonging to the lads. Fabian shone his torch inside, surprised no one was asleep in there, yet it was still full of personal belongings including two sleeping bags. "Bloody strange this, Eryk. Whoever was in this tent can't be far away. We'll split up and look for them. I've a feeling they could well know where Chinwe is."

For ten minutes they searched, finding no sign of anyone. Now they were back together by the side of the tent.

"This isn't right, Fabian. Who just walks away from their belongings, unless there is a real reason? I wouldn't mind betting Chinwe came across this tent and persuaded the occupants to take her to someone who could help."

"I'm thinking the same," he answered, pulling out his smartphone and switching to the maps. "There was no other vehicle in the car park when we arrived, so they've got to be on foot. My guess is they will head for the A1 and try to stop a car. What do you think?"

Eryk looked at the map. "Their nearest route to the A1 by road is through Cheswick. Unless they decide to avoid the roads and keep to footpaths heading toward Haggerston. Let's go, either way we'll overtake them before they get to the A1."

Running down to their vehicle, already loaded with the last three girls, they set off. Already the sun was beginning to rise, making the search that much easier.

***

Jonathan, as Fabian surmised, had stayed off the road, keeping to the footpaths by the edge of the fields that would take them towards the A1, with the intention of thumbing a lift. It would be far quicker. They passed a number of houses, but all was in darkness, the occupants asleep. They even found a bed and breakfast, but Chinwe wouldn't let them knock on the door. She was convinced they wouldn't believe she'd been abducted and maybe send her back. In her mind the only adult she would trust was Karen Harris. If they could get to the police, Karen would collect her. Jonathan didn't push it, or try to convince her otherwise. The girl was terrified and in her frame of mind, with Cheswick and the A1 being less than three miles ahead, they would be far better going there rather than trying to explain to someone who had just got out of bed.

Coming out on the A1, they turned right, walking in single file, looking for a lay-by where a vehicle could stop to pick them up. This was a fast road and few vehicles would take the risk of stopping, effectively blocking a carriageway and risking a collision. But Jonathan was not discouraged. A number of vehicles had passed so he was confident once they found a place for one to stop safely they would easily get a lift.

In less than a mile, they found a pub with accommodation but more importantly, a parking area at the front where a vehicle could pull in. With no intention of knocking up the owners of the pub, the three of them stood a short distance before the pub and began to thumb for a lift. Jonathan had even thought up a reason why they were out so early and wanting a ride. Whoever stopped was bound to ask, with all of them obviously young.

Quite a number of vehicles passed without stopping, then a lorry-driver sounded his horn before slowing down, coming off the carriageway at the pub entrance. All three of them ran to the passenger door, and the driver wound down the window.

"Where are you heading?" he asked.

"We're trying to get to Berwick."

"No problems. If I drop you off at the top end at the roundabout close to the supermarket, is that okay for you? I don't want to drive through the centre."

"That would be brilliant, thank you," Jonathan answered. He knew where the driver was suggesting. This was a supermarket they often went to, with a McDonald's restaurant next to it and around a quarter hour's walk to the police station.

Once inside, the driver asked why they were up so early.

"My brother and I took Chinwe, who's staying with us on

an exchange visit, camping. We'd intended to go birdwatching on Holy Island, except the tent got a bit damaged in the wind last night, so we've decided to call it a day and go back home. We'd have got the bus, but it's not due for another hour, so decided to see if anyone would give us a lift."

"Did a bit of camping myself when I was your age. Do you do a lot?" the driver asked.

"Yes, I love it, Ryan's the wimp, if he can't get on the internet, then it's not for him."

The driver gave a knowing nod of agreement. "Yes, the internet has got a lot to answer for."

They all fell silent and very soon the lorry pulled up at the roundabout to let them out.

They'd walked less than a hundred yards before Ryan stopped outside McDonald's. "I've got my spends with me, let's get a breakfast muffin before we go to the police. They could have us there ages and besides, I'm dying to go to the toilet."

"Why not, half an hour won't make much difference and I could do with a toilet break myself. Have you ever had a McDonald's, Chinwe?" Jonathan asked.

She shook her head. "I don't know what you call a McDonald's, but we are wasting time, shouldn't we find Karen Harris so I can go home?"

"We will, but at least have a drink, then we'll find your Karen Harris," Jonathan told her confidently. He knew they wouldn't. The police would take her away and that would be the last they'd see of her.

Chinwe refused to go inside. Such a place scared her with all its lights, so she sat down on one of the outside table benches to wait for them.

"Are you sure you don't want something to eat, Chinwe?" Jonathan asked.

"No, water is all I need."

"Water! Why not a Coke, when did you last eat?" Ryan butted into the conversation.

She looked at him. "Please, Ryan, you get your food, so we can go and find Karen Harris. I'm very used to going a long time not eating, we have very little at home. On the boat we would only get a stew with a little bread once a day. Water is all I want."

"Well, see you don't move till we're back, and don't talk to anyone," Ryan told her, then went inside the restaurant.

Jonathan reiterated what Ryan had said and followed him in.

***

A little earlier, the van Fabian and Eryk were travelling in arrived at the A1. In fact, they saw the three of them thumbing a lift, a short distance away, on the far side of the road. They were at the point of crossing the road to snatch Chinwe back, when the lorry that did pick the children up passed their van, before they could turn onto the A1. Now they were following the lorry.

"With them on the other side of the road thumbing a lift for vehicles heading north, my guess is they're heading for Berwick-upon-Tweed. Maybe Chinwe has convinced them to take her to the police station there," Eryk commented, looking at the map.

"That's all we need, particularly if they're dropped outside the station, then we're fucked."

They followed in silence. Eryk, looking at the map on his smartphone, was surprised the lorry didn't turn into the town, but kept on the A1. "You know, I think the driver of the lorry intends to drop them at the top end, he's missed the road leading in."

"Possibly, after all it's a huge lorry, so he wouldn't want to take it through the town centre."

"Looking at the map, the station is only a bit of a walk from the other side. That'll give us an opportunity to grab her back before they can get there," Eryk commented.

When the lorry came to a halt by the roundabout and dropped the children off, Fabian kept going and headed towards the town centre, past a supermarket and coming down to another roundabout, before turning right and actually parking up in the McDonald's car park. They knew the lads, along with Chinwe, would more than likely remain on this side of the road and virtually pass them. If they didn't and crossed to the other side, they would still see them. Then it would be a simple task of collecting Chinwe by the side of the road.

Eryk climbed out of the van and headed on foot past McDonald's in order to intercept the three of them. The idea was that Fabian would come up from behind. Eryk would snatch her as she walked past, or if Chinwe hesitated and turned back, she'd walk directly into him.

Fabian watched from the vehicle as the lads, with Chinwe, came to the McDonald's restaurant and stopped. Then Chinwe actually sat down outside while the lads went in.

'I don't believe that, bloody typical of kids these days, burger restaurants are like magnets, and kids can't walk past,' he said to himself, then called Eryk on his mobile. "Come back quickly. The lads are inside McDonald's, she's on a bench outside, collect her, then we go," was all he said.

Heading back towards the entrance, Eryk vaulted the low wooden fence surrounding the restaurant and ran down the side towards the outside tables. Fabian had climbed out of the van and gone round the back, unlocking the van door, ready to open it and push her inside.

Chinwe had seen Eryk vault the fence and head directly towards her. While he could just be a customer making his way into the restaurant, in Chinwe's mind alarm bells were ringing. If it was or not one of the searchers, she'd no intention of staying around. She did her best to get herself off the bench seat and run, but the distance was so short for Eryk, giving her no chance. Eryk literally dragged her off the seat, putting his hand over Chinwe's mouth, preventing her from screaming and frogmarched her to the van, before throwing her in the back.

Ryan, coming from the toilets, had decided to give Chinwe one last chance to accept something to eat, emerging from the entrance as Eryk grabbed Chinwe. In an effort to stop them taking her, Ryan ran after Eryk, grabbing at him, shouting at him to let her go. However, once Fabian had taken control of Chinwe, Eryk turned his attention to Ryan. Seconds later, he too was grabbed and pushed into the back of the van, with Eryk following them inside and Fabian slamming the door shut. He then ran to the front of the van, climbing in. Seconds later the van left the car park, heading towards the A1.

In the back, Ryan was still shouting at Eryk to let them out. That was before he received a hard thump to his stomach, doubling up in pain. His arms were quickly dragged around behind him and his wrists tie-wrapped together, followed by his ankles. Chinwe had cowered in the far corner of the van, terrified of what this man would do to her for escaping. But all Eryk did was secure her, the same as Ryan.

***

Jonathan came out of the toilet and looked around. He had expected

Ryan to be standing at the counter, but he was nowhere to be seen. Going back into the toilets, he called his name, with no reply.

Then he went outside, deciding he must be with Chinwe, but of course she was missing as well. Now he was in a panic, running to the main road and looking either way. Back in the restaurant, he went up to the counter.

"Can you call the police, I think my brother and a girl with us have been abducted?" he blurted out, obviously in a state of alarm.

The lad, not much older than Jonathan, looked at him for a moment. "That sounds a bit over the top. Who'd abduct two people outside here? I'll have to get the manager."

"There's no time, every minute they will get further away, I need you to call now," he came back at him, his voice rising to the point of virtually shouting at the lad.

The lad shrugged. "Either way I can't, the manager must decide. Wait here," he said, then sauntered off into the back.

The minutes ticked by, Jonathan stood there with a feeling of helplessness. Having no working phone, he had to rely on this lad, but he'd looked at him as if he was some sort of loony.

Soon the manager came through. "You want us to call the police?" he asked.

"Yes, my brother's been abducted along with a young girl."

"You saw this happen?"

"No, I was in the toilet and when I came out he'd gone, along with the girl we were with."

"So that makes him abducted? Could he not have just walked away?"

"No, we found the girl wandering around. She claimed she was being chased by traffickers. We were taking her to the police station. Please, call the police, let them help me find my brother."

"Very well, but if this is some sort of hoax, you are on camera and the police will prosecute you for wasting their time. Would you like a drink, on the house?" The manager had taken this tack because of the time of morning and the nature of the lad's claims. Already he'd asked other staff if they'd seen him with another lad or girl. None could remember. So hoax or not, he wasn't prepared for the lad to become agitated or even violent towards the staff. It was better to placate him and have the police sort it out.

"Thank you, coffee please."

The manager turned to the counter assistant, his voice low so Jonathan couldn't hear. "Get him a coffee, I'll call the police. Don't wind him up in any way, he could be on drugs or whatever. I want no trouble."

The lad nodded and the manager returned to his office.

***

Soon the police arrived. They sat with Jonathan, listening to his story, with one taking notes.

The note-taker turned to the other. "Have a word with the manager and ask him to rewind his security cameras. Let's see what has been happening outside." Once he left, the policeman glanced at his notes. "You say Chinwe mentioned Karen Harris? Does she know her? You didn't make that clear."

"No, she doesn't know her personally, only by reputation. Apparently she's looked on as some sort of god in Africa and Chinwe was convinced if she could talk to her, she would take her home."

The policeman shrugged slightly. "Hardly likely to be Karen Harris herself, more like her charity would send her home.

I understand the police refer victims of slavery and trafficking to the charity and not directly to Karen. They sort them out."

The other policeman came back. "You're needed in the manager's office."

The note-taker stood, looking down at Jonathan. "Stay here, will you?"

As they walked through, a policeman who had come from the manager's office lowered his voice. "The lad could be correct. It's on camera. A coloured girl and a white lad of around thirteen, both being bundled into a white van. This is serious, Mark, we need to make the desk sergeant aware."

"Shit, it's all we need when we're just about to go off shift. See if you can get the registration number from the footage, while I make the call."

"I'll try, but would you believe they've got a spider's web across the camera lens with the bloody spider sat in the middle?"

He smiled. "I would, happened to me at home. The spider kept tripping the alarm every time it moved."

Chapter 3

On the day Chinwe attempted her escape, Karen Harris had arrived in the UK. Aged thirty-six, and single, Karen was an attractive woman, tall, slim, with shoulder-length brown hair. She had joined the army at the age of eighteen, quickly rising up the ranks to colonel. She was now the commander of an EU military unit called Unit T, formed to combat the increasing threat in the EU of human trafficking and slavery. Her rise to the top was not without controversy among the politicians as well as senior officers in the forces. She had become a thorn in their side, with her conducting military operations in a manner as far away from convention as you could get, yet she obtained indisputable results; and to be fair, unlike military conflicts, the ones Karen was involved in were urban warfare, requiring informers, undercover operators, and powers to search premises that weren't normally available to local police without a magistrate's permission and a great deal of evidence.

There was also a consensus of opinion, among senior military personnel, that since Karen took over command, Unit T was out of control, accountable to no single EU country, given its powers of investigation and arrest surrounding human trafficking. Such authority even enabled Unit T to override local country laws. With an intelligence centre that rivalled EU member governments' own intelligence services, along with covert operators, the unit had grown to over two thousand personnel, and there were also an unknown number of informers paid by Unit T. While most of the complaints were in reality directed towards Unit T operations, the complainant would always cite Karen personally, as Unit T's commander. However, her public popularity and high-profile arrests of prominent people left many of the complainants scared of confronting her directly. Some even suspected if you did target her, she wasn't averse to setting up an operation to bring that person down, if she couldn't get enough evidence to convict.

Over the years, Karen had become wealthy in her own right. The money was made up of various questionable inheritances, with her as the sole beneficiary, along with the compensation she'd received when, while on covert operations, she'd been subjected to abuse - at times even ending up in brothels. These payments were tax-free and legitimate, because when Unit T brought a trafficking group down, they would seize their assets to pay damages to victims of the traffickers and Karen would often be classed as a victim. Human trafficking was also a billion-pound industry, so it was quite usual for assets held by traffickers to be well in excess of a million pounds, sometimes substantially more. In fact Karen, according to the media, had an asset base worth as much as seven hundred million, but no one had been able to prove it, and it was just a matter of speculation. There was another side of her wealth, unknown both to the media and the authorities. A great deal of money and precious goods had come her way, including huge sums of cash, diamonds and gold bullion, from illegal funds she'd come across in operations when working on her own down the years. This was all kept in various deposit boxes across Europe, as well as her own private safes in properties she owned. Of course, with wealth comes power and while Karen wasn't that bothered about exploiting such an advantage, she was very powerful. It never went to her head, where others coming into wealth would pay silly money for designer gear, or lavish parties. Karen spent very little on herself, would not eat in the best restaurants, and was often to be found in small cafés, or pubs with 2-for-1 meal deals.

While Karen had an apartment in London's Canary Wharf, with her doing so much work in other European countries, she rarely came to the UK. However, she urgently needed to see her solicitor and property broker to sign for a recent property purchase. There had also been a request for a meeting at the Home Office with a junior minister. Both meetings had prompted her to stop over in London on her way to her usual three to four days a month that she'd spend at the EU headquarters in Brussels. Such a diversion was not much of a problem. Karen had been a licensed pilot since the age of twenty and flew her own aircraft. At the moment she was flying a Gulfstream jet, currently owned by the EU after her own was sabotaged. Her long-time friend Sherry Malloy, a girl in her twenties who had worked originally at Unit T, but now looked after the charity LBNF [Lost but Never Forgotten], which was formed by Karen to help victims of human trafficking, had come with her to London. Sherry was due to go to London anyway and then on to Manchester, for her regular visit to the LBNF's two UK offices, but by scheduled flights. From there she would go to the Amsterdam office and the Berlin office before returning home.

LBNF was now listed among the top fifty wealthiest charities in Europe. Financed mainly by the proceeds of crime gained from criminals convicted of human trafficking offences, along with the EU government's contributions for looking after their own citizens, LBNF currently provided various levels of care for nearly eight thousand victims, besides directly housing over a thousand in ex-timeshare complexes that had become available following the property collapse in Spain. Karen also owned a number of apartments and villas which the charity used.

Karen's property empire was considerable and growing at an alarming rate. Even investigative reporters looking into Karen's true worth to write articles about her, which were readily snapped up by news groups, could only give tentative estimates of just how large her property holdings really were. Most articles gave wildly different estimates, from a hundred million to a staggering two hundred million, fuelled in part by the rise in value of property across Europe. Even so, they all agreed Karen was still on an upward trend, increasing her portfolio, which also showed no signs of slowing. Although they all missed the point - Karen had nothing else to do with her money and she enjoyed buying and sometimes selling properties. She even made a small profit.

Karen entered her apartment in Canary Wharf along with Sherry. She flopped down on a settee, while Sherry went through to the kitchen and made two coffees from the inbuilt automatic coffee machine. Both girls might have considerable skills in what they did, but when it came to basic cooking, they fell flat on their faces. At Karen's main home located in the south of France, she had a housekeeper, at the private apartment in the Marbella complex she used the complex's restaurant, but in London and her house in Corsica she had no one. So the food cupboard would be empty, apart from a few ready meals in the freezer.

Bringing the coffees through, Sherry sat down in another chair. "Where do we eat tonight, Frank's?"

Frank's was a small café close to Euston station, used mainly by people who lived on the streets. Frank did basic non-fancy food. That suited Karen, she couldn't stand the food offered in top restaurants and like Sherry, would sooner sit on a wall with fish and chips, or a burger. Even her wealth never made any difference to where she'd eat, the same as Sherry. Sherry was brought up by a mother who drank to excess, took drugs and fed her habit by prostituting; often the only food Sherry would get was the school meal. Sherry had vowed never to be in that position herself, squirrelling away every penny she earned and again, she was a girl with over a million pounds in the bank, since Karen had managed to obtain compensation under the proceeds of crime legislation from the people running an illegal brothel who'd originally abducted her. Not that she'd need to be so prudent about holding onto her money, as Karen had assured her she'd always be looked after. However, Sherry would not rely on that happening - in the past, they once had a massive bust-up, resulting in Sherry walking out. While eventually they did make up, it also opened Sherry's eyes to the fact that Karen was so unstable in her relationships, that to be beholden to her was in the long term not to be recommended.

"Why not, unless you want posh and we look for a 2-for-1 offer in one of the local pubs?" Karen came back at her.

Sherry rolled her eyes back in despair. "If that's what you consider posh, we'll give Frank the business. Besides, I've not seen him for ages. Last time I was in London, I was out with the owner of the contracting company that did this place up."

Karen frowned. "He was bribing you?"

"Bit late for that, he'd already finished and this was just a little thank-you to him and all the lads who had worked so hard. I was the token person who represented the client – you - besides buying them all a drink on your behalf out of my own pocket. Let's face it, if you'd been there, you wouldn't have joined them, or if you had you'd have taken them all to Frank's for his special with a mug of tea."

"I wouldn't, in fact, I'd have taken them to a pretty upmarket restaurant - after all, they had done a good job and I'd enjoy going out with a load of burly workers. It'd be like I was back with the army lads. But for you and I, we'll go to Frank's. Maybe use the underground, rather than drive."

Karen switched on the television, selecting the news channel. While she could speak and understand French, the EU versions were never the same as being back in the UK, where she was born.

The newsreader droned on with the usual news items before a breaking news notice in red came up along the bottom of the screen:

'Abduction of children in Berwick-upon-Tweed. Police to make a statement.'

The newsreader finished his current report, picking up a sheet of paper. "We are going over to our reporter in Berwick-upon-Tweed where earlier today, two children were snatched outside a fast food restaurant. The police have only just finished making a statement. Nigel, I believe you've more details of what the police have been saying?" the newsreader asked the reporter, who was on the spot.

"I do, Jeremy. Although it was first believed to be a spontaneous abduction, that does not now seem to be the case. The police are saying the abduction came about when two children camping across from Holy Island were approached by a young girl claiming she had been trafficked and asking for their help. With both their mobile phones not operating, they decided to take her to a police station. The police are appealing for the driver of a lorry who gave the children a lift to Berwick and for anyone driving along the A1 at around five o'clock this morning who saw three children thumbing for a lift, to get in touch with them. Additionally, they have put out an appeal for anyone who has seen a white Vauxhall Vivaro van with the registration AA61BTG. The police are asking the public not to approach the vehicle, but contact them. The occupants of the van are believed to be dangerous and may be armed." Then he hesitated. "Just one minute, Jeremy, I believe the parents of the abducted boy have come out of the police conference and are about to talk to the press, let me get closer and see if we can get any updated information."

"I'm here to make an appeal on behalf of our son Ryan," Mr Selby began, when a number of reporters had assembled. "The police didn't want me to make this appeal, but Ryan is our son and no matter what, we are prepared to do anything to get him back. Our other son, Jonathan, told us the girl they tried to help was called Chinwe and came from the Sudan. He told me she had the absolute belief that Karen Harris of Unit T would find her and take her home. We are begging our government to not delay in contacting Karen Harris, who we believe is far better placed to find Ryan as well as Chinwe and bring them home safely."

"Why did Chinwe think Karen Harris would help? Does she or her family know her?" a reporter asked.

"I asked my son the same question. He said in the villages of Africa, because Karen has returned many girls to their families, who were taken by roaming gangs snatching children for the human traffickers, Karen is looked on as their only hope in locating missing children. So when Chinwe found out she was in the UK, she asked Jonathan to contact Karen so she could take her home. Of course Jonathan had no idea how he could do that, but believed the police would do it for Chinwe." He hesitated a second, tears forming in his eyes. "It humbles me that a little girl so far from home, believed that only Karen Harris could help her. What society do we live in when the world has to rely on one person to do what we should all be doing. Looking after our children, who are, after all, our future? So if Karen Harris is watching, please, we beg you, take charge of the investigation, find our son and the girl Chinwe and bring them home."

Nigel turned to the camera. "There we have it, Jeremy. Ryan's father making a heart-rending appeal to the authorities to request that Unit T and of course, their commander Karen Harris, take over the investigation, even at this early stage. I will attempt to get a comment from the police and come back to you."

"Thank you, Nigel." Then the newsreader gave a contact number and reiterated the police appeal.

Karen turned off the sound and leaned back in thought.

Sherry looked at her. "I suspect you know who the police are looking for, don't you, Karen?"

"Why would I?"

Sherry smiled. "Because I have been with you for years and the way you nonchalantly turned the sound off and never commented tells me you know. After all, it's obvious that Chinwe escaped as the traffickers brought her ashore, which is how the other kids got involved."

"More than likely. I do know who the group probably is and possibly where the van's heading. It's been known for some time that the group in question had moved their operation further up the coast, to transfer their girls off a ship onto the mainland. Although if we'd known where the actual location of transfer was, we'd have already stepped in."

"So what will you do about it?"

Karen shrugged. "Nothing, I'm not risking destroying months of intelligence-gathering for the sake of two children. They, like many still in this group's clutches, will have to wait until we're ready to make our move."

"And the little boy, what will happen to him?"

Karen looked at her. Sherry had seen this look many times. One of disinterest; the usual sparkle in Karen's eyes was not there, replaced with the coldness of a girl who had seen and faced death so many times in her life, that she had become immune. Then, while Sherry owed her own life to Karen and loved her like a sister, she could never understand how she had been allowed to continue running Unit T. Karen had lost her parents, her sister, she'd been abused and dumped in brothels, some the absolute pits, yet each time she would fight her way out and not be averse to killing her keepers in doing so. While Karen had always been ruthless in her fight against the trafficking cartels, since the Soviet Union's collapse and countries in that Union had joined the EU, a new level of violence was emerging among the trafficking gangs. Sherry knew this life was tearing her apart, the pressures on her enormous, as she struggled to control and keep alive covert operators deeply entrenched in the criminal cartel groups in operations running seven days a week, making the demands on her time relentless. Now, once more, the eyes of the world would turn towards Karen to find one child out of thousands she already had on her books, because of the girl's absolute faith in Karen's abilities. Sherry knew the job was hard enough, without the added glare of the media watching her every move.

Karen brought her out of her thoughts. "If these people are part of the group I think they're from, they will have no use for the lad. That would leave them with the dilemma of dumping him, to be found by the authorities, or killing him. In my view he'll be dead already, or soon will be. The girl may well receive a good hiding for giving them so much trouble, but she's valuable and will survive. Can I intervene? No, I can't at this stage, first I'm not sure if it's definitely the group we're on to, or one we don't know about as yet. So to play my hand in the hope of it being the same group, may not only be a waste of time, but counterproductive. You of all people, should know that?"

"You're correct as usual, Karen. It's not my place to tell you your job and I can understand why you tend to avoid contact with parents. Their pleas for help will always be emotional, distracting you away from the big picture."

Karen shrugged. "I've been at it for a long time, Sherry. Sadly, there will always be collateral damage - I hope I'm wrong, but in this case I think the boy may become the collateral damage." Then Karen stood. "I'm having a shower, then we'll go to Frank's."

Chapter 4

Karen, along with Sherry, both wearing jeans, leather bomber jackets and baseball caps, came up from the underground station at Euston. Then they made their way past the arches and the homeless, who were already settling down for the night, to Frank's café. Karen, as usual, was armed with an ankle knife, along with a gun, located in an inner pocket of her bomber jacket. Since Sherry had left Unit T to work in LBNF, she was no longer licensed to carry weapons, but for Karen, it was essential she was able to protect herself. Over the years Karen had made many enemies and only recently an attempt had been made on her life. Such was the world she now lived in.

"Well, if it's not my favourite girls," Frank said as they walked into his café.

"Not only your favourites, Frank, but two very hungry girls," Karen added, giving him a hug, followed by Sherry doing the same.

"Get yourselves sat down. It's roast beef with Yorkshire's and onion gravy today."

"Sounds good, Frank," Sherry said, taking a seat opposite Karen.

Soon he came over with two mugs of tea. This was one of the only times Karen drank tea, since taking up the position of commander. Usually it would be coffee.

"So what brings you to the UK, Karen?"

She shrugged. "The usual, I've meetings with my solicitor, then one at the Home Office. Even so, I like being here, I've a nice new apartment, with an actual balcony. Admitted, it is only postage-stamp-size with a bit of artificial grass, but you can sit out, when the sun shines that is."

Frank smiled inwardly. He knew Karen wouldn't have anything that minute. This girl may outwardly look as if she lived like an average person, but behind the scenes all the homes she owned, her vehicles, her clothes, reflected considerable wealth. He had not forgotten the time she invited him to take a break and stay in her home in Corsica. The house was the first occasion that he'd realised just how far she had come, which was a very long way from the semi-detached house in the suburb of Manchester that she was brought up in. What she called her holiday home was a 5-bedroom ultra-modern house set in acres of semi-tropical gardens, with an infinity pool that blended perfectly with the blue sky as if it went on forever, and a private beach below. In his view it was a snapshot of the real world in which Karen now lived, but she was also a very special girl who deserved all she had.

"Don't let her kid you, Frank," Sherry cut in, confirming his own thoughts. "This apartment is nothing like the one she's just sold in Kensington. It's so big you need an intercom to communicate between the rooms. Mind you, the huge kitchen with every appliance known to man doesn't equate to half a dozen ready meals in the fridge. It would have been better if her interior designer had left her with a fridge and microwave. The rest will never be used."

"The coffee machine's used," Karen reminded her.

"Yes, how could I forget the most important appliance, even that self-cleans, Frank."

He laughed. "You two make a good pair and with you both being non-domestically inclined, it is good for us café owners at least. I'll fetch your dinners."

Dinner would always include pudding. And then, Frank

would never let Karen leave the café until she had eaten every scrap of the meal, believing she didn't look after herself, food-wise that is, when away from her main home in southern France.

Frank joined them for a few minutes, sitting down beside Karen.

"So how is my favourite new girl, Midnight?" Frank asked.

Midnight, aged eight, was in fact Karen's sister, Sophie's daughter. After Sophie died, following an overdose, Midnight came to live with Karen. For the little girl, it was a wrench from the way she was brought up. Sophie had always believed Karen's actions had resulted in their parents' death. That was true in a way, but the reasons were far more complex and Karen could have done nothing to prevent it. Sophie at the time had also been abducted, but Karen found her and brought her home. Sophie never forgave Karen and wouldn't have anything to do with her. Because of this, Sophie got in with the wrong crowd, had Midnight, and lived a life that at times forced her to prostitute to make ends meet. All those years, Sophie had constantly reminded Midnight of just how bad Karen was, so when the little girl first met Karen, her hatred for her and all that she stood for was firmly entrenched. But she soon found out what her mother had said about Karen was not true and slowly she became closer to Karen. Now both of them needed each other. However, Karen, at times living so close to the edge, couldn't cope with the hassle of a dependant and the demands of a growing child. That left Sherry to step in and remind Karen of her obligations to Midnight. Except reminding her would often bring discord and even Sherry would be in the firing line when Karen was 'on one'. At the moment, everything was calm, too calm in Sherry's view, but that was often the way.

"She's good, Frank. Apart from the fact she keeps growing,

so every time I want to take her somewhere important, nothing fits. Then we both end up arguing about what I want and what she'll wear. The girl's eight and telling me how she wants to dress, I ask you, what does she know about anything?"

"Maybe, but I think you love her all the same?"

"Bloody good job, or I'd have strangled her by now," Karen added.

"Well, as she's still alive, when are you bringing her to see me?"

"Next month, it's her mother's birthday. I plan to take her to Manchester, so she can lay flowers on the grave, then we'll come to London. I don't want her to forget Sophie, even if she and I never saw eye to eye - Midnight is Sophie's daughter and always will be."

"You're right, a child should never be allowed to forget their roots."

"I'd rather forget mine, all I ever experienced was drugs, alcohol and prostitution," Sherry cut in. "Besides, my mother was so useless, she couldn't even think of a real name for me, finally naming me after a bottle of booze."

Karen smiled. "Well, at least it's a great name, Sherry, what if she'd had a brainstorm and ended up calling you gin or scotch? Whatever your mother had to do to bring you up, I'll bet you still loved her."

Sherry shrugged. "I suppose, and then, mum did her best, she never had anything, was often beaten up by a drunken client. But you're right, I still loved her."

"Of course you did and if she knew just how far you have progressed, Sherry, I bet she'd be very proud of her daughter," Frank added. "Anyway, I've a bit of news. I decided after my time in Corsica that I should have a regular holiday, it reinvigorates you, so where do you globe trotting pair recommend?"

Karen gave a hint of a smile. "I assume you want sun, sea, great nights out, with perhaps a little female company thrown in?"

"Of course, what more can a man ask? Although I already have my favourite girls visiting me often."

Sherry turned to look at Karen. "You're not thinking what I'm thinking, are you?" she asked sternly.

"Why not?"

"What," Frank asked, already worried as to what these two would cook up.

Karen smiled. "Marbella, Spain. It's time you lived a little, Frank. I've an apartment to die for, besides, the complex has a restaurant so you've no cooking, and a private beach."

"And don't forget to mention the fact he shares this with over two hundred girls, Karen, with birthday parties every week and barbecues on the beach."

"I was coming to that. So how about it, Frank?"

He sighed. "I didn't mention my proposed holiday expecting you to put me up, Karen. You know me, I'm not one to take advantage of our friendship."

Karen slipped her arm around him. "I know that, but we're all friends and these places I own can lie empty for weeks. So you're more than welcome to take your break there. Besides, Odette and now Spuds are in that area and they would be really put out if you didn't go to see them."

"Odette's with LBNF?" Frank asked.

Odette Boyer had worked as a covert operator for Karen. They met during an operation when Karen was attempting to take down an Irish gang that virtually ran both north and south Ireland.

The gang was involved in drugs and prostitution along with other criminal activities. Her cover was blown after she ended up in the clutches of an Italian criminal group called Circulo, requiring Karen to step in and negotiate her release. However, her use as a covert operator came to an end with that and Karen had moved her on to LBNF.

"She is and runs our new Tossa del Mar apartment complex. Once fully operational, it will house over six hundred victims of human trafficking."

He shook his head. "I really don't know how you do it, Karen."

"She doesn't, I do it these days," Sherry cut in.

Karen said nothing, just gave a smile. No one, not even Sherry, knew about a large operation, running in the background, that handled all Karen's purchases, sales and rents as well as the repairs and renewals that went on constantly. Everyone seemed to believe it all happened automatically with no intervention. It didn't, Karen employed close to fifty dedicated workers, housed in offices in London, working in the background, who handled all that.

"Anyway, Frank, are you going to Marbella or not?" Karen asked, avoiding any more discussion on the operational side of LBNF.

"Yes, of course, it sounds idyllic, but I insist that I make some contribution."

"That's fine, but to the charity, although it's unnecessary. You will be a guest staying somewhere not only owned by me, but in my private apartment."

Chapter 5

The following day, while Sherry had gone to LBNF's offices, Karen was on her way to the meeting with a junior minister at the UK Home Office. Karen's vehicle, a Range Rover with bulletproof glass and a blast plate underneath, was driven by Darren, her driver from Unit T, a soldier attached to her strike force named Dark Angel. They pulled up outside the Home Office and she went inside. Immediately she was shown through to a plush office on the third floor where the MP Carl Wright, a junior minister, was waiting.

"Colonel Harris, it's good of you to find time in your busy schedule to see me," Carl said, shaking her hand.

"That is no problem, Minister, although I'm usually in Brussels at this time of the month and will be leaving the UK later today."

"I understand completely, shall we sit down?"

Coffee was brought and soon they were left alone.

"Bad business up in Berwick-upon-Tweed don't you think?" he commented, while stirring his coffee after adding sugar.

The casual way it was said gave Karen the impression he was attempting to strike up a very low-key conversation in a relaxed way, except she suspected this was not the reason why she was here. She decided to remain low-key in her response so as not to involve herself in speculation.

"It doesn't sound good - then, I know little about the circumstances. But I don't believe you have asked me here because of that?"

"Of course not, the police are handling it. I've every confidence they will find the children soon. Yet I'd be interested to hear your immediate thoughts?"

"I have none, Minister. Like I said I don't know the facts, apart from the press reports, which are usually useless for forming a professional opinion due to the lack of fine detail and their own speculations."

"Understandable. As it is, the reason I've asked you here is to talk about the Knights."

Sir Robin Knight and his father Sir Richard Knight had engaged contract killers, through a Russian gangster called Alexie, to eliminate Karen as well as Ale Bassani, the leader of a criminal group known as Circulo. The devastation the contract killers had left in their wake during the attempt on both their lives, shook not only the British government, but Unit T. Such was the effect on Karen personally, it led her to question if the time had come for her to step down as commander to concentrate more on her charity. Since then, although she hadn't completely discounted giving up, she still hadn't made a move that way. As for the Knights, with the use of an informer Karen was able to prove they were behind the attempt on her life, which led to their arrest. Karen could have arrested them earlier than she did. It wasn't really necessary to use an informer to add more incriminating evidence before their arrest, except for one very important reason. Under EU law, a person convicted of human trafficking faced not only a minimum ten-year sentence, but under proceeds of crime, after paying compensation to their victims and Unit T's costs, Karen's charity LBNF received the balance and not the public purse. These two men, particularly Richard Knight, made Karen's own fortune pale into insignificance, so she wanted their conviction to be a charge related to human trafficking. This was one of the important ways Karen financed her charity, so she had no issue in ensuring that was the case before she made a move, otherwise she'd get nothing, as opposed to everything. So when Karen found they were not only targeting her, but were involved in human trafficking, she went for them on that basis, assisted by the informer.

"I'm sorry, Minister, I cannot discuss ongoing prosecutions. You must direct all your comments and observations to the Unit T legal department. Is there anything else you want to talk about? If not - I should leave."

"Colonel Harris, you are the commander of Unit T and have the power to dictate policy as well as decide who to prosecute. With regard to the Knights, I, or rather Her Majesty's Government, require Unit T to stand aside and leave their prosecution with our Director of Prosecutions."

"I may, as you suggest, have the final say on a number of issues. Until, that is, I've passed the documents of the case to legal. They are like your Directorate of Prosecutions. They look at all documentation and decide if the prosecution is a valid human trafficking violation and meets the criteria laid down by the EU with regard to Unit T's scope of operations and my rules of engagement. To pass the prosecution back to the UK may only be done if I have breached such rules, or human trafficking violation conditions have not been met. In this case they had."

Carl seemed to ignore her words and kept to his own agenda. "Let me explain, Colonel Harris. I'm given to understand that Sir Richard was working on behalf of the British Intelligence Service MI6 to find out the true people behind the transportation of immigrants into mainland Europe and on to the UK. In view of this, the British government has requested the EU drop all charges concerning human trafficking by Sir Richard, which the EU has indicated they would agree to, except their hands are tied unless

Unit T withdraws charges. The UK also wants you to drop criminal charges against both Sir Richard and his son Robin, relating to their allegedly engaging contract killers."

Karen sighed inwardly. She'd expected an attempt to be made by someone senior in the government, after all, the Knights had many powerful friends, but to claim they were working on behalf of MI6 sounded far-fetched. And then, she had already been in discussion with her legal team as to what she should say if approached.

"When you say the EU, who in particular is making that decision?"

He gave an indifferent shrug. "I'm not sure, but I would imagine it originated from the committee that oversees Unit T. I was just given that information."

"I see, as it is I am meeting the chairperson of the Unit T committee while in Brussels, I will talk to her. As for Sir Richard working with Security Services, that may be the case, after all, we also use covert operators and informers, so while I'm not discounting they were running a covert operation, I'm not sure what I can do for them now. Charges were laid over two months back and I know of no approach from any UK department to Unit T clarifying the Knights' position. I can assure you if such an approach had been made, I would have acted. I suggest whoever in MI6 was controlling the Knights, send the new evidence direct to legal. Legal may request that Unit T's intelligence unit look into the claims, but because of the delay in us being made aware of these facts, legal could decide such proof is required to be submitted to the court for direction."

Carl was obviously frustrated with her answers, in his view she was skirting the decision. He decided on another approach. "Come off it, Colonel Harris, let's get to the real facts, shall we? You set both him and his son up, on a trumped-up trafficking charge toward Richard Knight and rape of a minor by his son Robin. Both for your own personal gain and that of LBNF - you and your charity now stand to make many millions from proceeds of crime. Neither of them interest you beyond that. As for passing it to the courts, even I know at this late stage that you could claim new evidence and withdraw from the court. You could also downgrade the charges sufficiently for our DPP (Directorate of Public Prosecutions) to look into the facts and prosecute, if necessary."

Karen took a moment to sip her coffee without comment. Then looked directly at him watching her as she replaced her cup on the saucer, sighing as she did.

"Have you any idea just how many times such accusations are directed against me across all EU countries when I prosecute under EU human trafficking legislation? I can assure you it happens often, particularly after the criminal realises the very real threat of losing all their assets, often putting their families out on the streets. In the Knights' case, under EU law a conviction will almost certainly be followed by a proceeds of crime order. LBNF, after Unit T's costs and damages, will as you say profit. There is nothing I can do to prevent that, nor would I want to. As for claiming I set Robin Knight up… Are you suggesting I supplied a trafficked underage girl, took her into a bedroom that Robin Knight was inside, besides giving her instructions to bend over the side of the bed with her knickers down so Robin could fuck her and we could get photos?"

"Of course I'm not."

"I hope not, because that's slander and you'd end up

explaining your accusations in a court of law - and you can be very certain I would win with costs and damages that could bankrupt you. So if you're not suggesting I set Robin Knight up with an underage girl, what are you suggesting?"

"You'd already picked up the fact that a child was being transported to the hotel, you could have stepped in at that point and not allowed it to go as far as it did. As for Richard, again after obtaining a recording of his conversation with the Russian Alexie, you could have arrested them both at that point. So I stand by my accusation that you did nothing in order that it would escalate to a trafficking offence where you stood to gain millions."

"Hindsight and conjecture, Minister. All we logged while watching the Knights was a child entering the hotel with a man in his forties. There was no reason to believe it wasn't the perfectly innocent act of a father and daughter returning to the hotel, or booking in for the night. If we arrested every man with a child, accusing the man of trafficking, we'd become a laughing stock. Then, most children under such circumstances, if confronted, are often scared of their minder. Experience tells us they would only recite what they'd been told to say, if questioned, and nothing more. As it was, we had no idea Robin Knight was with the child. We were waiting outside to arrest him and his father, but only his father came out, which instigated a search of the hotel. It was then we found him with a child."

Karen had in fact twisted the truth, she knew that the child was trafficked and the man was her minder. So the minister was correct in that she was out for a conviction under the EU's laws concerning human trafficking, requiring that their prosecution remain with Unit T. Then, she also had an answer to his other accusation, of wanting the Knights' money, not that she didn't want it, in reality she did, but again she downplayed that fact.

"As for personal gain, why should I take such a route? I don't need their money, I've already hundreds of millions in the bank I don't know what to do with, earning me close to twenty-five million a year in interest and that's without my rental incomes. Then LBNF has a capital base of around thirty-seven million along with substantial assets, so while the Knights' funds will be absorbed if they are convicted, LBNF and of course, myself, can comfortably survive without their money."

This time Carl took a moment before replying by taking a drink of his own coffee. He was aware she had a considerable fortune, but even he hadn't realised just how much annual income it generated for her and how large a capital reserve the charity held. A simple statement in front of the court would blow any argument the Knights' defence could claim that she was pushing ahead for her own personal gain. After all, it would be plainly obvious she had no need of it. Then, her claim Unit T had been waiting outside was the truth as he understood it, because the father was arrested outside. It was obvious she had tied them up very tight, giving no wriggle room for accusations of allowing a child to be raped for her own financial gain, even if she had set that up. He replaced the cup back on the saucer.

"May I be candid with you, Colonel Harris?"

"You can, provided it is not another claim I condone rape and abuse of a minor for my own personal gain, otherwise I'm leaving and the next time we meet, it will be in court."

"It isn't, I can assure you."

She shrugged with indifference. "Then be candid, not that I can see that by being candid it could change the facts of the case."

"The point is, the matter has been discussed at a very

high level. The government is fearful of the press blowing their involvement out of proportion with the Knights being on so many committees as well as in the Lords. Or at the very least it could be extremely embarrassing; at a time when the country is already in turmoil because of Brexit and there's a need for clear leadership. They suspect that the attack to your vehicle on the streets of our capital and the loss of life, once in court would unavoidably expand to include the attack inside a London hotel by the same contract killers. Again, that could move on to the loss of life after the same contract killers apparently shot down an aircraft. The public currently believes that particular accident was caused by an aircraft malfunction. I'm certain you can understand this cannot be allowed to happen, Colonel Harris?"

"I understand very well, after all I was there and the plane very nearly landed on top of me. Tell me, do you have a wife and maybe children, Minister?"

"I do. Two children in fact."

"So if I paid a stranger to go to your home and shoot them both dead, or as the Knights' contract killers preferred, threw a grenade into your house and your family were left with life-changing injuries, you'd be happy to walk away? Before you answer that it would be a ridiculous scenario, I'll remind you the attempt on my life left a good friend of mine and his wife dead. An innocent woman who had three children under ten was shot in the head. Police were killed in a hotel the contract killers attacked and many civilians sustained life-changing injuries. Most, if not all, have loved ones. Then, if you're unaware what life-changing really means, such injuries could include loss of limbs, being confined to a wheelchair or left badly disfigured, both mentally or physically, for the rest of your life. I could go on and bring up the air crash that killed many and left others with, yet again, life-changing injuries, but I think you understand where I'm coming from."

He looked at her, saying nothing. It was one thing pontificating to make excuses for what the Knights had instigated, but to have the consequence of their actions spelt out in graphic terms left him at a loss for words. It was Karen who broke the silence.

"I note you don't have an answer - because there is none. I enforce EU law, Minister. The consequences of prosecution, be it a government collapse, a failure of a business or bankruptcy of an individual, is not my problem. If like you suggest, Her Majesty's Government has civil unrest concerns over the prosecution going ahead, the decisions to reduce, suspend or withdraw charges must be taken by people well above my pay grade, or a decision could be made for the prosecution to be conducted behind closed doors."

"So you are indicating if that happened you would not object?"

Karen shrugged. "I am not suggesting, or as you say indicating anything. I'm also not a politician, judge or in the police service, I'm in the military. So while what happened sickens me to the core just thinking about it, my personal objections don't come in. A level of objection is limited to the rank you hold. So yes, like every other soldier, I will have the opportunity to make my case in front of senior officers and with me holding the rank of Colonel along with being the Commander of Unit T, I very much hope I would be carefully and seriously listened to. Whatever they decide I will abide by, because like every enlisted soldier, you lose the right to make decisions, you follow orders. Why, you may ask? That is very simple to explain. If every soldier sent to the front line attempted to dictate what he or she considers right or wrong, there would be no military... just anarchy. Now I think it's prudent that I leave. Although I must warn you under current EU law, human trafficking violations can carry many penalties, including one very important aspect."

"And what is that?"

"Human trafficking does not limit prosecution towards just the perpetrators, it extends to users of such services, for example Robin Knight, along with those who attempt to pervert the course of justice. To align yourself alongside the Knights could be construed as the latter and you risk losing your life savings, your home, with your family put out on the street, as well as ten years behind bars - and yes, as you so blatantly pointed out, LBNF will take it all. Keep that in mind."

After Karen left, the minister's Permanent Secretary came into his office.

"You have sorted her out, then, Minister?"

"I wish, Archie, but this is the first time I've met Harris and her arrogance is beyond belief, she even suggested I could be dragged into court by attempting to pervert the course of justice. I ask you, just who does she think she is, threatening a Minister of the Crown?"

Archie didn't answer, he was all too aware just how powerful Karen was, along with being popular with the public. Then, no matter what the minister believed, if any of his colleagues felt they were being drawn into a possible face-to-face conflict with her, particularly after the devastation the Knights' actions had created, they would first be looking at the ballot box and running the other way as fast as they could. Because of those thoughts, he refrained from answering the open question. "So what was the outcome, or wasn't there one?"

"While she's not playing ball, Archie, and hiding behind her legal team, she has admitted, if ordered by a senior officer, she'd not stand in the way of the prosecution being handed back to the UK," he answered, playing down the cold facts of life Karen had pointed out.

"How would that work, Minister, Harris is no longer part of the UK military."

He frowned. "How can that be? I understood each country supplied personnel to Unit T as a posting and Harris is a British subject?"

Archie shook his head. "They do, but not Harris. It's all very complicated. Harris apparently in the past resigned following a UK military tribunal where she was accused of going beyond her remit. We all firmly believed we were rid of her, but Unit T was suddenly brought under EU direct control, with a new multi-country steering committee in Brussels. The next thing we knew, Harris was reappointed by the EU."

"But the EU doesn't have an army, nor do they have military personnel."

"They don't and technically, Harris is classed as a military adviser for the EU, retaining her military rank and title. Because of that anomaly, while military personnel stationed temporarily at Unit T answer ultimately to their own country, she only answers to the committee that oversees Unit T at the EU."

"So she's winding me up and she technically has no senior commander over her?"

"That's right, apart from you making representation to the committee who can issue recommendations to her. However, it's unlikely that would happen. They would normally only be involved in operational considerations. Any interference could leave them open to serious questioning as to why an EU steering committee overrode a Unit T prosecution by Unit T's legal department, which would technically be beyond their remit."

"If what you are saying is true, it's a bloody joke. Harris has more powers than the elected representatives of all the EU countries."

"Precisely, Minister, but no one in the EU governments seem to understand, or wants to go down the road of asking such questions. She also has a military force behind her along with an intelligence unit, but we nor any other country have access to their records. To take her on, you need to be squeaky-clean because you can guarantee if there is anything to be known about you, she will know it. After this meeting and with you pushing to have the Knights' charges dropped, she will be asking her intelligence unit who you are and what is known about you and your family. Have no doubts about that."

"She'd better not, I'm vetted by Her Majesty's Government, which is the best. Talk to the Security Services lads, off the record, and have them cobble something together for me to place in front of the Cabinet and let's sort her out once and for all."

"MI6 will need to be very convincing. The PM's bound to want Unit T to look at their report. You do know he's a good friend of hers, I assume? Then, Harris knows a great deal about the criminal groups operating in Europe, so they will struggle to deceive her."

Carl grinned. "Friend or not, Harris is an illiterate working-class school kid who's not even been to university, or risen through the service to achieve the rank of colonel in a recognised military way. Then, she's not even capable of investing the money she's filched off people over the years, beyond leaving it in a bank. What idiot does that? If our people can't run rings around her they shouldn't be in the job. Many influential people want her off this case, so make sure it happens by talking to Max Hart at MI6 off the record."

"What should his direction of approach be?"

"Just tell him from me to crush the little parasite by fair means or foul if he wants to keep his job and fat pension. He'll know what to do. Richard's bloody annoyed with the way she's gone on, so you can guarantee he'll not hand over a penny for her to squander on that two-bit charity."

"Even so, Minister, I advise caution. Karen Harris has not got where she has by acting the fool - as many have found to their cost. She is also very dangerous and more than capable of retaliating with extreme violence against anyone who takes her on."

"Maybe so, but to take that route will be her downfall. As it is she's gone too far this time in messing about with the influential and the very rich for us to be cautious in dealing with her, just do it."

Archie left the office. All he could do was warn him. In his view, like most of the politicians, given jobs as a public voice for a department, they suddenly had the notion in their mind that they had capabilities beyond their experience. They listened to influential people who promised them even more power. If they got it wrong and fell flat on their faces, so be it, another would take their place with similar aspirations. So to take on Unit T just as a favour for the Knights and in particular, their commander, when human trafficking was involved, was asking for repercussions with only one winner - Unit T and particularly Karen Harris.

***

A tweet among a group of aircraft enthusiasts stating that a Unit T aircraft flown by Karen had landed at Biggin Hill airport, would have gone unnoticed in the usual run of things if Mr Selby, Ryan's father, had not made his heart-rendering appeal to involve Karen. The tweet, which included #KarenHarris for those who liked to follow her movements across Europe, was picked up by a reporter, who - with the help of his news desk - was able to find out her departure time through a flight plan lodged with air traffic control. However, he was not the only reporter who had found this information. By the time Karen arrived at the airport, there were close to twenty reporters clamouring to talk to her.

As usual her car swept through security to the hanger where her aircraft would normally be stored. Except by the time she arrived the aircraft had been brought out and made ready for departure. The car would sometimes be left inside the hanger and the weapons on board transferred to the plane. Although with Karen flying on to Brussels on this occasion, the car would be taken back to the secure garage in the basement of the block where Karen had her apartment, with the driver returning to Unit T on a service aircraft.

A senior employee of the airport walked over as she climbed out of her car.

"Lady Harris, may I have a word?" he asked.

"Of course. Got a problem?"

"We have. As you know we're a small airport, but in the airport hall there are a number of reporters causing quite an inconvenience for our passengers, all wanting to talk to you. Are you prepared to talk to them, or should I have security ask them to leave?"

"I'll have a quick word. Then at least they will go."

"Thank you, Lady Harris. I will have them shown into the boardroom."

Karen went into the room, it was packed and she struggled to get to the front.

"I've only a few minutes, I'm already close to my departure time," Karen told them once they had fallen silent. "First question?"

"Daily Mail, Karen. Are you involved in looking for the two children kidnapped in Berwick-upon-Tweed?"

"Unit T will have been informed that they are missing, believed abducted, however, at this moment we have not been approached to assist. Next question."

"Independent, Karen. Are you saying you will ignore the father of Ryan and his plea for you to intervene and find his son?"

"I understand that the UK police are currently treating this as a kidnapping. While, like everyone, I feel for the family and know what they're going through, Unit T will not directly get involved until the UK government has reason to suspect, or evidence, that this is an abduction by human traffickers who operate beyond UK shores. Then we will assist."

"Moses Jabari, editor of the online magazine, Africa Today."

Karen looked at him. "I have never heard of your magazine, are you Europe or Africa based?"

"We are an international magazine highlighting the inequalities for black people in today's society, particularly in the free world."

"I see, not that I can follow how any question I may answer might be based on that premise or could be relevant to the children's plight. Because of my time contranint may I have only relevant questions about the children's abduction please?" she said, directing her answer to the assembled crowd.

"Then it seems you really have risen above what you've stood for since forming your charity. Is this because Chinwe is a young black African girl, thousands of miles from her family and in your eyes valueless? Even when her one belief, in fact, her only belief is the absolute conviction that you, Karen Harris, will find her and take her home. Yet you discount her beliefs publicly, preferring to hide behind the UK police, who you know are out of their depth when it comes to international human trafficking groups. Maybe now you're so wealthy, such people are a nuisance and you prefer to sit on your private beach in Corsica sunbathing, rather than help those who believe you are the one person who can offer hope - that you will come for them?"

The room fell silent, everyone was interested in Karen's response. Karen on the other hand was very aware this question could be a minefield for her and her reputation. To reply off-the-cuff would be risky and all the time she was at this press conference, the clock was edging closer to her logged departure time. London area was, aircraft-wise, very busy, so to lose a departure slot could delay her considerably. Yet she must say something.

"It's unfair as well as untrue to accuse me of hypocrisy, as well as showing a complete lack of understanding as to who I am and who I work for. I am a military commander and work directly for the EU, not independently or for any individual EU country. Any crime committed in the EU, we cannot become involved with, or take over the investigation, unless it is a human trafficking offence and the perpetrators operate across the EU, such as an international criminal group. If a crime meets those conditions, any EU member country may request our assistance, but they are not required to do so."

"What of LBNF? A charity you began and still run. Are you telling us they will not help the little girl as well?" the man persisted.

"Again, you are distorting the truth to suit your thinking, Mr Jabari. You and everyone else watching or listening to this impromptu press conference need to understand both Unit T's and LBNF's roles regarding a child who is reported missing. All EU countries will automatically inform Unit T of a child's disappearance, along with EUROPOL and other European agencies if the time a child is missing exceeds twenty-four hours. Of course, with babies and very young children not of an age to walk, time is of the essence, so the twenty-four-hour delay is ignored. Unit T, like other agencies, holds databases, allowing us to identify a child when we come across children during our general investigations. LBNF does not investigate, they look after the victims of human trafficking. The Unit T database of children under sixteen is over twenty thousand, which does not include children who have gone missing that are from outside the EU, like Chinwe. If we add those and ones over sixteen that are reported to us - though I can assure you many are not - it is well over two hundred thousand. That, Mr Jabari, is the extent of the problem, but there is good news. This year alone, at least two thousand children under sixteen, who were victims of human traffickers, have been found by Unit T and returned to their families. Within that number, close to eight hundred were from various African states. You mention LBNF. Already it has approximately a hundred children from across Africa in its care, who for one reason or another cannot be returned, mainly because of continuing civil wars displacing not only families, but complete villages. Such problems make locating parents slow and difficult, often impossible. LBNF looks after those children, educates and gives them a future. Only this last month, Unit T pulled out twenty-five victims of human trafficking in the UK, twenty-one of them under sixteen and from Africa. Soon many will be on their way home. Again a number cannot return and they will be looked after."

She hesitated for a moment to take a breath, everyone was listening intently. "On average, I personally oversee at least a hundred ongoing investigations. It requires me to work seven days a week, with many days finishing late into the night. Yes, I try to have a break and yes, like most people, I try to get away, in my case to my home in Corsica. What more do you want me to do? Would I, as you suggest, turn my back on any child, or victim of human trafficking that needs help? Of course I won't and never have, but to do that I first have to rely on local police to complete their lines of enquiry, before furnishing me with the results of their investigations. Until that happens, I would only be going over the same preliminary work, when the country's own police force can do that just as well and at times, far better than me."

Many in the room were taken aback, not realising the scale of the problem Karen was attempting to contain – and yet here they were, pushing for one little girl.

"BBC, Karen. It is good that you remind us just how difficult your work is. News often concentrates on the happenings of the day, where you are constantly looking at the overall picture. We know, if the police ask, you will do your best for Chinwe and Ryan, like every other missing child."

"You can be certain I will and at times we come across children who we haven't been asked to look for. I'm also - with the input of the media - now aware of the abduction of Chinwe and Ryan. If I can help in any way, I will," she said, then hesitated, glancing at her watch. "I'm sorry, but I must leave, thank you for your time."

As she left, some began firing even more questions at her, in the hope she'd answer, while others began to clap. Very few in the room had realised just how much time and effort Karen put into her work, believing she now lived the life Moses Jabari accused her of, that of a multimillionaire, indifferent to how she had got there.

Many reporters were streaming out, one stopped. "Good question, Moses, putting Karen on the spot, but may I suggest somewhat naive? Karen is very astute and you wouldn't be able to put one over on her without being very certain of your facts. Even so, it's not often we get so much current information from her, my editor will love it."

Moses gave a weak smile as the reporter walked away. He had been convinced Karen would fall on her face and struggle to answer his accusation, openly admitting by default she was no longer interested in helping black people. He thought he'd had the chance to show up this high-profile woman's complacency, when it came to the plight of black people in the world, to get his magazine to the top, yet as the reporter said, this was not a woman you could get one over on that easily.

Karen flopped down in the pilot's seat and began to go through her pre-flight checks. Satisfied all was well, she started the engines and began taxiing to the runway. Pausing for a moment, while the engines came to full power, Karen released the brakes and in seconds she lifted off. In her world, most of her travel was by private aircraft. She had been flying for over ten years, racking up thousands of flying hours, yet she still got a buzz when taking off, or landing. This visit to London had been stressful and she could have done without it. Now she faced three or maybe four days in Brussels, and the problem with the Knights would certainly be raised.

Chapter 6

Ryan was in complete shock as to what had happened to him. People only got kidnapped in books, not pushed into a van outside a fast food restaurant. At any time he was expecting to hear police sirens and the van door to be suddenly pulled open by armed police, allowing them all to go home, with the criminals marched away to prison. But as time went by, his belief that this was about to happen began to diminish.

He also felt he should say something to Chinwe, after all, it was his stupid fault for wanting to eat. "I'm sorry you got caught, Chinwe," he whispered, so Eryk, sitting at the back, couldn't hear.

She shrugged. "We'd never have got to the police station, he'd have taken me off the street. But Karen Harris will come for me, you'll see."

"You truly believe that - will she come for me as well?"

She looked at Ryan in the dim light. "She will come and take us all home, Ryan. Now with you taken as well, she will know I am here."

Ryan said nothing, he couldn't understand her absolute faith in someone she had never met and who in reality may not be interested in one girl over the thousands that went missing. After all, like most people, even at his age, he couldn't help hearing his mother and father talking about this mega-rich woman who flew her own aircraft and travelled backwards and forwards across Europe, battling criminals like the heroes do in video games. And yet, as they travelled on, he also began to believe that if the police didn't help, his future rested in Karen's hands, as for everyone else in the vehicle.

***

The van continued on before turning down a narrow private road in Slough, west of London, coming to a halt outside a double set of wooden doors seven feet in height. Along the top of the doors was razor wire looped in coils. Fabian sounded the horn of the van and the gates were opened. It revealed a large yard and as soon as he drove inside the gates were shut.

A man walked over, having locked the gates, as Fabian climbed out of the van.

"Help Eryk get them inside, I've a call to make," Fabian told him.

Going through into the building, Fabian ran upstairs and into a room he used as his office. Taking a pay-as-you-go mobile out of a drawer, he dialled one of his customers for the girls.

"Jedrej, Fabian."

"What do you want?"

"We've your delivery ready for collection."

"We need to talk first, the usual place in an hour," he said, then cut the call.

***

Jedrej Mazur originated from Poland and now with the help of two sons, ran a successful prostitution operation using girls from both the old USSR countries and Africa. When Fabian arrived his car was already in the car park of a local beauty spot. At this time of day, no other vehicles were parked there.

Fabian walked over and climbed in the front passenger side of Jedrej's car.

"What the fucking hell have you been up to?" Jedrej began, ignoring any sort of welcome banter. "You assured me by dropping the girls further up the East Coast, it would avoid the problems we get south of London. Now the press is full of it and demanding Unit T's called in."

"For a start it wasn't our fault. We arrived to find the small tender from the ship was already on the beach. One girl couldn't have been properly secured and she'd done a runner. So after loading the ones bound for Glasgow and Manchester, Eryk and I had to go and find her. To cut a long story short, we picked her up outside a fast food restaurant, and a kid intervened, screaming at us to let her go. What could I do but take him as well? Then you forget, we've done this drop like eight times with no problems. Now we have a kid of thirteen that needs to be got rid of."

"He's your problem, we can't use him. Talk to Fillip and see if he'll take him to work on his cannabis farm, he'd keep him in check by feeding him the product," Jedrej suggested with a grin.

"That sounds an option, he could pay for him with a few bags of weed. But he couldn't use him permanently on the farm. What of the paedophiles on your books, would any be interested, even if it's in a month or so, when press interest dies?"

"They might, I'll make a few enquiries, but the kid's currently dynamite, even they could be too scared to touch him."

"When do you want your girls delivering?"

"Tonight, but again, don't include the one called Chinwe with our lot. She's trouble, so send her somewhere else."

"No problems. Blackthorn will take her. But you're losing a good girl. The supplier told me she was intelligent and speaks good English, meaning she can converse. Very rare with what is currently being supplied."

"Maybe, but a bit too intelligent if she was able to escape. As it is, we only want them for one thing and not to strike up conversations with clients. So we take three with the usual payment method."

***

After leaving Jedrej, Fabian returned to meet Eryk, telling him what had been arranged. "I've also called Fillip, he's agreed to keep the lad for a short time," Fabian finished.

"One month, if he can't be placed then we bury him, agreed?" Eryk decided.

"Agreed, you and Charlie can take him to the farm, while I sort out Blackthorn for the girl."

"I'm not going to use Charlie, I don't trust that man. He asks too many questions for my liking."

Fabian frowned. "You know, Jedrej said the same thing a couple of weeks back. I thought he was pushing for using one of his drivers in an attempt to get more knowledge of our contacts, so I discounted it. But I've an idea that will give us an indication one way or another, leave it to me."

Eryk just shrugged. "Better not use him again, then it wouldn't matter either way, rather than play detective."

"True, but if he is talking to others, we need to know who they are. We've a good little earner going on, it relies on being one step ahead in the game, not one behind. Then, you know the press is pushing to get Karen Harris involved, to find the kids?"

"What's that matter? It seems any kid that goes missing these days, the press scream to involve her, why's this time any different? Although she did do us a favour by taking the Nigerian gang down some years back, who were our major competition for bringing girls in from Africa."

"It has a lot to do with it. That woman uses informers, pays good money - in fact, without them she'd be stuffed. So you can be very certain if she does take on the investigation, she'll be pushing hard in the UK. So you sort the kid, and I'll make sure the people who do work for us are not in the queue to take money off Harris.”

Chapter 7

When Karen came out of the airport terminal in Brussels, she found Jasmin sitting outside on a low wall. This was a slim girl with blonde, shoulder-length hair, in her late twenties, dressed in tight jeans, T-shirt and wearing a baseball cap. She was also very attractive, with soft features that most men liked, in the belief she would be naive in the way she responded and acted. Yet Jasmin was a very long way from being naive and was not a girl to become involved with. She had worked as a contract killer since the age of eighteen and in the past had taken on some of the most dangerous and violent criminals. Even so, as far as Jasmin was concerned, Karen was no different. Although, they operated very differently in that she was paid to kill by contract, where Karen was effectively licensed to kill by the EU. That said, even Karen had overstepped the mark at times, by operating on her own volition, making them both cold-blooded killers. Since Jasmin had joined Unit T, she too was now licensed to kill, except Karen at times would call on her unique skills in a covert operation not authorised by Unit T, and then she would revert to type and her contract killer role.

Jasmin had come to Brussels to find a permanent home and because Karen, who was now coming to Brussels every month for at least four days on EU business, had agreed to buy an apartment or house with her.

Jasmin would normally live in hotels, although in Amsterdam, she did have a small one-roomed flat in one of the many properties she owned and rented out - but now she wanted something larger, more upmarket and away from the city's red light district.

The two girls hugged each other before walking through to

the car park, where Jasmin had left a hire car.

Once in the car, with Jasmin driving, Karen checked her mobile for messages, then leaned back. "I hope you've not done a Sherry on me and left the key to your piggy bank in Amsterdam, Jasmin?"

Jasmin smiled. Sherry was renowned for spending nothing, squirrelling all her money away. "More to the point, have you got a fat wallet with you? We're not going cheapskate, Karen. I want a pad that reflects wealth. So the ones I've set up for us to see are not cheap."

"That's fine, I no longer do cheap, although don't expect me to agree to pay a premium because it's a minutes' walk from the EU offices. I want something I can live in, that includes a swimming pool. I also want gardens, secure parking, as well as not falling out of the front door into the street."

"You don't want much, do you? I'm not as wealthy as you, I've got to live as well. Your pay is pathetic to what I'd earn doing contracts."

"It's you who wanted us to share the cost of buying somewhere - you're not having second thoughts now you've seen the prices around here are you?" Karen mocked.

"No, but it's not that easy to turn gold bullion into legitimate cash for buying property. So spend too much and you will drain my cash resources, then you get gold in part-payment of my share. See if you can get rid of it."

Karen was aware that Jasmin, although wealthy, had most of her legitimate wealth tied up in properties, along with a little cash in the bank. Her illegitimate wealth, paid by clients using her services, was in gold Krugerrands. They were easily cashed in any country, so long as it was just for general living, but changing large quantities into millions of euro, that was another thing altogether because of money laundering regulations.

"Don't worry about how to pay, Jasmin, we'll sort something. But first things first, let's find a place we both like, shall we?"

They fell silent, the traffic was heavy and slow-going.

"I hate coming here, everyone looks down on you. Well, they do with me," Karen commented, gazing out of the car window.

"Jealousy, Karen. No man likes to see a woman come good, it dents their ego. Then, since you sold the Sexton Shipping line, they can't even match your wealth, it must really stick in their craw."

"I suppose, but money only buys you problems. Everyone thinks, because you're loaded, it's okay to rip you off all the time. That's why I like going to Frank's café, it brings everything back into perspective."

Jasmin grinned. "I don't think they'd rip you off. God, even the restaurants struggle to actually sell you a dinner beyond egg and chips. You're a nightmare, especially when they are forced to smile, when you decide that you're not prepared to select anything off their posh menus."

"Yes, well, it's a bit pointless presenting a meal so small I end up stopping off at a takeaway on the way home because I'm still hungry. But forget all that. There's a possibility, later in the week, I'll need to go back to London. Stanley's on one of his 'look after me' rolls again, and will almost certainly insist on a Dark Angel unit being there if you're not with me. You've nothing on at the moment have you?"

"God you're a wimp these days, Karen. You're supposed to be in charge and they tell you what to do."

"I may be the commander, but when it comes to security I don't have much say. There's procedures to look after a commander when on an operation and even I've got to keep to them, otherwise it would soon become chaos, with everyone doing their own thing."

"That's a bloody joke, you're always doing your own thing."

"At times I have to. So are you with me or not?"

"I suppose having little to do at this moment in time, I may as well keep you alive until you at least sign a purchase agreement and pay your share of our new pad. After all, our agreement was if one of us dies the other gets whatever we buy."

"Bloody hell, Jasmin, you're a bit mercenary."

Jasmin frowned. "I'm supposed to be, after all my work is usually the other way round, I kill people, I don't keep them alive. So it's a departure for me, although I may just get the odd pop at some weird or nasty looking person who has the idea you'd look better in a coffin."

Karen smiled to herself. The girl may act in a cavalier way, but she was reliable and the sort who would stand between her and the adversary without a thought for her own safety.

"Right, that's sort of sorted. After I check in, we eat, then we spend the rest of the day and tomorrow morning looking for somewhere to live. After that I'm pretty booked up."

***

Karen had already attended a number of her regular meetings with different groups within the EU that required the input of Unit T. On the third day she was requested to attend what was known as an adhoc committee, appointed for the specific purpose of submitting a report on Sir Richard Knight. This had been formed at the request of the UK, although it wasn't made clear to Karen who had made that request.

Karen wandered past endless offices in the EU building before finding the meeting room. When she went inside, a number of people were standing around holding coffee cups talking among themselves. Emil Meyer, the chairperson, broke away from two people and came over to welcome her, before introducing her to the other members of the committee.

Once they had all sat down Meyer began proceedings. "This meeting has been brought about to consider the actions of Sir Richard Knight and his son. Both are currently awaiting trial. Perhaps, Colonel Harris, you can give the committee Unit T's current position regarding Sir Richard Knight?"

"Sir Richard's prosecution is with our legal team. Before attending this meeting, I did contact the team, but the person I needed to talk to is in Italy on another case."

"But you're their commanding officer, surely all departments report back to you on a daily or weekly basis?" a committee member wanted to know.

"You are correct, however, I'm overseeing close to a hundred operations at any one time, so unless there are particular issues needing my input, I receive short bulleted internal reports of operations, mainly about progress and points arising. As for our legal department, currently I understand there are around thirty outstanding prosecutions and the last report I received concerning the Knights' case, was that our team is awaiting a date from the court to discuss legal arguments before it goes to trial. Mrs Leonie Vogel is our legal director and when she returns from Italy, I can arrange for her to come to Brussels and talk with this committee."

"So to make it clear to the committee, you are not prepared

to discuss Sir Richard Knight on any basis?" Meyer asked.

"I'm not saying that, Mr Meyer, you asked for the current position. I'll happily assist in clarifying the background and basis of the charges, but his prosecution and the legal points I'm not qualified to answer, it would only be my opinion. Then, as I was one of the targets of contract killers arranged by the Knights, I could be accused of being biased, so it is prudent that I keep personal opinions to myself."

"We understand, Colonel, and have no intention of placing you in a difficult position. We are here looking at the facts surrounding the UK government's request to allow them to prosecute and not the EU. We are also aware that the Knights may have committed a breach of EU human trafficking regulations, which is why the prosecution remains with Unit T. Is that your understanding?"

"It is. Although the UK has already requested that Unit T withdraw the charges of human trafficking violations on the basis of fresh information, I can't, only the legal team can do that - although I have informed the UK government I'm prepared to allow our intelligence unit to look at the evidence and send a recommendation to legal."

"I don't believe we can ask more of you. Thank you, Colonel. But please look at this new evidence very carefully as a matter of urgency. The UK's situation with the EU is at this time very precarious and to bring additional confrontation between the EU and UK is not what is wanted. Having said that, these are very serious charges, that resulted in the loss of life of not only UK citizens but citizens across the EU."

"I am fully aware of the implications, Mr Meyer, and will do as you ask. But you must understand the evidence submitted will require verification acceptable to a court. But from what I understand in regard to new evidence submitted by the UK, to verify such would place the Knights in a very high-risk position. I will need them to sanction such an investigation. If they refuse, then the legal position remains."

After Karen left, Emil Meyer looked around the room. "It would seem the UK has got a fight on its hands. I don't sense movement on the part of Unit T, from believing the Knights were working with the UK's Security Services. Also, the French government has made it clear they want to see the Knights prosecuted. They lost citizens as well because of the contract killers the Knights supposedly engaged. Then if it wasn't for Unit T, the contract killers would have escaped justice. We will reconvene when I receive their report."

The committee broke up, leaving only one man and Emil in the meeting room.

"What's your opinion, off the record, Francis?" Emil asked as he collected his papers together.

Francis sighed. "The problem I can see is evidence. While the EU courts will accept covert recorded evidence, in cases of human trafficking, in the UK courts, unsanctioned recording is not accepted as evidence. On that basis, the Knights would walk away. Is that what we want? I'll tell you, the French won't stand for it even if it eventually comes down to Colonel Harris being overruled by a vote in committee."

Emil shook his head slowly. "That is not a route I want to go down, she is far too unpredictable."

"She certainly is. If you remember the last time there was an orchestrated effort to have her ousted, it backfired when she took it personally and decided to investigate her opponents."

"I remember only too well. The fear among the ones playing the system when they heard Karen had ordered Unit T to investigate was unbelievable. I always say you can't cage a lion without the risk of it lashing out at times and she's very capable of that."

"True. Except at this moment it's been downplayed, leaving the press in the dark. If they caught wind of a cover-up, it could all blow up in our faces with only one person coming out on top, Karen Harris."

Emil sighed inwardly, Francis wasn't far wrong there.

***

Karen returned to her hotel. She was meeting Jasmin later for dinner. At that moment Stanley, her senior intelligence officer, called on her mobile phone.

"Hi Stanley, do you need me?"

"I do, I've a quick update that may change your plans going forward. The UK has just been in contact and formally requested our assistance in the disappearance of the two children. Apparently the registration number was false and turned out to be on the van of a builder who lives and works in Birmingham. He's been eliminated, after all, his van was plastered with his adverts. The picture of one of the kidnappers is fuzzy, spoiled would you believe by a spider deciding to make its web across the camera lens and sitting waiting for its dinner. They have come to a dead end and their hope is we may have intelligence on groups in the UK who could have taken the children. We do, but it's down to you as to where we go from here."

"I need to talk to a number of informers. The problem is, most of the trafficker groups in the UK who would take the girl would not want the boy. He'll either be dead, or put up for sale to a paedophile circle in the UK or Europe. Hopefully whoever has him will first make an attempt to sell before cutting his throat. If they do offer him for sale, I'll find out pretty quickly."

Stanley never ceased to be amazed at just how many contacts she had, in addition to all the ones Unit T knew about, in the criminal underworld, but didn't make his thoughts known. If Karen was talking to informers, they would be the ones she had recruited but not logged at Unit T. He had no issues with that. Every organisation had leaks, it couldn't be stopped. But if only Karen knew who the informers were, there could be no leak from his end.

"Very well, I'll leave it with you. On another issue, we've not talked as yet about how you got on at the Home Office?"

Karen told Stanley all that had been said.

"I have it all recorded as usual. Then, I expected the father to attempt to use his contacts to get the prosecution dropped. So it was no big surprise. What did surprise me is taking it as high as a junior government minister getting involved. At this moment in time he's very close to the charge of an attempt to pervert the course of justice."

"From what you have told me, I'd agree. I'll reserve judgement until I hear the recording. Do you want legal to read a transcript?"

"Most certainly, I've got to protect myself and Unit T against any charge of collusion. I've also had a meeting here in Brussels with a committee put together to consider the UK's request. To tell you the truth, I've hidden behind legal. Now they are waiting on me to look at the new evidence that Knight was working with the UK's Security Services, before reporting back to them. I intend taking Leonie with me. In my view, this is more for the legal people than me."

"Very wise, leave others more qualified to make a decision on this one, Karen. As far as the children go, will you be coming back home, or returning to London?"

"I'd like to say home, but it's looking more like London, now we're involved."

"Are you still with Jasmin?"

"I am. We've agreed to go halves on buying an apartment. She wants a base rather than Amsterdam, which would be useful to me, and better than sitting about in hotel bedrooms each month. Why do you ask?"

"If you do return to London, will you be taking her with you? If not I'll have a Dark Angel unit waiting there. Let me know what you decide."

Karen suspected this would be the case, as she had told Jasmin. "I've already talked to Jasmin about coming to London and she's agreed. I want to remain under the radar. The informers I need to talk to wouldn't take kindly to a lot of burly soldiers standing behind me."

"Very well, keep in touch, and take care, Karen."

Karen cut the call. To actually come out and request she take Jasmin was not like Stanley. He didn't trust her, believing she was a loose cannon. Understandable, she thought, after all in Jasmin's world, you died, you didn't go to prison.

***

Karen was on her way back to London with Jasmin. While in Brussels she had talked to a number of informers by telephone and among them, one had information which sounded not only interesting but worth investigation. She had made arrangements for a face-to-face as soon as she arrived in London, but not with her, with one of her covert operators - not that she told the informer that. In the meantime the informer was going to keep his ear to the ground.

Jasmin was sitting in the co-pilot's seat. She was looking through sales brochures at places she and Karen had seen.

"So out of all the properties we saw, you like the house set in twenty-five acres? Which would be the largest, besides most expensive, although pretty cool for a pad to crash out in?"

"It is, then it was the only one with an indoor swimming pool, sauna, cinema room – and had a massive garage and fantastic gardens. Importantly for me, it could also be made secure."

"Yeah, but something like twenty rooms is a bit over the top, don't you think? We'll be rattling around."

Karen shrugged. "It's not much larger than Corsica and smaller than France. I like my privacy these days, Jasmin, I've also got to think of Midnight. You can't have a little girl locked up in an apartment all day with nowhere to play. I've already got three apartments with balconies not really suitable for a child to play on. I don't want another, or I may as well stay in hotels. I'll employ a gardener and housekeeper. It'll be all right, you'll see."

"Okay, I'll let the agent know. But one point five is my maximum in cash, the rest, like I said, you get in gold."

Karen looked at her. "Have them set the sale documents up as a fifty-fifty ownership, but you pay one million and that's it, I'll cover the balance."

"Are you certain, Karen, I'm only winding you up and can pay my share, besides, it's a beautiful house so I'm more than happy to do that?"

Karen shrugged with indifference. "I know you can, but I was the one who wanted more of a home, rather than a pad to crash in. Then, it can also be used to host parties for the elite of Brussels. I've been advised I need to change my image somewhat and look as if I'm part of the 'in-crowd', even if I'm not. So I can hardly have people turn up to a two-bedroom apartment."

"You have a point there. Are we buying all the contents, which is optional?"

"Why not, it'll save traipsing around the shops. Then, neither of us are interior designers. I'll have the building contractors who look after my other properties paint the walls to brighten it up."

Jasmin sighed inwardly, there was no way Karen's cowboys were going to paint a house she partly owned. "No, I'll look after all that, it'll give me something to do, when I've little on." Then she quickly changed the subject, knowing Karen had too much on to mess around getting her contractors involved and would be more than happy to leave it to her. "I also picked up a British paper in the airport, it seems the world now knows you've taken over the investigation for the children,"

"Let's have a look at it."

Jasmin handed Karen the paper.

Karen looked at the headline. 'KAREN HARRIS CALLED IN - AT LAST' it said, along with the mandatory stock photo of Karen that seemed to always be included whenever her name was mentioned. This was followed by a report of a press conference with Sir Hardy Melcher, her police liaison contact. Karen read on.

Police are still baffled as to the whereabouts of thirteen-year-old Ryan Selby and a girl known only as Chinwe, who were abducted outside a fast food restaurant in Berwick-upon-Tweed. Sir Hardy Melcher, Unit T's liaison to the British government, announced late yesterday he had formally requested the assistance of Unit T. Asked 'why the delay', when for the last few days the press has pushed for Karen Harris, Unit T's commander, who is experienced in this type of crime, to be brought in, he told the assembled reporters that it had become increasingly clear an international trafficking gang was at work and under EU rules, the British government was required to inform Unit T.

When quizzed as to why Karen Harris hadn't been involved at the outset, particularly with her being in the UK at the time, he replied, "Procedures had to be followed before any approach to Unit T could be made. The most important being an initial local police investigation, with a report submitted to Unit T to indicate a suspected international criminal group could be holding the children. This suspicion supported the request for assistance. As for Unit T's commander already being in the UK when the crime happened, that was not unusual as she comes to the UK regularly. Even so, her presence would not have accelerated Unit T's involvement." Ryan's family also expressed their relief that Karen will now be involved and have requested a meeting with her. Sir Hardy discounted a meeting between them and Karen Harris, adding that the family already had police liaison officers keeping them abreast of any progress in the investigation. They would pass on any progress as far as Unit T is concerned. You can read the full story along with the entire interview on page two.

"Melcher always seems to get a hard time with the press. I'll have to call later to give him a shoulder to cry on," Karen commented putting the paper down.

"What's your plan going forward?"

"On the two children snatched?"

"Yes."

"I'm hoping the little boy is not dead but offered for sale.

I've an informer who has contacts within paedophile rings. He'll tell me if a child of Ryan's age is being offered around."

Jasmin looked across at Karen. "If you know of such people, as well as the dealers bringing in kids to service their depravities - why don't you do something about it? After all, if the legal option is a no-no, you could always raise a contract with me. The world would be a better place without those types of people."

"You think? It wouldn't, Jasmin, believe me. I know of these people's existence mainly through informers. Most gangs have their roots in the countries migrants are fleeing from, and then, those who pick the kids up are effectively scouts for the gang leaders. They prefer to operate at arm's length, keeping out EU jurisdiction. The next factor is cost. My funding is primarily to tackle criminal gangs based in the EU, Unit T would need to triple or even quadruple its operation to extend into Asia or the Middle East. So with those criminal groups we can only chip at the edges when they stray into the EU."

"And you're happy doing that?"

"I am, there's only me at the end of the day, Jasmin. I'm expected to coordinate everything, and there's not enough hours in the day for me to expand. Although having said that, I have on occasion covertly taken a little trip out of the EU to curtail the operations of certain criminals, if you get my meaning?"

"Then give me the job of getting shut of the odd nuisance out of reach. I've worked in most countries."

"I could, but you'd be on your own, I couldn't help like I can in the EU."

"I know, except before we met I was on my own anyway, so it would be no different."

Karen didn't comment, distracted by air traffic control

calling her and changing their heading.

"That's all I need, they are placing us in a holding pattern, we'll be late landing."

"Doesn't Unit T get priority?"

"Only the C4s and my aircraft if I am with them, but normally air traffic are very good and will, if possible, sneak me down even when it's busy, so I can't complain."

"No worries, at least this aircraft has all the facilities, including great coffee. Want one?"

"Good idea, black and no sugar please."

Jasmin had only been gone for a minute when Stanley called on her mobile.

"Hi, Stanley. I'm currently in a holding pattern over the South Downs of the UK, so I may drop off quickly if air traffic call. Have you anything important?"

"I've the report from the UK Intelligence Services. You'd laugh, Karen, it looks like a junior has written it and is treating us like fools."

"I half-expected that. Put it in my cloud account and I'll have a look. Also add your comments to save me wading through. While I'm in London, see if you can arrange a meeting with them along with Leonie from legal. I just want to get it over with and concentrate on real work."

"I'll do that. When will you be contactable?"

"Not sure yet, if I am it will probably be late at night. Depending what I can find out about the two children."

"Well, take care, and keep Jasmin close. I'll get off and talk to you tomorrow."

Chapter 8

Wearing jeans, bomber jacket and a baseball cap, with a hint of heavier make-up than usual, Kale Martin, a girl of twenty-eight with long black hair and a slim build, left the underground at Camden Town, before heading down the high street and making her way down to the towpath running alongside the canal. Kale was one of Karen's new covert operators, who had replaced Odette Boyer after her cover was blown in an operation with Circulo. She was a girl who came from a military family, began her career in the regular army and after a few overseas postings, including Afghanistan, applied to and was accepted by Unit T. There she had proved her worth, joining the elite Dark Angel unit before moving to covert operations. Now she was here on behalf of Karen to meet an informer.

The time was coming up to eleven at night and the high street was still a busy area - even so, the towpath at this time was not somewhere for a woman to be alone. Yet in Kale's world, this is what she had been trained for and she had no fear. Although to be fair, she was well armed, with a Glock handgun and an ankle knife, besides knowing Jasmin would be very close as her backup.

She walked past a number of street people huddled up and asleep, most looking like a heap of rags. A short distance down the path, a man around six feet tall, in a heavy black coat and sporting a beard, was leaning against the wall, cigarette in his hand. He turned his head to watch her approach.

As the informer was where Karen told her he'd be waiting, Kale approached him. "Charlie?" she asked.

"You're working with Karen?"

"Yes, I'm Kale."

"Where's she then?"

"I'm not sure, I never get that information," Kale lied. No Unit T operator would tell anyone where Karen was, even if they knew. "But while you can still talk to Karen by mobile, I'll be your personal contact for face-to-face meetings."

He smiled. "Since when has Karen begun fearing the streets? It's not how she's operated in the past."

Kale shook her head slightly. "Believe me, Karen does not fear the streets, but being Unit T's commander has curtailed unnecessary risks to a degree. Is it okay to call you Charlie?"

"I'm fine with that. Are you one of her Dark Angel soldiers?"

"For some years, before I was moved to work closer with Karen."

"That's good, it's a dangerous world you've entered, Kale."

"So I'm finding, but I'm cool with that. What are you up to these days, Charlie?"

He shrugged with indifference. "Still doing the odd job for the gangs, when they want a getaway driver that is. But it's not the same. Most robberies are done by young idiots on scooters. Then the big money is made by online fraud, there's nothing like the Brink's-Mat robbery today, you've got to be a computer whiz. That I'm not."

"True, and in my line of work, it'll never change and will always be hands-on."

"Yes and bloody dangerous for Karen, if the papers are to be believed over her recent operations?"

"Tabloid gossip, Charlie. But to business, what have you got?"

"Not here, walk with me. We'll get a drink at a late bar I

know, dressed as you are, no one would give you a second thought. And most knowing me, seeing me with a woman at this time, will think you're more than likely to be on the game."

Kale had no issue with that, in fact, it was better if people saw her as a pick-up, rather than talking in dark alleys. Even so, using her watch, which enabled communication between her and Jasmin, she had already pressed her winder once, indicating she had made contact and was safe. Now she pressed it twice to indicate to Jasmin she was on the move and needed no assistance. Three presses would require Jasmin to join her, four presses was a call for immediate assistance, and it was unlikely that she would be in any position to help. It also told Jasmin firearms were sanctioned if necessary. Even so, Jasmin was very good at melting into the background and Kale had had no sight of her since leaving the underground station. Yet she knew she'd be very close.

They headed to a local pub and while Kale took a seat in a corner, Charlie ordered two pints of lager at the bar.

"Who's the girl, Charlie?" another man standing at the bar asked.

He looked at him. "Fucked if I know, except she'd better be a good shag, after costing me a beer."

The man laughed. "Cheapskate, when all a girl's worth is a pint to you. Push her my way when you've had enough, at least she'll have real money in her hand."

Charlie smiled to himself. 'Yeah, like that's going to happen with a Unit T girl,' he thought. "Maybe, but don't hold your breath, I make them work hard - fucking hard," he answered, taking his drinks and walking over to Kale.

"What's he want?" Kale asked.

"Wants to take my place when I'm finished with you. Even

offering cash when all I'll pay is a pint."

"I'll bear it in mind if I'm ever caught short. So what have you found out?"

"Has Karen ever talked to you about the Mazur family?"

Kale thought for a moment. "I seem to remember a Polish group with a similar sounding name some years back requiring Karen to bring in Dark Angel support, if they're the group you're alluding to."

"Correct, in fact, it was close to all-out war between them and Karen, but they stepped back. In those days you didn't take Karen on if you wanted to live. As it is, the Mezurs are a large Polish family who originated from the north-east of Poland, which in fact was the old Prussia. This arm of the family found themselves in the area of Prussia taken by the Russians when it was divided after the war. When the USSR fell apart, most of the family moved to France, with some coming to the UK. They saw both countries as ready markets for using trafficked girls for prostitution, with weaker laws and indifference by the authorities to such activities. Of course they were pissed off when Unit T was formed and began taking an interest in them.

"It disrupted their supply and the running of prostitutes, but it didn't stop them, although they have diversified and purchased large amounts of cannabis, selling it through their massage parlours. What surprises me is Karen's fully aware of the Mazur family and their drug dealing, but she's never made a move on them, why is that?"

"It's not up to me to question what Karen is doing, Charlie, although our remit does not allow us to take down drug operations, unless it can be joined up with a trafficking violation. Maybe Karen has not made a strong enough link between the two yet, I wouldn't know. Tell me, the girls they use, are they from Russia, or Poland?" She was more interested in the prostitution side for Karen, rather than the drugs.

"Both, as well as Africa. But now mainly Africa. These days, most Polish as well as Russian parents have become far more sceptical when offers of lucrative work in the EU are made to their daughters, so the supply has all but dried up. Then, the Mazur family doesn't bring the African girls in themselves, they use groups that specialise in transporting such girls, as well as immigrants into Europe."

"You know about this because?"

He shrugged indifferently. "You need to know the way groups work, doing my job. I often move girls, already in the country, to other areas as well as new ones purchased by people like the Mezurs. I actually moved four new African girls only this week and I know of three going to the Mezurs here in London. Most are heavily drugged for ease of transport. It's how I make a living. Karen's aware I do this."

"That's okay with me, just don't get yourself caught. It's unlikely Karen could help you with the British police."

"I understand."

"As it is, Karen's interest is in a male child open to offers, as well as African girls. From what you told her over the phone, one such male child is available. Are the dealers still conducting auctions? I understood in our briefings at Unit T that was a thing of the past?"

"It is, most pimp operations in the UK, at least, order girls as required, specifying age and colour. They're not interested in standing around bidding. Even so, at times there's a cancelled order, maybe because the buyer has been arrested or killed. So the dealers ask around their clients. Buyers who want extra will make an offer over the phone after getting the photos and whoever offers the most gets the child, there's no going backwards and forwards between buyers, like at an auction. The dealer just wants to get shut."

"And you believe this is the case for the little boy?"

"Hold on - I said to Karen that I know a little boy has been offered by a dealer who uses me to deliver. Why he's been offered like this, I've no idea. Maybe it's a cancelled order, or there is another reason. I don't know, all I know is he's white and around twelve or thirteen. I don't have anything else, or any chance of finding out if he'd be the one Karen's interested in. But apparently the kid has been sold. They've been in touch with me and I'm their driver this Saturday."

Kale sipped her beer in thought. This was leaving her in a quandary. Would Karen want to snatch the child before Charlie collected, or would she allow the delivery to go ahead and take down whoever was using such children?

"Tell me, Charlie, so I can make it clear to Karen, while he's waiting to be moved to his new owner, will he be looked after by a minder, rather than the dealer?"

"Children are always with minders, so if a child is found the crime cannot rebound onto the dealer. For them, it's just a straight sale and holds little significance, beyond getting shut."

"In that case I suspect Karen will want to take down the buyer, she'll have no interest in a minder, they would be replaced. Then, with her knowing the Mazur family are still active in human trafficking, she will look closer at them," Kale told him, at the same time pulling out a gold sovereign from her jeans pocket and pushing it in his hand. This was the normal way informers would be paid for top information. A sovereign was worth around two hundred and fifty pounds and easily cashed in the many jewellery shops or pawnbrokers, leaving no paper trail. "Once you have the collection address, let Karen know and you're finished as far as the operation goes – then the balance of three more sovereigns will be paid. She will take it from there."

"You're a good girl, Kale. We'll meet more. I'll be in touch, give me a bit of verbal and leave."

They began a low-level argument, resulting in Kale standing up, ready to walk away and looking down at him. "And another thing, I'm worth more than a fucking glass of beer thank you," she scorned, then turned to leave.

However, she hadn't seen two men enter the bar and virtually walked into them. One grabbed her arm, while the other looked down at Charlie.

"We were told you were here, Charlie, who the fuck's this?"

Kale could see the shock of seeing them on Charlie's face. Who were these men? She decided to step in and give him time to pull himself together.

"So that's another lie, called himself Bert, besides expecting a shag for a pint of beer." Then she glared at Charlie. "I suppose the flat you claimed you'd take me to is yet another lie? Probably expecting to have me up against the back wall of the pub?" Kale cut in, shaking the man's hand off her arm and trying to leave.

"You're going nowhere, so don't move," the man told her.

The other man moved to prevent her leaving.

The man who had done the talking looked back at Charlie. "How much is she asking?"

"Fifty bloody quid for half an hour. I've not got that sort of money."

"I hope not, after all you owe Marcus a grand and you've been avoiding us for the last week. Marcus wants to talk to you."

"He's in debt as well. That's all I need. Now I am off," Kale added to their conversation.

The man spun around, his face inches from Kale's. "I told you, stay where you are, what don't you understand in that?"

She shrugged. "If that's what you want?"

Satisfied Kale wasn't moving, the man turned to his mate. "Take Charlie to Marcus, I'll join you later at the club."

Charlie left the pub with the other man.

Now they were gone, the man firmly gripping Kale's arm, propelled her to the bar, placing a ten pound note on the counter. "We'll use your upstairs, Stan, okay?"

Stan took the money and nodded his agreement. Marching Kale through to the back and up a short flight of stairs, he pushed her into a room with just a bed. Slamming the door shut, he stood looking at her.

"Prostitute are you? Why have I never seen you around?"

Kale shrugged indifferently. "How would I know, I've lived here long enough."

"Cocky fucker as well. You know what I think? It's a load of shit coming out your mouth and you're not a regular working this area - maybe trying to take work off the locals. Who's your pimp?"

"If I'm local or not, why should I worry what you think? As for naming my pimp, he'd kick the fuck out of me if I banded his name about to every John."

"Maybe, except with an attitude like yours he'd not be the

only one. But I like a girl with spunk," he came back at her, at the same time pulling out a wad of notes, counting out fifty pounds and throwing them down on the floor in front of her. "You've been paid - get rid of the jeans."

Kale sighed inwardly, this was getting heavy. She had already realised she'd made a grave error of judgement by going to the pub with Charlie. Adding to that, there was the dilemma of allowing this man to take her, or risk wrecking the operation and Charlie possibly losing his life. Then, she was all too aware in taking a covert job working with Karen, at times she could find herself in this type of situation, after all, her work surrounded human trafficking and paid sex. So to be coy about having to remove her knickers on occasion meant she should never have accepted the position. Even so, in this instance, did she have a need to sell herself and would it serve any advantage? After all, the information she'd been given would direct Karen to the possible holders of the African girl, leaving only the problem of a call from Charlie to locate the lad. To make that decision required a question to be answered.

"What will happen to Bert or Charlie as you call him? Are you going to beat him up if he doesn't pay this man Marcus?"

"What's it to you? Charlie knows the rules, pay or face the consequences. As for you, I've not got all night, so stop pissing around and get rid of the fucking jeans, before I rip them off?"

With the realisation that Charlie may well be unable to drive later this week and he'd be replaced, Kale could see no value in carrying the pretence on.

"I think not. I'm fussy who shags me, even for money, you don't come close."

The man's mood suddenly changed and in less than a

second he'd raised his hand and unexpectedly for Kale, slapped her hard across the side of the head, sending her sprawling. "You're fucking fussy, comparing me to that little shit Charlie," he shouted down at her as she pulled herself up to face him, but a lot further away.

While he'd been speaking, he had pulled out a flick knife from his pocket, snapping it open, with the obvious intention of hardening his demand with a threat. "As for that insult, if you don't perform, you'll be spending time in hospital after I beat the shit out of you."

Kale gave a hint of a smile. "I see, you expect me to grovel, because you're holding a pathetic little knife used by children, do you?" she said, at the same time backing even further away to the far wall, before reaching down and drawing the knife from the ankle strap under her jeans.

"I also have a knife, so let's see just how good you are, but be warned, unlike victims of the loan shark Marcus, like Charlie, I can defend myself and know how to use my knife." Then she shrugged with indifference. "I always fight with the intention to kill - not maim as you're threatening."

The man knew knives and a cold shiver ran down his back after she produced a British SAS-issue Fairbairn Sykes dagger. In the right hands, this was a far deadlier weapon than what he held. But that was if, as she claimed, she knew how to use such a weapon. Although from the way she stood, the way she held the knife, she gave every indication she did. He suspected he wasn't facing a prostitute attempting to defend herself, but someone far more dangerous.

Karen in the past had been given such a knife by an SAS soldier when she was first abducted and on the run in the Lebanon.

He'd told her this was a weapon of not only defence, but attack and used correctly, could save her life. After Karen's initial training, followed by her time in Unit T's Dark Angel covert operations unit, this weapon had on many occasions done just that and she always carried it. Now she insisted all her covert girls did the same and knew how to use it. With Kale, an ex-Dark Angel soldier, she really did know.

"Who the fuck are you?" he demanded.

"At this moment your possible executioner, but it's healthier for you not to know more about me, apart from the fact I have dealings with Circulo." Kale had of course bent the truth. While most of her work to date did surround Circulo, it was not as she was insinuating, for them, rather against. Circulo was also a name many in the criminal world would know and fear, being an Italian-run criminal cartel deeply entrenched in both human trafficking and drugs. Kale was certain the man would also be aware that to attack, injure, or even kill a Circulo girl, as she hoped he'd now believe her to be, was not advised. They would find out who she had been with, then his life would be worthless.

"You were watching Charlie for them?"

"Like you with Marcus, I don't ask questions, but do as I'm told. So do we fight, or do you drop the weapon and lie down on the bed. We'll wait a short time to give credence to your claim you got your shag, then I'll leave. Attempt to follow and I will kill you - have no doubt."

Convinced he would have little chance against such a weapon and the person holding it, he snapped the flick knife shut, dropped it on the floor and lay on the bed, all the time watching her, not sure if she would still attack him. As it was, what happened next made him even more certain he'd done the right thing not taking her on, as Kale returned the knife to her ankle strap and pulled out a handgun. This was one dangerous girl, quite prepared to take him on with a knife, possibly for the adrenaline rush of hand-to-hand combat, when all the time she carried a gun.

Kale, on her part, leaned against the wall, watching him and saying nothing, fiddling with the gun, at the same time pressing the winder of her watch three times for Jasmin to come. Eventually she replaced the gun in her pocket.

"Right, I'm off. Like I said, it would be better you never mentioned what happened in this room. I was a prostitute, we're going our separate ways after doing business," she stated, then left.

He stood, switched the light off and looked out of the window through a slit between the curtains. He saw her leave the pub and join another girl waiting across the road, before they both walked away. Smiling to himself, he selected a number on his mobile, the call was answered quickly.

"Yeah!"

"Marcus told me to call this number, if Charlie met someone tonight."

"Did he?"

"Yes, I at first thought her to be a prostitute, now I'm having doubts."

"Why's that?" the person asked.

The man related what happened, but finished with his own assessment. "I tell you, when she drew the knife and I realised this was no prostitute standing in front of me, with her talk of Circulo, I began shitting myself. The girl was a killer I've no doubt. And then, she wasn't alone, but met another girl outside when she left."

"Interesting, except Circulo talking to Charlie seems odd.

Tell me, was the girl she met, blonde, around five eight and slim?"

"Figure and height yes, not that I could see the colour of her hair, who is she?"

"A girl fitting that description did work for Circulo at times. A contract killer from South Africa. Except I heard she'd joined up with Harris of Unit T. Maybe she didn't. As it is, if you believe the girl you met is bad, the one with her is not one you'd pull a weapon on and live to tell your story. Neither would she have given you the option to drop the knife, she'd have gone for you, followed by putting a bullet in your head to make sure you were dead, before walking away."

The man shivered involuntary. "I hope you know what you're doing? These sound like dangerous people."

"Possibly, just tell Marcus I'll be in touch."

***

The person the man spoke to was in fact Fabian, who did a lot of business with Marcus. Marcus would over-extend loans to carefully selected vulnerable female clients, waiting until they could no longer afford the repayments. Then he'd introduce them to Fabian, who would exploit their debt and put them to work, either calling on clients at hotels or working the streets. Marcus had no issue in helping Fabian out with his suspicions of Charlie being a possible informer and his men going in to collect a debt had exposed a probable link. But also, this meeting confused Fabian, thinking it was Karen Harris Charlie was informing to, not Circulo.

Chapter 9

Karen and Jasmin were in Karen's apartment at Canary Wharf. Jasmin had gone out earlier and collected basic food items from a local shop. Now they were in the kitchen diner of the apartment, sitting at the table.

"So where do we go from here, if Charlie doesn't get back?"

Karen shrugged. "I'm not sure, mind you, thinking about it, Kale was lucky to be with him, at least I know his position with the loan shark. If she'd not been there, we could be waiting for a call that never came and not know why. Now we know the Mazur lot could be involved with Chinwe, I've asked Stanley to dig out all we've got and you and Kale will spend the next day or so nosing around."

"That's what I like to hear, action."

At that moment the mobile Karen used for informers rang. Looking at the caller, she pressed answer. "Charlie, don't tell me it's off, and you're in hospital?"

"Kale's told you what happened then?"

"She did, what was the outcome?"

"I've got till Sunday night to pay, convinced him I had a job and would settle, plus I'll give him a little more interest. I'm sorry Kale got herself compromised with one of his heavies."

"No worries, it's just part of the job. But you should have told me you'd a debt, I could have arranged something for you to pay it off."

"No, that's the last thing I'd want. He'd want to know where I got the money, after all I never have any – any obvious to my creditors, that is. So it was better this way. Anyway, it's still on, but there's a delay and they want me on Sunday now. I'll text the address where I'm to pick the child up and the time, once I know. Hope that's okay with you?"

"Better in fact, it gives me time to plan. When will you know the address of where you're delivering the child?"

"I never know that, Karen. A man will accompany me and he will know where we are going. I just drive."

"Very well, I'll keep the vehicle under surveillance. If the man with you suspects you're being followed - and really he shouldn't, our teams are very good - just press the brake pedal twice to flash the lights and we'll back away."

"That's no problem."

"Okay, we'll not talk again - your payment will be at our usual drop."

"Thanks Karen. I'll look forward to us working together again." He cut off.

"So it's still on?" Jasmin asked.

"So he says. I'll need Hanna to set up surveillance and follow the vehicle, we'll forget involving Dark Angel, I think between us we can manage, don't you?"

Jasmin grinned. "If we can't, we may as well give up and retire. Although thinking about it, lazy days on the beach followed by nights of passion after being chatted up by a hunk, are a good alternative."

"Rubbish, you'd soon be bored with that. Now we've work to do. I'll need to see Hardy, you can go and suss out the address the child is being picked up from after Charlie's texts. Just a general drive-past with a few photos as well as the back of the building. Then we'll all meet later, once Hanna arrives from Unit T, and discuss options."

***

"Karen, it's good to see you, take a seat while I pour coffee. Still black with no sugar?" Sir Hardy Melcher asked, after Karen arrived at New Scotland Yard and was shown to his office.

"Yes, please. I had a little time to read the paper on the flight from Brussels. Are the press still giving you a hard time then?" Karen replied, at the same time sitting down.

"It's more the tabloids, Karen. They have this fixation over you as some knight in shining armour riding to the rescue, more I might add for a boost to their sales, rather than a genuine interest in what you represent. Apart from that, it really winds up the senior police officers asking for your help, when they see your intervention not only as an admission of failure in the eyes of the public, but an affront to professional police procedures. It's understandable, when most have the belief that because you've never been in the police force you've little idea about how to conduct a professional and structured investigation. But of course, they don't have any comprehension about the size of Unit T, the people involved and what your intelligence unit already has on these groups. That can and does make a great deal of difference when conducting investigations. It all adds up to perpetuating the belief held by the press and often the victims' families, that only you can find their loved ones."

"Maybe, except they don't see the failures, only the successes. We're no better than your own police in many respects, it's just that we don't operate under a glare of publicity, unlike most police operations."

He brought their coffees over and sat down opposite Karen.

"So how are you these days? Last time we met you were obviously very tired and despondent. Not that I can blame you after an aircraft virtually crashed on top of you and minutes later, you were shot at by a deranged contract killer."

Karen smiled. "All in a day's work, Hardy. But I'm good, although I really could do with not having to work seven days a week, if only to bond more with Midnight. She's getting to the age when a child is becoming that little bit more grown-up, but is still a child and wants to experience and do everything. Being with her is like a breath of fresh air in the dark underworld I'm forced to live in. Mind you, taking holidays with her can be really stressful. Her constantly being on the go and me just wanting to chill out. I come back a complete wreck and very often to a number of stalled operations. No one seems to want to take the lead and make any sort of decision when I'm not there."

"Life and death decisions can never be taken lightly, Karen, at the best of times. I learnt that in the army. So it's understandable that people hold back for your input when you seem to make it look so easy. As for your experiences with Midnight, it takes me back to the time when my children were that age. Grab it with both hands, Karen, believe me it doesn't last long. They soon become teenagers, then your problems really begin."

"So I've been told, but she'll struggle to get one up on me, when most of the girls I deal with are teenage. Anyway to work. We've read the police report, they did a good job under the circumstances. On our side, we believe we know who the group is, but knowing and doing something are two different things."

He shook his head. "It never ceases to amaze me how you are able to pinpoint the perpetrators so fast, where we're still wallowing. Do you need assistance?"

"Not at this stage, but I've just one surveillance unit and only three combat-trained personnel in the UK, so I might need to call on an armed response unit, once I go deeper."

"Anything you want, Karen, you know that. Will you be attending any press conferences?"

"No, and you need to keep them away from me. It's bad enough them announcing to the world that I'm on the case, without getting more interference. The traffickers could panic and dump one or both children, although I'm also here for another reason, the Knight family."

Hardy looked confused. "I thought that was put to bed and is now with legal?"

"It was as far as I was concerned, but not for a senior member of HM's government. Let me explain." Karen went on to tell Hardy about her meeting at the Home Office.

"It's the old boys' network attempting to save one of their own, Karen. They live in a different world to us, with the belief they can control government thinking, as well as the civil servants." Then he smiled, adding, "But I suspect they have met their match with you, well I hope they have."

"Possibly. As far as the minister is concerned, legal have read the transcript of our meeting and they say it borders on an attempt by him to pervert the course of justice. I'll hold that in abeyance for the time being, pending my meeting with MI6. The report they've just sent in to back up their claims Knight was working for them reads like a poor novel. It seems to have been written by someone who believes he or she lives in the world of James Bond, and that I'm some sort of idiot. They will get a nasty shock if such an attitude persists."

Hardy sighed. "Take care, Karen, these are not nice people and can make your personal life very difficult in the UK. I suspect if you rock the boat, they would not be averse to setting you up for a gigantic fall."

"Probably, but what can I do? This was not a letter to me personally, it was an official report to Unit T. I may have a great deal of leeway in what I do, but there is a limit I can't go beyond before it's out of my hands."

"Yes, I have the same constraints and believe me, even in my mediocre position I've often had to walk a tightrope, risking being everyone's fall guy. In my view, with the UK virtually out of the EU, and still no firm commitment for even the police to carry on cooperating like they do now, let alone an agreement to keep funding Unit T, the Knights' prosecution could be passed back to the UK by default. Bearing that in mind, what's the chance of perpetuating matters as an ongoing investigation until it's certain just what's going to happen?"

"I could certainly push it close to the final day the UK actually crashes out, we're renowned for taking our time. Thanks for the advice, Hardy."

"You're more than welcome, although I'll miss you if we do split. You're so different to the people I deal with on a day-to-day basis."

They talked in general for a little longer before Karen left, heading back home.

***

Hanna Davis had been in Unit T for over seven years. She led the surveillance teams and would herself on occasion join a mission. So when Karen requested her team, this was to be one such occasion that she would work out in the field.

Hanna, with three others, arrived at the new apartment block in Canary Wharf, taking the lift to the top floor. They went into the apartment provided for security staff.

Andy, a lad who worked with her, gasped. “Wow, if this is our apartment, what must Karen’s be like?” he commented.

“Karen is your commander, Andy, and deserves your respect, always address her that way please and not by her Christian name. You also never talk about this apartment to anyone or its location.”

“Sorry, Hanna, I didn’t think.”

“That’s fine, now you and Michel, take the lift down to the garage and check out the two cars we’re using. Make sure they are full of fuel and the communications equipment is working correctly. We’ll eat in an hour. Arthur, you come with me, we’ve a meeting now and apparently Jasmin has already taken a few photos so we can look at the location and decide how we’re going to approach this operation.”

Chapter 10

Karen, driving the Range Rover, arrived at the MI5 building in Millbank, Westminster, for a meeting arranged by Unit T. With her was the head of Unit T's legal team, Leonie Vogel. They were directed to a parking spot in the underground car park, entered from the rear of the building. This was essential for a vehicle carrying weapons. It could not be left unattended on the street. After signing in and handing her personal weapon over to security, Karen and Leonie were shown into a meeting room on an upper floor overlooking the Thames. In the room were two men, one introduced himself as Max Hart, the other Charles Sutton. Both men were in their forties and in Karen's opinion looked ex-military. Coffee and biscuits were brought and they were left alone.

There were no pleasantries, Max was leading the conversation. "You have read our report and the work Sir Richard was doing for us, Colonel?"

"I have."

"Then we assume you're satisfied that he was indeed working for us and although his actions can never be made public, the allegations against Sir Richard can now be dropped?"

Karen shrugged with indifference. There was no way, as far as she was concerned, that the Knights would be allowed to walk away. However, she didn't voice such an opinion, but directed the answer away from herself. "That is no longer my decision. Miss Vogel from Unit T's legal department will explain to you the legal position Sir Richard and his son find themselves in."

"Thank you, Colonel," Leonie answered, opening a file in front of her before looking up at the men watching. "So I can have it clear in my mind as to what you are asking, Mr Hart. Are you seeking to have the human trafficking violations withdrawn, based on your claim Sir Richard was working on your behalf?"

"That is our position."

"Within this claim that you were working with Sir Richard, are we to assume it was also your department that asked Sir Richard to engage contract killers to assassinate Colonel Harris and apparently, the current leader of the criminal group Circulo, which incidentally, does not form part of the conspiracy to murder charges against Sir Richard?"

He glared at her. "Of course you can't assume we had anything to do with engaging contract killers. What do you think we are?"

"My personal opinion is not at issue, Mr Hart, I'm only requesting clarification as to what parts of the case against Sir Richard Knight and his son your department is asking to have dropped."

"We require only the human trafficking charges to be withdrawn. Criminal charges regarding the so-called collusion between Sir Richard and contract killers will then be transferred to the UK. Then the Director of Public Prosecutions will decide if there is a case to be answered under UK law."

Leonie looked at him for a moment, more for effect rather than any confusion. "I suspect by your words you don't think there's a case to answer?"

He shrugged, effectively brushing off her accusation, although he did know the Knights had made arrangements to have the charges thrown out. "I've no idea, that's nothing to do with me, the only evidence I know of is a taped conversation with him, his son, and a co-conspirator who has left the country. Whether that is sufficient evidence to lay before a court in the UK is anyone's guess."

"Very well, I'll give you my answer based only on the human trafficking charges," Leonie began. "I've looked at the report your department sent to Unit T, in support of your claim Sir Richard was working on behalf of the UK government. It is confusing in so much as the content lacks sufficient detail to place before the courts. Therefore, I've requested that Unit T's intelligence unit investigate and report back to my legal team based on your information. If they confirm there is sufficient evidence to support the claim that the Knights were working covertly, I will offer no supporting evidence to the court on the specific charges of human trafficking violations. Legally, there is no other method to have the charges set aside, with documents already lodged at the court."

He stared at her in obvious shock. "Are you mad, woman? For Unit T to make any sort of investigation would require them to talk to people. A word to the wrong person and it may get back to Circulo that Sir Richard was working for us. If that happens he's dead. Tell her, Colonel, am I not correct?"

Karen sighed. "Miss Vogel is not mad, Mr Hart, she is only clarifying the legal position. Although I cannot disagree with you that there will be risks for Sir Richard, but that's the chance all informers and covert operators take, when working both sides of the fence. We also operate with informers as well as covert operators and take a great deal of care in how we use their information so as not to place them at risk. In Sir Richard's case, he was given every opportunity in a private session with me, before the charges were made, to make Unit T aware of his circumstances. A transcript of our conversation can be made available to your department, if a formal request is made, in order to satisfy yourself that at no time did either of the Knights mention their involvement with the UK's Security Services. Although the reality is, your department also chose to keep us in the dark until this week. That's a delay of two months with the legal wheels already turning, when all you had to do was talk to Sir Hardy Melcher, Unit T's UK liaison officer, and he would have informed us. Now Unit T is in the position to find sufficient evidence to lay before the court and convince them of his collusion with your department. How you expect us to do that in any other way, when up to this meeting secrecy from your department and indeed Sir Richard has prevailed, I'm not sure? Personally, I think it is too late, you should stand away and let the law take its course, unless he and his family are prepared to go into a safe house under protracted protection until we can round up the groups he's been involved in. That could take months, maybe years."

"And in the meantime, you keep hold of his money, allowing him a pittance to live on," Max said with obvious contempt in his voice.

Karen didn't rise to his insinuation that all she wanted was the Knights' money. "I'm not sure if you are aware, under EU regulations, we are required to freeze the assets of any person who is accused of human trafficking, or in fact using the services of a person who has been trafficked, pending court appearance. On conviction we make a proceeds of crime application. In the meantime we have no issue in Sir Richard Knight requesting reasonable funds to live on, which he is already doing. Although he can hardly carry on a life in the public spotlight when under protection. It would be pointless. As it is, where do you want Unit T to go from here, regarding protecting your covert operator, Mr Hart?"

"You do nothing until I take advice. Your interference has caused enough problems, we will be in touch."

"Excuse me, I'm just doing my job, where you're meddling in areas where you have no experience. Such interference kills people. Besides, Sir Richard Knight's problems are of your making, not mine," Karen came back at him.

He glared at her, annoyed that his demand they step away had been effectively thrown in his face. It was obvious Karen had no intention of doing any such thing. His annoyance got the better of him. "When I need to seek advice from someone who the entire Security Services consider a laughing stock by the way she goes on, without even a level of education that would secure a job as a junior in our service, it's time I retired. So I reiterate, you wait - until we tell you what we want done."

Karen, along with Leonie, stood to leave. Karen looked down at him. "Then we understand each other, Mr Hart. Unit T will await your response with interest, but don't hold your breath we'll act in a positive manner. In the dangerous and unpredictable world of the human traffickers, you need us far more than we'll ever need you." Then they both walked out of the room, with Charles Sutton seeing them out of the building.

***

Later the same afternoon, once he'd returned to his own office, Max called Sir Richard.

"Have you sorted the idiot out?" Sir Richard asked.

"I haven't, you've let it go too far, Richard. She's hiding behind the legal lot and they are insisting the court makes an order. Then these accusations of you engaging a contract killer to take Harris out only add to the complications. MI6 can't be associated with an attempt on her life - far too many people, innocent people, died, we'd be castrated in the press."

"The contract killer claim is all hogwash, a set-up to line her own pockets. Just get this collusion with Circulo to be an official undercover operation that she wrecked by pulling me in, and once back in the UK courts, like I said, I've been assured by people in the know that the contract killer accusation will go away."

"Very well, but we must meet for me to really understand what was going on between you and Circulo's leader, Ale Bassani. I'm going to have to put a few top secret files together that even she cannot dispute without actually asking the trafficker groups and she won't do that."

"You'd better be very sure about that. Harris knows a great many people, and in the past has been on speaking terms with Ale. She'd not be averse to playing dirty and pulling us all down. After all, in her view, there's a great deal of money at stake, my money."

"I can only do so much, Richard, before senior people in the service want answers."

"Then we meet tomorrow. I'll let you know a location."

***

Karen parked up in the underground car park at Canary Wharf, after dropping Leonie at the airport, for her flight back to Unit T, and sat for some time in thought. The way she had been treated, it was as if she was the criminal, not the Knights. Then, while she was not convinced Richard Knight had been working for MI6, she had underestimated just how much clout and influence he had if people were prepared to perjure themselves on his behalf. Now she had a dilemma. Was she prepared to allow a man to walk away after he had managed to kill a soldier she considered a friend? Karen knew she couldn't, but how was she going to fight him? Leaving the car and going up to the apartment, Karen found Jasmin sitting reading.

"How did it go?"

"They intend to shaft me and let the Knights walk away scot-free. I need a drink."

"You needing a drink during the day - that's not like you Karen, you don't drink. But if you've been driven to it, I'll join you."

"Driven is a good word in this instance. As it is I have been known to have a few too many once or twice, particularly when I was a lieutenant. I'm not teetotal, you know."

Soon they were both sitting with a drink in hand and Karen told Jasmin what had gone on. She needed to tell someone, even if she had been an idiot believing she could bring the Knights down.

"It seems to me there are a few in the conspiracy. If you had a different hat on like that of a Circulo leader, they would all be dead by this time next week."

"They would, but I'm supposed to uphold the law these days."

"True, but this Max Hart guy, is he the kingpin and without him, would the cards begin to fall?"

"I don't believe so. He, in my view, is too low down in the pecking order against billionaires like the Knights. He could be in it for a nice cash bonus, for keeping the Knights out of prison."

"Then he's corrupt and holding a position of power. Raise a contract and let's see what comes out of the woodwork once he's gone. You owe it to Malcolm and his wife to have someone pay."

Karen sipped her drink. Malcolm had been her driver, killed by two contract killers the Knights had paid to take her out. "You know, if things get worse, I'll seriously consider giving you a contract. Because of the Knights, I reckon they are close to throwing me out of the UK anyway."

Jasmin smiled. "Never look at it that way, this is a war begun by the Knights. They need to learn not everyone will lie down and be walked over. So after we sort out whoever is taking the boy, then we sort out the Knights, one step at a time."

Karen smiled to herself. Jasmin's world was very black and white. You lived or you died. But no matter what, you couldn't fight the establishment, they never forgot and never went away. Very much like Unit T, once it had eyes on someone, it would watch and wait until they hung themselves.

Chapter 11

Charlie was confused when he arrived to pick up the child for delivery. A man he'd never met before was in the hall of the house when he was let in. This man was small but broad and well-built, with a constant scowl, giving a look of intimidation.

Fabian came out from a back room. "Ah, Charlie. This is Mongkol, he's going with you today."

"If you say so, what time do we leave?" Charlie asked.

"Now, the car's already loaded. I'll open the garage."

Charlie went through the entrance from the house into the garage. Climbing in, he glanced back to see something quite substantial in size on the back seat, covered with a blanket. Mongkol joined him in the car and after backing the vehicle out, they were on their way.

"So you work for Fabian?" Charlie asked, in order to make conversation.

Mongkol looked at him. "No."

Charlie was taken aback a little at his curt reply, expecting more of an answer. "Then, if not Fabian, why the fuck are you here?"

"You're paid to drive, yes?"

"Yes."

"Then drive. Who I am, who I work for, if I actually do, is of no concern for you."

Charlie said no more, yet this man did concern him. His accent pointed to South America, and he knew Fabian dealt among others with the Sinaloa Cartel, who, while Mexican-based, had extensive operations across all the South American countries. Fabian's dealings were with the Colombian part of Sinaloa. So could Mongkol actually be Colombian? Charlie shuddered inwardly, the Sinaloa didn't mess around giving a person the benefit of the doubt, as far as being an informer was concerned. They would kill that person, even if they were found later not to be an informer, it didn't matter, they were no longer a problem. Now very aware that Karen would be close by, he became nervous. If Mongkol became aware of them being followed, being a suspected informer could point directly to him. Charlie decided to pre-empt such a possibility by raising a concern.

"I've a feeling we're being followed," he commented.

Mongkol turned and looked back. "Which vehicle?"

"Two cars behind. It's been with us since we left the house, while other vehicles have come and gone."

"Take a few turns before coming back on the route and let's see if it follows."

He did as suggested. "The one I thought was following us didn't, but one behind it has," Charlie told him, in an attempt to convince Mongkol that he was not involved. Charlie knew the car behind must be one of Unit T's, taking over from the original car. He could have warned Karen by flashing his brake lights, but on this occasion he decided it was important to convince Mongkol they had been followed from the outset and hopefully direct any suspicion away from himself. His reasoning being that Karen may look as if she'd backed off, but she would still be following, of that he was certain.

Mongkol pulled out his mobile and called Fabian. They talked in a language Charlie couldn't understand.

"Looks like someone is on to us, Fabian. We turned off and a car kept with us. That one's gone now, but that could just mean they have changed over."

"Interesting. Was it you or Charlie, who noticed the tail?"

"Charlie, but I'm not sure how he knew so quickly, the roads are busy, unless he was expecting it to happen?"

"Yes, those are my initial thoughts too. Carry on as planned, let's see where this leads."

Mongkol cut the call and looked in the wing mirror, but being on a main road with a number of vehicles, he wasn't sure.

"You've told Fabian?" Charlie asked.

"I did, we carry on."

"I'm not sure, if it's the authorities I'm not risking arrest. We should abort and return, what's a few days' delay?"

"You don't make that call, Fabian does. Unless you want to get out of the car and walk? But don't expect any payment."

Charlie couldn't afford to walk away with Marcus on his back so he just shrugged. "Well, if you are still going, so am I," was all he said.

Neither said anything more about anyone following, with Mongkol restricting his conversation to giving directions by following the route on his mobile phone. Eventually they turned into an industrial estate, heading for a small unit at the far side.

Mongkol went inside and was soon out, telling Charlie to lend a hand in getting the box off the back seat and into the unit. Charlie was confused, he'd expected a drugged child under the blanket, but this was no fourteen-year-old and in his view, couldn't be much older than two to three to be put in the lidded box. But he kept his comments to himself, at least Karen would have a child, even if it wasn't the one she was looking for.

Once the box was in the warehouse, the man who opened the unit door made everyone drinks, delaying any early departure, which would be the norm on drop-offs Charlie made. Again,

Charlie was confused, this all seemed so laid-back, with no one even opening the box to let the child out. He wanted to say something, but was nervous of Mongkol. A man he didn't trust.

Chapter 12

Hanna called Karen. "The vehicle has just left the address you gave me, after backing out of an attached garage. There are two people in the front, but I can't see anyone else. The child may well be drugged and laid down on the back seat, or even in the boot area. I'll give you a running commentary as to the direction, speed and roads they're taking."

"Thanks, Hanna. We're on the move now."

"This is too easy, Karen," Jasmin commented, at the same time checking her handgun.

"I've got to agree with you. But just sometimes we get lucky and have an easy one."

Jasmin leaned over to the back seat, grasping hold of her sniper rifle and pulling it over. She began checking it, then attached the telescopic sight.

"We'll not need such heavy weapons," Karen commented.

"It's better to be ready for any eventuality than not. Besides, I've an uneasy feeling about this, so I think I'll suss out a location for me to watch the entrance. We should also position Hanna so she can report on any possible blind spot I have."

"If you feel that's how you want to play it, I'm cool."

"I do. Personally, I think you're far too trusting of the informer - and it's a set-up. Then who am I to say, I kill people for a living, I don't talk to them."

"Unfortunately, I don't have that option, I have to at least make an effort to follow the law. In my experience, if this is a paedophile who's purchased the lad, with the reality of being found out, they often end up blubbering like a baby."

"They are not delivering to a house, but have turned into

an industrial estate," Hanna's voice came over the walkie-talkie. "That discounts continued surveillance by vehicle, we'd be seen. We'll park and enter on foot."

"That's fine, we'll join you very shortly," Karen told her, then hesitated before a quick glance at Jasmin. "You may be correct this time."

Jasmin never answered, she'd not have been stupid enough to walk in with little or no backup anyway, no matter what the location was. Recently, Karen seemed to have been acting stupidly, particularly as to her own safety and risking others in doing so. In Jasmin's view, Karen's extensive experience should have told her nothing was adding up. Why she was acting this way, Jasmin couldn't imagine.

***

The unit on the industrial estate was located in a far corner, with two-metre high palisade fencing to the rear and one side, allowing just enough room between the fencing and building for anyone caught inside, in case of a fire, to exit a fire door. The frontage was a set of offices to one side and a large single-roller shutter door to the other. Two vehicles were parked outside. One, a small van, the other a car.

Karen joined Hanna, while Jasmin wandered off to find an observation point where she could target the front of the building.

"The car belongs to the people delivering the child. We have photos of the two men who were inside the car, carrying something with a rug wrapped around it through the main door. We could only see one person inside who opened the door," Hanna told Karen.

"They've picked a good day, the estate is deserted," Karen commented. "Once the men who delivered the child leave we'll give it half an hour and if the other vehicle's not left, Kale and I will go in."

Hanna looked at her. "Kale I can understand, but you shouldn't be taking risks."

Karen just shrugged indifferently. "Jasmin said the same, but it's what I do, besides, there's very few of us and Jasmin wants to stand back with her sniper rifle. I need to seriously talk to that girl, when I have time, she's too trigger-happy."

"Sensible, more like. This isn't right, Karen. I've been on too many not to smell a set-up. I agree there should be two going in so I'll replace you if you want? I'm fully trained to handle and use a firearm. Then, I'm more than happy, knowing Jasmin will be watching my back."

"This is not what you do, Hanna, you shouldn't be risking your life."

"We all risk our lives in the business we're in, Karen. I'm no different to anyone else here."

"You're not, and I'm not for one moment questioning your competence, Hanna. But you're not front line when people like me and Jasmin are around, this is what we're paid for."

"At one time you were, Karen, but you've moved on and shouldn't be risking your life unnecessarily. You give us all a purpose for being here, apart from carrying responsibility for hundreds of victims in LBNF under your care, the safety of your troops at Unit T and then, there's a little girl at home who also depends on you."

With Hanna's mention of Midnight, Karen suddenly had a realisation. "God, with you mentioning Midnight, I'd forgotten it's her birthday tomorrow. I'll have to try to be there."

"No, Karen, no matter what, you go home. Don't leave

her alone on her birthday. We'll keep you up to date with what's happening."

At that moment Jasmin called them on a walkie-talkie. "I've sorted a position, Karen."

"Okay, now it's just watch and wait."

***

Half an hour after the car driven by Karen's informer Charlie had left, with Mongkol beside him, there had been no movement from inside the building. Kale, accompanied by Karen, walked up to the main entrance door and pressed the intercom. This was to be Kale's operation and she would lead, leaving Karen as backup.

"What do you want? We're closed," came a male voice from the speaker.

"We're from Unit T, with a warrant to search these premises. Open the door," Kale demanded.

The electronic catch on the door clicked.

"It's open," came the man's voice again.

The two girls looked at each other, Karen lowered her voice. "This is not right, draw your weapon and release the safety. If we meet a deadly response, you hit the floor no matter what and call Jasmin for assistance. I'll protect you."

Kale just nodded and pulled her gun out.

Kale pushed the door open. She also took a small strip of plastic from her pocket and pushed it into the latch of the door, making the lock ineffective.

Jasmin, covering the entrance door from her sniper position, would, if Kale or Karen pressed their watch winder four times to indicate they were in trouble, need to enter the building. The open door would allow her to do just that.

The entrance door led into a small reception area with

an office beyond. Inside the office a man was sitting at a desk, a computer on in front of him.

"Come through," he shouted.

They both pocketed their guns before going through.

The man, thin-faced, with heavy glasses, leaned back in his chair to look at them. "So you say you're from Unit T and have a search warrant? Why you'd need one I've no idea, you only had to ask to be let in. But with your presence seemingly being official, I suppose we'd better go through the motions - you show me the search warrant along with identification."

Kale came forward and showed him the warrant as well as her ID. Followed by Karen flashing hers, not that he could read her name on the ID. Karen didn't want to introduce herself, she wanted to remain low-key and let Kale lead.

"Well, everything looks genuine enough, but don't you lot deal in human trafficking and the like? You're not going to find an illegal immigrant or trafficked women here, unless you've read about us on the internet and are really here for a wood burner, we do an extensive range?" Then he shrugged. "Even then, we import and sell to retailers, not the public. But seeing as you're from Unit T, I'll make an exception, for cash that is."

"A child was brought into this building only three quarters of an hour ago. Where is the child?" Kale asked, ignoring his offer.

He frowned, shaking his head slowly. "Three quarters of an hour ago you say? No, I don't think any child was brought here, I'd remember."

"The car that was here earlier, they brought something into the building covered with a rug. You're telling me it wasn't a child? We will search the premises, so it would be in your interest to cooperate, even if you believed you were just looking after the child for their father," Kale persisted.

"Ah, now I understand, but I think you've got your lines crossed somehow. A cash customer and his mate brought back a stove, wrapped in a blanket to keep the dirt off the seats of his car. Only a small one mind, for his canal boat. You wouldn't move a larger one so easily." Then his face lit up. "You didn't think their stove was really a child wrapped up in the blanket, did you? The wife will never believe this when I tell her, loves a bit of a giggle with others on their social media pages."

"Abduction of a child is never a giggle," Kale came back at him. "But if our information is incorrect, so be it. I'll still need to search the premises. First of all, your name and identification, please."

"The same name as on the plaque at the door, S and J Jones Importers. I'm the S bit for Sam, the wife's the J for Jean. So you're really serious, a child's been taken and you think it might be here?" he asked, at the same time pulling out his wallet and removing his driver's licence for Kale to see.

"There are many children taken, Mr Jones. Our job is to find them and take them home, besides arrest the perpetrators. My colleague will look around while I take your details."

"No problem, the code for the locked warehouse door is the wife's birthday, 2310. She put it in so I didn't forget it. Missed one year and got a right earbashing."

Karen wandered around. She suspected it was an obvious trick by traffickers in making whoever was following believe this was the destination, when in reality the child would have been in the boot of the vehicle and taken on to the actual drop-off point. All she could hope now was that surveillance still had eyes on the car and the real destination would soon be known. Then there was another alternative, but far more sinister. Had her informer been compromised after the events in the pub requiring Kale to pull a knife? Then, did they change the day in order to do this inept run just to confirm their suspicion of him? If that was the case, he'd likely be found dead in the next few days. Either way, she was back to square one and no closer to finding the two children.

Karen returned to the office and shook her head at Kale.

"Thank you for your cooperation, Mr Jones," Kale said. "You should understand we have to follow up information received regarding possible human trafficking activity. Even if on this occasion it was misinformation."

"You're welcome. Can I interest you in a log burner, then?"

She smiled. "Sorry, I don't have that sort of house."

Sam looked towards Karen, passing over his card. "How about you? You can't beat cuddling in front of a real fire, on a cold winter night. I'll give you forty per cent off retail."

Karen gave a hint of a smile. "I'll keep it in mind," she answered, pocketing the card.

Kale thanked him for his time and they left.

Sam watched them on the CCTV camera located at the front of the building. They seemed to be waiting for something. Soon a black Range Rover drew up. The two girls climbed into the Range Rover and it sped away. Then he dialled a number with a mobile phone he'd taken out of his pocket. It was answered quickly.

"Unit T, as you suspected, turned up shortly after your people left."

"Karen Harris herself?"

"I'm not sure, I didn't read their IDs close enough. But there were two girls, one in her mid twenties, around five eight, with dark hair and doing all the talking. The other older, five ten, slim, attractive with shoulder-length brown hair. But she stood back and said very little. Both entered with guns drawn, but soon holstered them. They left in a car driven by someone I couldn't see. So they hadn't come alone."

"Was it a black Range Rover, tinted glass and looked like it was heavily loaded?"

"Yes."

"Then that's Harris's armour-plated and bulletproof vehicle, so one of them could well have been her, or she was driving. If they return, call me. Thanks for your help, I owe you."

"No problems, I'll see you at the gathering later in the month."

***

Kale and Hanna returned to the apartment next to Karen's in order to make out their reports, while Jasmin and Karen went through to Karen's apartment. Jasmin poured them both a drink, then flopped down on a settee. To make matters worse, one of Hanna's surveillance teams following the car after it had left the industrial unit, reported it had returned to the same house it came from.

Karen considered raising a search warrant for the house, but discounted it. She had no real intel that gave her the basis for a search - only suspicion. So to show her hand at this stage in an investigation, could well be counterproductive. In the meantime. Hanna, using her team, would remain watching the house just in case the child was still there and the real run was to be made later.

"Well, that's an informer who won't be informing anymore," Jasmin said drily.

"You don't need to rub it in, I messed up, it happens."

"No Karen, it doesn't happen. Once Kale was compromised

in the pub the operation was doomed. The men we were following are not stupid, as you seem to think they are. Alarm bells would have been ringing over Charlie and Kale, leaving them little choice but to test out their suspicions and your operation just served to confirm them. I don't know what's going on in that puddled brain of yours, but you're not acting like the Karen I know you to be."

Karen sighed. "You're right, my actions have probably killed Charlie. Even so, he's a criminal, the same as them and has been moving victims around for years, so why should I bother?"

"You don't kill people, Karen, you're not like me," she came back at her.

Karen shrugged. "You really believe that, or you're just saying the words to placate me? Because the reality is, I really am like you and additionally I couldn't care less, Jasmin. My entire adult life has been surrounded by death. I'm immune to the consequences of people's actions, both for themselves and for others, because if I wasn't I couldn't do the job. Charlie could have had alarm bells sounding himself and bailed, but he didn't, the money was far too powerful. The same as the times you took your contracts. If you once stood back and had any empathy for the victim, you'd be finished as a contract killer. We both live in a spiral, always going down until one day we will hit the bottom, and the day we just give up, or we're dead. It is also the time I will finally meet our maker to explain why, since the age of eighteen, I turned my back on him. That frightens me more than you can ever imagine because I know he'll turn his back on me."

Karen hesitated for a moment, the tone of her voice changed, her eyes wetting. "My spiral is coming to the end. I've had enough, Jasmin, I can no longer think straight. I thought my last break with Midnight would give me the rest I needed, but that was a waste of time, kids don't let up from morning to night and it just added to my stress, watching where she was, what she was doing. Then this thing with the Knights only shows no matter how much I try, the real money men behind the scenes, I can never touch. Now I'm close to being kicked out of the UK, the cartels will be rubbing their hands with glee. We all eventually fail, no matter what our original grand plan was. People, some just jealous of your success, or criminals, because of your hounding, conspire against you. Then you're no longer flavour of the month. My life has become a personal monster, uncontrollable. The lines between right and wrong have been crossed so many times, making me no better than the criminals I take down."

Jasmin sipped her drink, looking at Karen. "I hope all this hogwash is not directed towards me, to make me feel sorry for you? Because I don't. After all, it's obvious you're burnt-out. So why are you messing around, call it a day and walk away? People rely on you to give direction, and it's clear to me looking from the outside, you can't. Not to do that places the lives of your own people at risk. As for the Knights, the day they paid money over to kill you, they threw down the gauntlet. So unless you're prepared to turn the other cheek and walk away, relying on the courts to obtain your pound of flesh, when it's increasingly looking like the charges will be watered down so much they will just walk away laughing at your naivety, say the word and I'll sort them out."

"I know you would, but it would point towards me being the instigator."

"True, but like with them, the reality is proving it, not just a belief. Alternatively, call Circulo and talk to Ale. He, like you, was targeted and left crippled. Believe me, if the Knights were working with him or not, it would make little difference. He won't pussyfoot around, he'd be bringing a contract killer in, or even send his own men and that would be that."

"I need to think, at this stage Circulo cannot be part of my strategy, but all that could change. I also believe if the Knights are working with Circulo, even if I talked to Ale, unlike you, I don't think he'd do anything. As it is, if people have an idea I can be made a fool of, they are playing a dangerous game. I will get at the truth - one way or another."

Jasmin didn't comment further, convinced even more that Karen was falling apart, when in the past, she'd be all fired up and looking for new leads. Even so Jasmin knew Karen was no fool, maybe at times making a bad judgment, which everyone does on occasion, and her final words 'one way or another' were not words to be ignored. She had the capability, the contacts and the clout to tilt the scales back her way, which often might not be strictly legal, but when did that worry her?

"I think it's time we had answers, I'm considering you utilising your particular skills and talking to this Sam Jones," Karen finally said after messing about with her smartphone for a few minutes.

"You have his home address?"

"I'll find it."

Jasmin stood. "I'll look forward to his reactions when he finds that getting into bed with human traffickers, he becomes a target."

"The same as we're their targets?" Karen asked.

"Maybe. Except when the waters are muddied, who are the hunters and who are the hunted?"

Chapter 13

Mongkol joined Fabian after leaving Charlie. "Was the unit visited by Unit T?" Mongkol asked.

"It was, but this is where it gets confusing."

"Why?"

"After what transpired in the pub between Charlie and Marcus's man I didn't expect Unit T to actually turn up, when they did I'm asking myself, how's that happened? And where does Circulo come into all this? Or do we still have an informer talking to Harris, and it's not Charlie."

Mongkol shrugged with indifference. "What's it matter if he's in with Circulo, or it was an elaborate plan by Harris to throw you off the scent, he's blown anyway, so get shut and let's move forward. My people are becoming restless over the delays."

Fabian leaned back in the chair he was sitting in. "We do need to move forward, I agree, Harris has been a thorn for some time, and if the name Circulo was as you suggest a red herring to confuse, I've a mind to give Harris a bloody nose."

"Explain?"

"I'm going to give Charlie something really juicy, which could well have him wanting to talk to the girl he met in the pub again. This time, whoever turns up, we take. Then, beat the truth out of her before sending what's left back as a warning to stay away."

Mongkol frowned. "Then you're a bloody fool, neither Unit T or Circulo would put up with that shit. Particularly Harris, she does not back down with intimidation such as you're suggesting, it would only serve to direct her considerable resources against any threat, particularly if one of her covert operators was injured.

Then you mentioned the other girl Marcus's man saw in the street - even from the weak description, if it is Unit T this could be the South African contract killer Harris uses. Sinaloa's already had dealings with that contract killer, when she was with her partner Nick. After he was killed we suspected she'd given up. That was until a Romanian group, operating in Ireland, told us about two girls the Murphy gang captured. Circulo believed one to be the contract killer who killed their previous leader. Before Circulo could get to her, she'd killed the two brothel owners holding her and fired their building. The Romanian lads insisted that both girls worked for Harris. If that's true and Harris raises a contract using her, you can guarantee it won't be a retaliatory beating from her, she kills for a living and you will die, have no illusions. She is far more dangerous than Harris herself and that's saying something."

The Sinaloa cartel in the past had indeed faced Unit T a number of times, often with costly results on their side. Mongkol knew the danger Karen posed when even against a Mexican-based international organised crime syndicate and one of the most feared, she never backed down. Sinaloa's origins were as a drug syndicate, which had since expanded into trafficking, money laundering and kidnapping, which was why they were originally targeted by Unit T. Mongkol was one of the cartel's police, meting out justice to those, internal to the organisation, who believed they could take more than their share. Retribution was swift and violent to both the perpetrator and often their family, serving as a warning to others to keep in line.

Fabian looked at him confused. "Since when has Sinaloa been afraid of the likes of Harris?"

Mongkol shook his head slowly. "Never believe we have fear of such a woman, we don't and given the nod, I would be more than happy to kill her. But Sinaloa has a great deal of investment in Europe, which is now becoming more lucrative than the States and far easier to operate in. Take Harris out and Unit T will seek the perpetrators, using their accumulated intelligence and powers to take apart the entire criminal operation in Europe, which would require many years to recover, if it ever could. While Harris is in charge, we all make money, but operate in an uneasy stand-off. Why, you might ask? We believe her methods are all about how the charity LBNF is funded and that, my friend, is Harris's baby, who has personally pumped in millions of her own money. But once Harris goes, Unit T would ignore LBNF and go all-out to destroy the syndicates."

"You're suggesting that the only reason Unit T does nothing is because Harris likes to nibble at the edges to fund her charity, without smashing the golden egg? That's not the Harris we know, if she can find an in to take us down, she wouldn't hesitate."

Mongkol laughed. "You think? I'll tell you this. Already she'll have so much on you and the ones who work for you all, if she really wanted you'd all be languishing in cells. But Harris has made a quiet fortune backpedalling, and while she's delayed, her status and personal wealth have grown at an alarming rate, even larger than that of the criminal groups she takes down. So who is the criminal here? Harris, almost certainly, but of course with money comes power, as all cartel leaders find. Except Harris's wealth ostensibly comes from legitimate funds which give her power. More than enough to dictate how much or how little she needs to do to keep hold of that power. The authorities mock her, the cartels do the same, treating her like a clown. But look at her actions, by my way of thinking, you see a very different woman. She's no clown, but smart, clever, often ruthless to get where she has."

"If what you say is correct, what do we do with Charlie?"

"You kill him. Harris will already have written him off, knowing his cover is blown and she was set up. She'll expect it and believe me she'll have no issues with that. For her, unlike covert operators, there is no allegiance to informers, with most in the trafficking business making a living as Charlie is, with his driving. If he lives, she'll know he could be used as a set-up to lure in her operative. Harris won't fall for that and will throw in everything she's got to protect her. Better kill him, rather than have her turn a contract killer towards you for taking out one of her covert operators."

"You seem to know a great deal about what Harris will be thinking and what she'll do. Why is that?"

Mongkol gave a hint of a smile. "To study your opponent is to know your opponent. You may have the impression Sinaloa is just a bunch of gangsters ruling with the gun? In a way it is, but it also employs the best brains available, like scientists, to find ways of hiding drugs during transportation, bankers to convert illegal earnings into legitimate funds, and strategists, to study your opposition, learn how they think, how they react. We have studied Harris and believe me, we know how she thinks, how she reacts, when to avoid action and her weaknesses."

"And the conclusions?"

"That is for us to know, but I will tell you one thing. Harris sits on the border of sanity and insanity, caused partly by the violent world she lives in. Such people, when holding unlimited resources, particularly military, can swing from logical to illogical in their actions, like you get with dictators. You don't throw the gauntlet down to such people, just to be bloody-minded, because you have no idea which way the pendulum will swing. Then, Harris has shown many times that she's not afraid of striking back with violence well beyond her supposed Unit T legal limitations. So where are those operatives and are they part of a private army? That, my friend, where Harris is concerned, is the million-dollar question."

Fabian took two cans of beer from a fridge and handed him one. Over the years he had managed to avoid reverting to killing a suspected informer, where with Mongkol, it was a way of life. Also, Mongkol was only here to look over their operation with a view to supplying. His journey with Charlie was to understand yet again how they coped with a possible threat from Unit T. In his view they had contained it, so would the death of Charlie have any real advantage? Even so, he could not afford to look weak with Mongkol if they wanted the increased business which the Sinaloa cartel was offering.

Mongkol on his part sensed hesitation, he didn't like weakness. If a job needed to be done, just do it and move on. "You're not in agreement?"

"This isn't America, we don't go around murdering people, the pigs would never let it go and we'd be hit on both sides, with Unit T on the other."

Mongkol shook his head slowly. "Then you shouldn't be in the business. While someone lives they can always talk, be it for money, or the offer of criminal charges being dropped, making Charlie always a risk and even more so, now we know there's the possibility of a direct line to Harris or one of your competitors, Circulo. Take the route you prefer and Sinaloa will walk away. If they do, you could well find they decide to close all routes leading to them. If you get my meaning?"

Fabian didn't need a veiled threat spelt out, he was regretting having any association with Sinaloa, but there was no turning back if he wanted to live. "You're right, he must go. I'll talk to Eryk and see it's done."

"No, you and I will do this, we involve no others. Have you paid Charlie?"

"Not as yet. I need to call him and make an arrangement as to the time and place."

"Then call him as normal. In the meantime, we still have the meeting with Blackthorn. That can be very lucrative, with your farm already supplying weed and now their supply of hard drugs from us."

"I'll do that. Although we're currently struggling to keep up with the demand on our side, the new farm should be online later this month, the first crop is close to harvest time."

"Yes, Eryk was telling me you've found a way of decarbing the cannabis in quantity, so taking bags of weed around, in his view, is a thing of the past."

"We have, and gone is the smell the police associate with people taking it in cars. Particularly if you don't smoke it and use our tablet under the tongue as an alternative. Then, using the method with other drugs added to the cannabis in preloaded capsules, for many ailments, such as migraine and pain, it's unreal, with up to a thousand per cent mark-up. We have so many outlets for this new approach, we're even flogging it for clients making up pain salve using oil and beeswax. Others are doing massage oils. I tell you, Mongkol, this decarbed method is the way to reduce our risk going forward."

"I can understand, but the farms are still high-risk locations."

"You're correct, except we're now growing the crops among other legal crops such as tomatoes. They in themselves are pungent and serve to mask the cannabis. It's the Asian gangs who are the idiots, turning private houses into farms and bypassing the meter to get free electricity. The companies that supply the electricity are getting wise to it and monitor excessive loads in areas to pinpoint illegal usage, followed by the police sending up drones with heat-seeking cameras. That sort of operation is losing out to technology and becoming costly."

"If this is so good, why not grow abroad where the law is more lax?"

Fabian gave a hint of a smile. "Using the UK has just been for trials, but the real lucrative market for the weed is mainland Europe. So very soon we'll be pulling out of the UK for the growing and concentrating those efforts in countries where the authorities are less interested in cannabis production. After all, we can transport the product back without detection, which in the past was always the stumbling block."

"I must see the operation before I leave."

"And you will, next week we will have a load ready to take through the decarbing operation. You'll be impressed, it's like a mini-factory."

Chapter 14

Chinwe, for the third time in a week, was bundled out of a van, which had backed into a yard where the entrance gates had shut. Around her neck was a strap, the other end gripped tightly by her minder. If she held back, or tried to run, the strap would tighten around her neck, choking her.

She had been purchased from Fabian by the Blackthorn group and put to work immediately, Blackthorn used their girls for parties arranged for visiting overseas businessmen, stag dos and birthdays. All the time the girls were with clients, their minder was always close by. The clients who took underage girls, such as Chinwe, were told in no uncertain terms of the risks of using such girls in the UK and to not only keep their mouths shut, but ignore anything told them by the girls and to report what was said back to their minder. All the girls were aware of this and all had been forced to witness punishments of other girls for opening their mouths. Some had even disappeared and were never seen again.

Chinwe, a strong-willed girl, had at first objected to being used as a sex object for men, receiving a number of beatings in an effort to force her into this life. However, all efforts using this method just strengthened her resolve. The traffickers, if they'd taken the time to understand Chinwe's life before she was taken, would have known she'd often receive beatings from her father, who drank in excess at times. Such drinking was an attempt by her father to forget the frustrations of a hard and difficult life he'd had to endure after leaving Nigeria and struggling to keep the family together, which then overspilled, to be taken out on his children. Of course her father's beatings were not as severe, but she took whatever Blackthorn did and never flinched. When the minders found they were getting nowhere, they resorted to drugs until finally tying her down to be offered to clients who paid for the privilege. One night of that approach broke Chinwe, who realised no matter what, for the time being, she had to do as she was told. However, even with all this going on, she was still convinced Karen would find her and she'd go home.

When they were not being taken to parties, up to ten girls were kept in a large room on the first floor of an old house, except Chinwe had no idea where it was actually located. The van they travelled in to so-called parties had no windows, the yard behind the house they left and returned to had high walls, giving no clues. When they were not working, they would sit on their bed, sleep, shower and eat. There was no means of recreation, television or radio. Not that there would be much time, with the mornings filled with getting themselves ready before leaving for their first job of the day by twelve. Now they were back for food and tidying themselves up before the night work, which often finished around one or two in the morning.

Chinwe took a large muffin filled with cheese salad and a plastic beaker of coke from a table laid out for the returning girls, and went to sit on her bed to eat. Another girl known as Shelly, originating from Romania, sat on the next bed along to Chinwe's.

"Still here, are you? It seems your friend Karen Harris has decided to let you rot. You'll never go home, so just accept it. The likes of her wouldn't be interested in a nobody who doesn't even own the clothes she stands up in, besides being miles from home?" she mocked.

Chinwe looked at her. "Mock all you want, but she will come, you'll see, even for someone like you."

Shelly, who relished winding up the girls, placed her half-eaten muffin on the bed and stood before coming over to Chinwe, who'd carried on eating. "Someone like me, what do you mean by that, you piece of black shit."

Others in the room also stopped eating. Shelly wasn't one to be insulted, she had a short temper and had beaten up two girls. Fortunately not to the point where they couldn't work otherwise Martin, who looked after the girls, would give Shelley a good hiding as well as extra hours to make up his losses. In his view, low-key aggression between them was good for the girls to let off steam, it kept their frustration over captivity in check. However Chinwe didn't react, but carried on and finished her muffin. For her, food was, and always had been since she was born, more valuable than gold. She would refuse nothing, eat everything, even if she didn't like it.

"I'm talking to you," Shelly shouted, annoyed she was being ignored, at the same time giving Chinwe a shove.

Chinwe stood. "You are, what do they say - an idiot. Even if you don't want to go home, I do. My mother was crippled, after she'd been beaten many times by sticks from soldiers demanding food we didn't have. My father, a drunk and weak-minded, ran away and hid, only to be found, then killed in front of us. Without me, my little brothers and sisters would find it very hard to get water. It is a very long way from our village and dangerous to walk alone. Every time we went, they'd risk being taken the same as me."

"Oh, I'm so sad for you, can't you see the tears?" she mocked. "But you'd better get used to being here - because no matter what, you'll never go home."

Chinwe gave a hint of a smile. "I will go home, you can be very sure of that." Then she collected her empty beaker to return it to the table and began to walk away.

"Where the fuck are you going? I want an apology," Shelly shouted after her.

Chinwe ignored her.

Shelly ran after her and thumped her hard in the kidneys, sending Chinwe sprawling across the floor. Following her, she began kicking and screaming at Chinwe. Chinwe knew how to protect herself and rolled up in a ball. That was until one blow from Shelly's shoe caught her head. Chinwe suddenly stopped trying to protect herself and became still.

Shelly stopped kicking, looked down at her inert body. "Get up!" she shouted. But Chinwe didn't move. Other girls were now taking a deeper interest and one came over, kneeling down at Chinwe's side.

"What's wrong with the bitch?" Shelly demanded.

"She's not dead, no thanks to you, Shelly. But you're fucked when Martin comes back and finds she can't work," the girl answered.

"Then we say nothing, tell him she tripped and hit her head. Anyone objecting to my story will get the same as her later?" Shelly demanded with aggression in her voice.

Most nodded their agreement.

At that moment Martin came in the room. He looked at Chinwe and the girl at her side. "What the fuck's been going on?"

"She fell and hit her head," Shelly cut in before anyone else could reply.

Martin said nothing and came over and knelt down to check Chinwe over. "Think I came on the last banana boat?" he commented after a minute or so. "Fucking fell, my arse. You, Shelly, can take her work over and expect a good hiding when you come back later. You two, get Chinwe over onto her bed."

Once on the bed, Martin threw a blanket over her. "Right, the rest of you get yourselves lined up for checking. We're going to be late, with pissing around like this."

"Are you just going to leave her?" the girl who originally went to check Chinwe asked.

"I'm not a fucking hospital, she lives or dies, that's the name of the game round here. Now move."

Soon the room was empty, the door locked and Chinwe was alone. She opened her eyes, allowing a hint of a smile to cross her face - how often had she feigned unconsciousness when her father was in one of his moods? Now she had the night off and a plan forming in her mind since she came here was coming to fruition. Chinwe had considered how she could effect an escape. She'd been surprised that the room was not that secure, held shut by only a small bolt screwed on the outside of the door. It gave her the belief that fear of severe punishment, if caught, from Martin or the other minder in the house was the main deterrent. Chinwe had also found the beds, after making her own, were steel-framed with a mattress on top and that had given her the idea they could be dismantled simply, giving her items that may be used to force open the door. To this end, and now with an opportunity to escape, she dragged the mattress off her bed. Quickly dismantling the bed frame, she ended up with not only the top and bottom ends but two steel bars that ran the full length of the bed, along with wooden laths which stretched across to support the mattress. Wrapping a blanket around the end of one of the bars, she gripped it, directing the other end towards the door. Starting at the far end of the room, she ran towards the door. Seconds later the end of the bar hit the door square on, smashing a hole directly through, before she pulled it out slightly, so the end of the bar was just through enough to jam behind the undamaged outer frame of the door. Then using the bar as a lever, and with the other end now firmly wedged behind the frame, she pushed her end of the bar towards the wall. At first the door resisted, but a small bolt was no match for the force a long bar could exert. In seconds the door gave way, ripping the bolt from the frame. Now the door, or what was left of it, swung freely on the hinges.

Chinwe dropped the bar, before walking over to an old cupboard at the far end of the room. Inside was a bundled heap of clothes at the bottom, consisting of items discarded by girls, including jeans, jumpers and coats. Quickly sorting some that more or less fitted, along with trainers, she slipped on the coat she would wear when going out to work and left the room, making her way down the stairs and out of the front door to freedom.

Chapter 15

On the day of Chinwe's escape, Constable Clifford and his partner Constable Smart had been handed a number of international arrest warrants for the London area. Both men were in plain clothes, rather than uniforms, with the idea from senior officers they would be less conspicuous in the sort of places they would visit. For nearly a month they had been working through the warrants, calling at last-known addresses, or following up intelligence-led information to where suspects were thought to live. In his late forties, Clifford had been on the force since he left school and loved it. Six feet two and well-built, married and with a child at university, he was really happy with the way his life had gone. This year they had booked a cruise for their annual holiday. He had never been on a cruise before and was counting down the weeks till they left.

"This man Eryk Kowalski, wanted by the Romanian authorities to serve a sentence following conviction on two counts of rape, do we have a known address?" Clifford asked, looking at the final two on their list.

Smart looked at his computer screen for a moment. He, like Clifford, was married, but in his early thirties and unlike Clifford, he had ambitions, with his sights on being a detective. Both men considered working on international arrest warrants to be a cushy number, allowing them to go home at night, with no weekend shifts, for this month at least.

"He moves around a bit, but we have one in Ealing that comes up a number of times on the database. Why not take a ride out and give it a go? Then all we'll have on the list is slippery Jason, who for the last month always seems to have just left every address we call at."

Clifford glanced at his watch, it was coming up to three in the afternoon. "We'll get slippery, later, I've a few informers keeping an eye open for him. In the meantime, there's just enough time to wrap this Kowalski guy up, if he's there, and be back for a quick one in the local before meeting the wife."

"I'm with you on that."

***

Using an unmarked police vehicle, they arrived at the last-known address of Eryk Kowalski, Clifford was about to release his safety belt when their target came out of the house, carrying a suitcase and climbing directly into a car that had just drawn up.

"Would you believe it, that's Kowalski, with a suitcase. You don't think he's heard we're coming and already packed?" Clifford commented.

Smart sniggered. "Unlikely, but at least we know our man is around. I vote we follow and take him by surprise."

"Why not, like you say, we know he's in the vehicle, he won't lose us, that's for sure, even if we need to call for support."

They followed the car Eryk was travelling in through the London streets and into the grounds of a number of derelict buildings that were in the throes of being demolished. His car pulled up outside one of the still reasonably intact buildings and Eryk, carrying the suitcase, along with the driver, went inside.

'Got him,' Clifford mumbled to himself as Smart pulled up a short distance away.

"Should we call for support?" Smart asked. "They could be meeting others."

Clifford glanced at Eryk's details. Then shrugged. "He's no form in this country for violence. We'll never get back in time for a quick drink, before going home, if we have to sit around waiting."

"In that case, let's go and get him."

Both men left the car, heading for the entrance to the building.

"I wonder why they've come here?" Smart commented.

"Yes, I was thinking the same thing myself," Clifford answered as he grasped the door, pulling it open.

The building was an old store for the site and around a thousand square feet in size. Already everything of value had been stripped out, leaving a heap of rubble in one corner as it awaited final demolition. Inside the two policeman were confronted by four men, including Ryker Blackthorn and Eryk. On top of an old upturned packing case, the suitcase was open and alongside it were six packages, each the size of a house brick. A man wearing glasses had two small bottles in front of him and was currently holding a small container with a little liquid in. Both policemen knew the man was testing what was almost certainly a drug, probably heroin. This was bad, to walk into a drug deal unarmed and with no support, or even a call to control as to where they were.

However, it was too late to turn back, as when they entered one of the men had spun around.

"Who the fuck are you two," he demanded.

Clifford took the immediate lead, deciding to brave it out, what else could he do? "Metropolitan police. What's going on?" he answered, at the same time walking towards them and pulling out his warrant card for them to see.

Eryk had also turned. "Just a bit of business, what do you want?" he answered calmly.

Clifford grinned. "Business eh? I suspect the bit of business you refer to is drug dealing. You're all under arrest. Call control," he told Smart.

The man who came in with Eryk and now watching the drug test was in fact Sokna, another man from the Sinaloa cartel, who had come to the UK with Mongkol. He was small but well-built. "Are you having a laugh?" he came back at Clifford, then looked directly at Smart. "Touch that radio and it will be the last thing you do on this earth," he said very calmly, at the same time drawing a gun. "Both of you, turn the radios off, then on the ground, face down, hands above your heads. Delay and you're dead."

Clifford had no doubt if either of them delayed doing as he demanded they would be lucky to get out alive. The man holding the gun had a South American accent and was obviously very comfortable around weapons. All he could hope was that Eryk would be more realistic and not want to be involved in any action that could lead the police directly towards his involvement.

"Do as he asks," Clifford said softly to Smart. Once on the ground, Clifford decided to throw in the reason they were here and an offer. "Eryk, we're only here to serve an extradition warrant on you. We'll forget everything else, including the drugs and in particular the weapon."

"We should talk," Sokna cut in, curtly dragging Eryk away by grasping his arm and out of earshot of the two policemen and everyone else. "There's close to a million street value there, I'm not risking that sort of money in the hope they will walk away and keep their mouths shut. We should get rid of them."

Eryk stared at him, somewhat taken aback at the callous way he could kill in cold blood. "This isn't America, we don't kill policemen here," he came back at him. "Besides, they don't know you or any of the other lads for that matter and they'd struggle to make it stick with me without evidence."

He gave an indifferent shrug. "In the countries I work in, any policeman stumbling on dealers with even a tenth of what's here, unarmed and without support, would be either completely stupid or have a death wish. But if you want to let them go, that's your problem. If your buyers pay up, I walk away, leaving you to sort them out. But mention Sinaloa or my name to anyone and you're dead, my friend."

"I'll sort it somehow," Eryk responded.

They both returned to the group.

"It is your lucky day. Eryk here has pleaded for your life and you're now his problem," Sokna told them. Then he looked at the other two men, one who'd been testing the drugs. "Satisfied, have we a deal?"

"We do," the man testing the drugs answered.

"In that case settle up and we'll get on our way." Sokna keyed in a number on his mobile. "Bring the car," he said curtly and cut the call.

At that moment Mongkol entered the building. Sokna walked over to him as the suitcase was repacked and carried out, with Eryk following.

"Who are the ones on the floor?" Mongkol asked.

"Bloody police, hold some warrant to arrest Eryk and kick him out the country."

"That's all we want, do you reckon Fabian is in the same situation and we're wasting our time dealing with them?"

Sokna shrugged indifferently. "Who knows, but after we're paid for this shipment, we're out of here either way. So you sort this mess out while I check the payment."

After Sokna left to join Eryk outside, Mongkol stood behind the two policemen. Lying face down, neither saw him pull out his gun and screw on a silencer. Then, without delay, or even a comment, he raised the gun and shot them both through the head. Pocketing the weapon, he left the building to see the buyers driving off. Sokna was putting the suitcase, which had the drugs, and now contained payment, into the boot of the car Mongkol arrived in.

"It's been an interesting few days, Eryk. Sinaloa will be in touch very soon," Mongkol said, at the same time shaking his hand.

"It has, I'll soon get this problem sorted out with the police and then, while I'm gone Fabian will be dealing with you."

"You should, in our business there is no place for weakness. Such people never last long." Then both Sokna and Mongkol climbed into Mongkol's car and it sped away.

Eryk returned to the building, resigned to being extradited.

"You can get up and take me now," he shouted. But of course the men never moved. Eryk could only stand and stare at the pool of blood around each man, increasing slowly in size. He called Fabian in panic.

Fabian listened to what had happened. "Fuck, that's all we need. Get out of there and sort yourself an alibi smartish. The pigs will be all over everyone with two of their own dead."

Chapter 16

Following on from Karen's instruction for surveillance to continue watching Charlie and the man who travelled with him, Hanna called her with a problem. Charlie had left the house alone, and with only one surveillance team available, they needed to know who to watch. Karen had already decided that Charlie's continued surveillance was unnecessary, after all, he had led them to the next step towards the people possibly involved in the abduction of the children. Photos of the man with Charlie, which had been taken by surveillance at the stove warehouse, had been sent to Unit T and identified him as Mongkol, a known drug trafficker for the Sinaloa cartel. Karen was concerned, this was a very violent and dangerous cartel and one she had dealt with in the past. She called Jasmin.

"I'm shortly leaving for Unit T, Jasmin. With the Sinaloa cartel's possible involvement – you, like me, know them of old - it makes me concerned for our surveillance team's safety. Can you and Kale join them and watch their backs? I'll get a few Dark Angel troops over in the next day or so for more permanent support."

"Yeah, okay. Usual rules of engagement?"

"No, you don't challenge anyone to do with the Sinaloa - if you're confronted shoot to kill. Any delay, you could die."

Jasmin had smiled to herself. "That's what I like to hear, decisiveness. I'll keep in touch."

A little time later Stanley called Karen.

"Where are you, Karen?" he asked.

"At this precise moment I'm just taxiing my aircraft to the runway. Can I call you back, after I get airborne and onto autopilot?"

"No problem."

Karen never came to a complete halt after she'd turned the Gulfstream jet onto the main runway. Already given clearance and after lining up, she increased the engine speed and began the accelerated run. In seconds she was airborne. For her, such takeoffs were regular, so she didn't even think about it, although she still enjoyed the few seconds as the huge acceleration of the aircraft pushed her back into the seat, with the rumbling of the wheels on the ground suddenly giving way to silence as she lifted off. After being passed across to French air traffic control and setting a course back to Unit T, she switched to autopilot then wandered into the passenger cabin, making herself a cup of coffee, which she took back to the pilot's seat before settling down, coffee in hand.

"I can talk now," Karen said, once she'd called Stanley back. "Anything important?"

"Just a little concerned with surveillance watching Mongkol. We don't do drugs, Karen and that man is a hit man for Sinaloa."

"I'm aware of how dangerous anyone belonging to the Sinaloa cartel is, particularly Mongkol, I've had dealings in the past with them, but he could well be mixed up somehow with the people holding the two children. To tell you the truth my contact didn't come good, so I'm clutching at straws. But you and I know trafficking and drugs often go hand in hand. I've had Jasmin and Kale join them until we can sit down and figure out what's going on, besides, I've a mind to get Dark Angel over as support."

"We should do that earlier rather than later, you know I'm not comfortable with Jasmin. She's just as dangerous as the Sinaloa lot and she'll not hold back if there's a problem. I don't want Kale anywhere near if they begin shooting. The girl's still in training."

"True, but Kale has to learn what she's got herself into and Jasmin will keep her safe. But we do need to get troops over as soon as. See if you can get six on the next transport or service aircraft to the UK."

"I'll do that. Why are you coming back? Could you not have delayed and stood in for Kale?"

"That's a first."

"What?"

"You actually suggesting I revert to a combat role, you're normally dragging me away from what I was trained to do and in my view am very good at."

"Maybe, Karen, but if you insist on taking on such people you don't put inexperience in the field, you use trained covert operators well used to dealing with these people. Anyway, you've still not told me why you're on your way back."

"Midnight, it's her birthday tomorrow, I can't keep not being there for important events in her life. Then to be fair, I didn't think we'd be facing the Sinaloa cartel, just low-grade traffickers."

"Yes, I'd forgotten Midnight's birthday myself. You should be back. I'll sort out Dark Angel and relieve Jasmin."

"Okay, got to go - French air traffic's calling with course adjustments. We'll talk when I'm back."

Karen cut the call. In fact air traffic hadn't called but she didn't really want to carry on the conversation. She was fed up of being told Jasmin wasn't suitable for the work she was getting. In her mind, she was. She was a girl like herself, who could think on her feet and take appropriate action, rather than work within the rules of engagement all the time.

***

Nearly an hour into the flight, Jasmin called Karen.

"You've a problem?" Karen asked.

"Not personally, but I'm thinking we have a situation."

"Tell me about it."

"We followed Mongkol to an area where old buildings were being demolished and he went inside one. Three cars were parked outside one of the buildings, one of the cars a little further back than the others. Checking registrations, that car was a police pool car from the Met. Then Eryk Kowalski along with three other men came out. One was carrying a suitcase. They opened the boot of one of the cars, unloaded what was in the suitcase and filled it with something else from the same boot, we weren't close enough to see with what. Soon Mongkol came out and they all shook hands and went their own ways apart from Eryk, who went back inside, but he's come back out and driven off. The police car is still parked outside."

"Could they have exchanged drugs or cigarettes for payment?" Karen asked.

"The suitcase was certainly too small for cigarettes, I'd plump for drugs."

"So the policemen could be on the take?"

"I was thinking that, and they could well have delayed leaving until the others had gone. Kale's already left, with surveillance as support, to see where Mongkol goes. I've remained with Eryk and whoever arrived in the police car. Now Eryk's left and the police car is still here. Should I check it out or just go?"

Karen thought for a moment, then made a decision. "You need to check inside the building. Protect yourself and approach with caution. Use your Unit T ID if it is the police inside and call me so I can speak to them."

"Will do."

A few minutes later Jasmin called. "Two men are dead, Karen. Shot through the head. They are not in uniform, if it's the police."

"Professional kill in your opinion?"

"Possibly, but it was certainly carried out by someone who can handle a gun and must have used a silencer. I never heard any shots from outside and whoever shot them, from the angle of entry, would have been standing at the victims' feet end. Normally a killer would shoot to disable and finish off with the head - this one didn't, so they were pretty confident in their shooting and accurate enough to make a head hit first time in both cases. They must already have had them both lying face-down, their hands above their heads; the shooter killed the second man before he had time to turn his head. Worth remembering if I'm ever facing him."

"Let's hope it doesn't come to that. You've not touched anything have you?"

"No. Not even checked if they have ID."

"Then don't, just leave, there's nothing we can do. Let the UK police sort it out."

"Do you not think we should report the shooting?"

"Why should I tie you all up answering inept questions? You can be very certain they'd mess up the investigation on our side and maybe even get the kids killed."

"You dislike the British police that much?"

"Yes, well - when they take every opportunity to pull me down, besides treat me like shit, you can understand there is no love lost between us. Now get out of there."

"No problem, I'll catch up with Kale, just in case."

"I think not, just leave Kale protecting the surveillance operation, I want you to lean on Sam Jones. In fact, frighten the living daylights out of him and find out what he knows. I need to know if this is purely a Sinaloa operation and they are moving into Europe, both trafficking and drug dealing, or if this Eryk and others are just buyers of drugs from Sinaloa. I prefer the latter, Sinaloa would bring a completely different level of violence to the show and it's something I don't relish."

"This Sam Jones interview is off the record?"

"Yes, but first let me check on the Companies House website for his home address. If as he claimed, he and his wife are directors of S and J Jones Importers, they will be listed. Then I'll text it to you."

After cutting the call, Karen leaned back deep in thought. This operation was becoming too wide, maybe taking in drug smuggling as well, while she just wanted to concentrate on the missing children. Although she could see the obvious link between human trafficking and drugs, which was usual, the level of violence was disturbing and why were the police there? Then, if it was an official investigation by the police, why was there no backup and why would they have just walked into a possible drug deal with all the risks that posed? All she could hope was that Jasmin could glean information from Jones that would help to join some of the jigsaw pieces together.

Chapter 17

Chinwe's break from captivity was more opportunistic than thought-out. Her time in the UK since recapture had been spent in the back of a van, or at a private venue, so she had no idea what city this was. All she knew was if it was night or day. However Chinwe had a distinct advantage over the other girls working with her, she knew how to survive under some of the most adverse conditions a child could ever face. Her life to date had been a daily test of survival with one alternative, death - there were no half measures.

After leaving the building through the front entrance, Chinwe found herself in a side street off a busy main road. The light was failing so she decided it must be early evening. Beyond that she couldn't tell what day or time it was. Each day had been the same, her life dictated by sleep, breakfast, relaxation, when they were expected to shower and tidy themselves up, then following lunch they would begin work, returning like they had for food and a short rest.

She turned towards the main road and was soon among crowds looking in shops, intermixed with busy bars and cafés that seemed to stretch forever. With no money and scared of asking someone for help, she walked slowly, gazing in awe at the items in the shop displays. At a fruit and vegetable store displaying stock on the pavement outside it, she didn't even know what most of the items were, recognising only the basic foods like potatoes, apples and oranges. Further on and passing a newsagent, she suddenly stopped dead, staring at newspapers in a rack. Most of the papers had a picture of Karen. Alongside the picture on one paper was the headline 'KAREN HARRIS TAKES OVER', followed by a smaller sentence: 'At long last Unit T confirmed today that the police had asked for Karen's assistance in finding Ryan and the girl known only as Chinwe.' While her reading and writing was mostly home-taught, she could read and understand most words, except she couldn't read any more as the writing had become an article, mostly hidden by the folded paper. All of a sudden she felt an overriding sense of relief, that no matter what Shelly had said, Karen knew she existed and was coming for her.

A man in scruffy clothing, walking ahead of her, tried to snatch the bag of a woman looking into a shop window. She realised it and began screaming at the man. Others in the street also realised what he was attempting and two younger men ran forward, dragging him away, pushing him to the ground and kicking him in the ribs. The man was shouting abuse at both of them, the woman spat at him and walked away, the other two men melted into the crowd. Chinwe watched as the man stood and shuffled off. She followed and soon he turned into a side street towards an elevated part of the motorway. Underneath it among the pillars were tents, heaps of belongings and a few men sitting around a small fire in an old oil drum.

"Fucking bastards, fucking bastards," the man who'd been set upon was mumbling as he approached the others.

"What's up with you, Harry?" one asked.

"Fucking nearly had a woman's bag, I did," he said, then grinned. "But I got her purse out," he carried on, waving it in front of them.

"How much?" another asked.

He pulled it open and stared, obviously annoyed. "Tight-arsed bastard. A few fucking coins, not even a note."

Another laughed. "Always the same, no one has cash

any more, plastic's taken over. It's mobiles or nothing." Then the same man saw Chinwe stood watching them, from close to a wall. "Don't be shy kid, if you're cold come closer and get warm, we don't bite," he urged.

With the lure of the fire and the urging of others, she eventually moved closer.

"Where are you from, girl?" one asked.

"Sudan."

"That sounds a bloody long way from here, did you get on the wrong bus," he asked with a smile.

She looked at him, tears trickling down her face. "I was taken by a gang of men who came to our village and brought me here, to be raped every day. I just want to go home."

"Bloody hell, did you hear that lads, the girl's been abducted."

"She needs to go to LBNF, they will look after her," another commented.

"Is that where Karen Harris is?" Chinwe asked.

"You know her?"

Chinwe shook her head. "No, but everyone in our country knows to ask for her and she will bring you home."

"She would, but she's one powerful bitch these days and no longer lives in England. LBNF is the best for you. They will know where she is," Harry cut in.

"I'm not sure about that, Harry," another man added. "LBNF has gone from Kensington. I don't think they are even in London anymore. But I've seen Karen recently down at the arches, walking the streets, looking for children. Then, she goes to Frank's café a lot. She may be better making her way there, Frank knows Karen well and he'd be able to get in touch with her."

"She still does that?"

"Of course, like she's always done. Took Mandy, the twelve-year-old who used to hang around the arches after she ran away from home last month. You must remember her?"

"I do," yet another man listening to their conversation answered. "She'd not have lasted much longer after getting food poisoning. Didn't John go to see Frank and get him to call Karen?"

"He did. Karen came the same night and convinced Mandy to go with her."

"In that case, you could be right, we should see Frank," Harry said after a few seconds' thought, then he turned to Chinwe, who was standing listening to the conversation between them. "You'd better stay with us tonight, the streets are very dangerous for a young girl. I'll take you tomorrow."

"Thank you, but I must tell you the men who held me will be looking for me. I ran away and they won't be happy if I'm found with you."

Harry looked around at the others stood listening. "Fuck them, they don't know the streets like us." Then he looked around. "We need to hide her lads. Donations."

In minutes, coats, plastic covers and even a blanket appeared, as if by magic. Soon they had her snuggled up among some of the people there, hidden from view as if there was a heap of rags. One gave her half a sandwich, another a refilled bottle of water. For Chinwe this was more than sufficient and she thanked everyone for their help. Soon everyone settled down for the night.

Chinwe lay there. She was looking forward to going home, her nightmare very nearly over.

***

Martin was sitting in the van, waiting for the girls to finish their time at the private party, when his mobile began to ring, It was Giovanni, the other minder.

"All right, Gio?"

"I was going to ask you the same and why you didn't call me to have the door repaired."

"Excuse me, what are you on about, what door?"

"The door to the girls' room. It's in pieces and looks like someone's taken a sledgehammer to it."

Martin went cold inside. "Chinwe, is she still there?"

"There's no fucker here, why, isn't she with you?"

"Shelly was on one, not sure what happened, but Chinwe was left unconscious on her bed. I'm thinking now she wasn't that unconscious, more feigning it with a plan of her own. We have to get her back Gio. Get out on the street and ask around some of the street people. She's young, black and will stand out, besides, she will want help. She won't trust anyone but could well associate herself with those sleeping rough."

"I'll do that, but you call Ryker, I'm not taking the rap for this. He'll go ballistic."

"Yeah, whatever, just find the girl."

Ryker Blackthorn had been operating with girls for over ten years. He had begun small-time and well under the radar of Unit T, which was more interested in international groups. However, as time went on his operation grew and now he had five groups of minders looking after girls across London. But Martin and Giovanni's group were special. All under sixteen, in big demand and earning him a great deal of money.

His mobile rang. Looking at the caller, he answered, "What."

"We've had a runner, Ryker," Martin told him.

"How did it happen?"

Martin told him what had happened and about Gio's call.

"Not her again. This time when you find her, give her a hiding she won't forget. Then put her with 'Big Tom' for the night. An hour or two with him will bring her in line."

"I'll do that. Can you put your feelers out as well, she won't have got far?"

"I will, call me when you have her."

Chapter 18

The same day Chinwe made her break, Sam Jones, as usual, locked up the unit at five and stopped for a quick pint with his two workers before going home. Coming through the front door, throwing the car keys on a side table, he shouted to his wife.

"I'm home, Jean, what's for dinner?" he called out, at the same time entering the lounge. There he stopped dead. Jean was sitting on the settee, she looked terrified. He could immediately see why. By the window a girl in her mid twenties was standing watching him, in her right hand a gun, with a silencer attached. She was wearing tight black jeans, black T-shirt, her hair tied back with dark-tinted glasses. This was Jasmin back to doing, besides killing, what she did best - intimidation.

"We've been waiting for you, Sam, if you don't mind me calling you by your Christian name - after all, you won't know who I am but I know a great deal about you? So take a seat next to Jean and then we're going to have a nice little chat. Well, perhaps not so nice on your part, because there's a sting in the tail. If I don't believe what's coming out of your mouth that will be very bad for your wife. She dies first. Persist in your lies and you follow."

Sam couldn't believe what he was hearing, in his world, people didn't carry guns and even more they didn't threaten to kill. "Is this a wind-up? Because if you're after money, you're fresh out, we already owe a bundle to the bank, so get in the queue. Anyway, who the hell are you?" he demanded, but didn't sit down.

"The only thing you need to know about me is that I kill for a living. Think me soft, believe I have any compassion for the victims, think again, because in order to do my job, that is a luxury confined to a movie script. Exactly the same as there's no knight in shining armour coming to your aid. Again, believe me, apart from the movies, they don't exist. So you answer my questions or you die. Either way I receive payment for the job."

Sam had read in novels that such people existed, but this was not fiction, this was reality. "You're a hired gun - a contract killer?" he gasped. "Who sent you?"

"Label me in any way that makes you comfortable. As to who sent me - that's nothing to do with you. First question, Unit T came to your unit, why?"

"What's to stop you killing us even if I answer your questions?" Sam persisted.

"Nothing, except you're not my target, just a stepping stone. So yes, there's always the risk of becoming collateral damage, but that is the chance you take. The only certainty you should be concentrating on is how to remain alive."

"Sit down and answer her questions, Sam, this is not only yours but my life you're risking," Jean cut in.

"You have a sensible wife, Sam, what is it to be - you've five seconds to answer."

Sam sat down, but never took his eyes off Jasmin. "Unit T came looking for a kid that was supposedly delivered by two men half an hour earlier. How they came to that decision, God knows, we deal in log burners. Besides, what would we do with a kid? Our life doesn't include them."

Jasmin gave a sigh. "Believe me, Sam, Unit T doesn't make such basic mistakes, there had to be a reason why Unit T were there? Because of your visitors, or your involvement in human trafficking," Jasmin came back at him.

"My visitors brought a fire back and neither my wife or I are into human trafficking, so they got it wrong this time," he came back at her with obvious arrogance in his voice.

Jasmin was all the time watching him and his body language, before and as he spoke. "You know, in my line of work I meet many people. All believe that if they make up a convincing story I'll accept it and go away. But you see, I'm not that gullible. When I come to see someone, I'll already have been given a great deal of background information. That means when I hear the answers to my questions that don't stack up with what I already know, it requires me to revert to memory prods that become more and more painful in their execution. This often leaves people for dead after I squeeze out the real truth. In your case I do have names and associations which are bad news for you and the idea that the men who came to your unit were returning a wood burner is a lie. So I will ask once more - my client wants to know why Unit T had been directed to your particular industrial unit?" While she spoke, Jasmin raised her gun and had it pointing directly at Jean. The tone of her voice had also changed to one far more intimidating. "Think carefully before you answer, Jean's life now depends on the next words that come out of your mouth."

Sam was sweating, while he wasn't initially convinced this girl would carry out her threat, her persistence that she believed he was lying was casting a nagging doubt in his mind. If he pushed her further, he suspected neither of them would survive.

But it was Jean who changed his mind. "Tell her everything, Sam, we've done nothing wrong and I'll not die for Fabian," Jean urged.

Sam sighed, all he could do now was hope this girl believed him this time. "You're right, we were told to possibly expect a visit from Unit T. We know a man called Fabian Nowak. He runs swingers' parties every month in a country house about thirty miles from here. We've been going for around a year and got to know him and his mate Eryk Kowalski. Fabian rang me out of the blue on Friday night and asked for a favour."

"What sort of favour?" Jasmin asked, lowering her gun.

"He told me he'd been having trouble with Unit T. They had this belief he was dealing in underage girls. He said it was rubbish and we knew ourselves all the extra girls at the swingers' parties were at least twenty and there voluntarily. I couldn't disagree with him because what he was claiming was true. So providing what he was asking wasn't illegal we agreed to help out, although Jean was really concerned when I told her Unit T was involved. He said it was very simple. A car would come to my unit and drop off an empty box wrapped up in a blanket. If Unit T came later and asked what was inside, I was to claim it was a small wood burning stove that had a problem. It seemed simple enough and only a white lie about what was delivered, so I agreed. The only other thing he wanted me to do was if Unit T did come, to call him after they left."

"Did you not question why Unit T would be bothered about him delivering a box to a wood burning stove company?"

"Jean did, but he told us he suspected he and his employees were being followed and because of Unit T's suspicions, it was affecting his business and worrying for his family. So he needed proof to give to his solicitor to have them stopped."

"Your mobile, prove to me you telephoned Nowak after we left."

Sam pulled out his mobile and scrolled down to the call he'd made. Jasmin took a note of the number and the time of the call, then stood back, looking down at them.

"That wasn't too difficult was it? And not worth the risk of dying for. As it is you would be advised to forget I ever came to your house and get on with your lives. Call this man Nowak and mention I've been to your house and my client will know. Then I'll be back, but next time my contract will be very different. Have we an understanding?"

"We'll say nothing to anyone. We only did what we thought was an innocent favour for a person we knew. If we'd any idea people like you would be involved, we'd have refused," Jean cut in before Sam could answer.

"And you, Sam, those are your thoughts as well?"

"Too bloody right they are, we just want a quiet life."

"Very sensible, no matter what Nowak tells you, he's part of a criminal group that deals in drugs along with being involved in other criminal activities including trafficking. They use innocent people like you in their constant war between other criminal gangs that want a slice of the action. You are expendable in their fight, always remember that. Switch off your mobiles and leave them on the coffee table, then both of you upstairs and into your bedroom. Remain in there for at least fifteen minutes. Come out earlier, I may still be here, then you die."

"Will Fabian ever find out you got information from us?" Jean asked, at the same time turning her mobile off.

"To find my target often requires me to lean a little on others. How and what information I get remains with me, no other. Now it's time you both went upstairs."

Sitting on the bed with Jean in the bedroom, Sam slipped his arm around her.

"How did she get in?" Sam asked, once Jasmin had left the bedroom.

"I've no idea. I came out of the kitchen to find her standing at the lounge door, gun in hand. When I confronted her, she ignored what I was saying, only asked when you were due home. Then I was told to sit on the settee and say nothing. She terrified me, Sam, I was wondering what we'd got ourselves into. Do you think she'd have used the gun?"

He sighed. "We'll never know, but by the way everything seemed so casual with her, it was as if she'd done it many times, so I'd have to say yes."

"I'm not going to any more of Fabian's swingers' weekends."

"I'm with you there, particularly if what she said was true and he's into drugs and human trafficking. But what's confusing me is how did she know Unit T came to our unit? Then, how would she know our home address?"

"Could she really have come from Unit T?" Joan asked after some thought.

"Unlikely. If they really were investigating human trafficking and suspected we were part of it, they'd have pulled us into a local police station. They have the power to do that, you know. Mind you, Unit T is so well-known because of their association with Karen Harris, so to actually send a hired gun to threaten people, they'd never get away with it, there would be a public outcry."

She looked at him. "Maybe you're right, and if we went to the police or press, Fabian could find out, so our problems wouldn't just be with the girl but Fabian," she said, then shrugged. "Even so, who'd believe us that someone had actually come to our house threatening to kill us? It's not exactly something you read happening in the papers, it's more like something on telly or in a movie. I know I'd be sceptical if Madelyn from next door told us such a story, after all this is suburbia, nothing happens around here."

Sam sat for a moment. "Anyway, she's gone, let's hope she doesn't return. But we say nothing, not even to Madelyn. If Fabian calls, this never happened. Agreed?"

"Yes."

***

After leaving the house, Jasmin returned to Karen's apartment and called Karen, who'd returned to Unit T. She listened to a recording of the conversations that had gone on between Jasmin and the Jones's.

"You did well," Karen finally told her.

"It was easy, they were pussycats. Except it proves they must have been on to your informer and were testing their suspicions. But does it move us on?"

"I need to think, Jasmin."

"You do that. I'm just watching the news channel with the sound off. On the breaking news stroller along the bottom it seems two policemen have been found. They're almost certainly the two men I saw."

"I agree, I'll talk to you tomorrow. Now I've got to play the dutiful aunt for Midnight."

"My heart bleeds for you. Kids aren't my bag and I don't presume they're yours?"

"You're right, like you, I live in a world where emotional ties play no part. Having said that, it's good at times to stand back and see the change we can make in a child's life. After all, Midnight was pulled out of the gutter and given a chance after my dear sister was pushing even her, a seven-year-old, towards prostitution."

"Why do you say that?"

"Just the odd chat with Midnight and my sister's introduction of Midnight to her clients. I think she saw Midnight as an additional means of income. What type of mother would do that to her own child?"

"One who's desperate and failing?"

"Oh come on, the woman only had to pick up the phone, if just for her daughter's sake, no matter how much she despised me."

"And you would have done that in her position? Bearing in mind that because of your actions she'd ended up in a brothel after watching her parents killed. I don't think so somehow."

"That's not fair, Jasmin, I was fighting for my life and full of a drug that was destroying my memory. Then, I've helped thousands of victims, some in far worse circumstances than my sister. I don't judge, just help."

"Whatever, like I said I'm not into kids. Call me when you have decided on the next stage."

"I will, I'm also relying on you, Jasmin, to keep our people safe."

"That goes without saying, After you go off I'll go and check on them."

"Thanks, I'll talk to you tomorrow."

Chapter 19

Chinwe had slept very little. While these men had promised to look after her, she was still worried about Martin. He'd not be happy that she'd escaped. Because of this, she kept hidden under the old clothes that had been lent her, not even attempting to look out. It was the right thing to do because Blackthorn's people had come very close to finding her, but none wanted to search a heap of old rags, or even hang around the homeless. With a number of the homeless drunk, or high on drugs, the men from Blackthorn's moved on.

Early the following morning, Harry gave Chinwe a shake. "Come on, time we weren't here."

Chinwe stood and stretched. After handing the bottle containing water back to the man who gave it to her, she and Harry made their way through the still deserted streets.

"Is it far?" she asked.

"Five stops on the tube."

"I've heard about trains that run in tubes, is it free to go on or do they charge?"

He shrugged. "This is London, you get charged even to shit. But there are ways to travel and not pay. Today, it's slightly different, the kind lady who let me take her purse left her Oyster travel card inside. So providing she hasn't reported it yet, I can swipe it going in, and if it works we'll know if it can get us out. Just keep close as I go through the barrier when we leave the station and you'll get through at the same time. If we're sussed, run, they never follow you out the station, believing they will get you next time you try to use a dodgy card. Fate took over you see, to set you on your way home."

They turned into the local station, going through to the trains. Chinwe had never been in an underground and as they went further and further down, she realised what was meant by a tube and began to panic, tightly gripping Harry's hand. The wind on the platform they arrived at added to her fear, followed by a train thundering out of a tunnel, which terrified her.

"Don't worry, you get used to it," he told her as she began backing away, until she was hard against the wall, terror showing in her face.

Even so, it took a great deal of effort on his part to drag her onto the train. Sitting her down, with him beside her, he grasped her hand as the train set off.

"You never told us your name, what do I call you?" he asked, in an effort to take her mind off the noise and rocking of the carriage.

"Chinwe."

Harry stared at her. "You, you're Chinwe?" he gasped. "Everyone's looking for you. Even Karen Harris knows you're missing, along with a little boy. It's a bloody good job no-one realised just who you were last night. There would be many who would have turned you in to the Blackthorns. His people were bandying around a hundred-quid reward for information. If you're on the drugs or the bottle, that's a few days of fixes. You can't blame them, they live from day-to-day."

"Are you still taking me to see Frank, now you know?"

He sighed. "I wasn't always on the street, in fact, I have two children. Okay, since I lost my job and kicked out of my flat, my ex won't let me see them, but it doesn't mean I'd push any child into the hands of traffickers, no matter what I was offered. They are parasites, preying on the vulnerable, the ones who have nothing, like a woman forced into prostitution because of a loan shark. You see it all on the street, Chinwe, even in the so-called affluent West. Karen Harris has bucked the trend and turned the tide on these people, taking everything from them and locking them up for years. People on the street respect her for that. Even though she's mega-rich, the girl will still stop and talk to you and has never looked down on anyone I know of. That means a lot, believe me."

"She's famous in England as well?"

Harry sniggered. "You'd better believe it, but not just England, Europe, Asia and as you know Africa - maybe the world. I don't think there's anyone living on the streets who doesn't know about Karen. While all of us respect her and know she'll do anything for you if you're in trouble, you don't cross her if you've any sense. That girl, since she was eighteen, has lived in a world of violence and it's rumoured she's SAS-trained, carries a gun as well as a knife and would not be averse to using either to protect herself. Even the likes of Blackthorn and other groups would not go up against her. They back away until she moves on. Once we can get you under her care you'll be safe, I can promise you that."

"I know, although loads of people laughed at my belief, saying she wouldn't be interested in a nobody." Chinwe hesitated for a moment, still gripping his hand and looking at him with her huge deep brown eyes. "You don't think Karen would walk away because I have nothing and would only be a nuisance?"

"All of us on the streets have nothing, Chinwe, the kids like you live in constant fear, some offering themselves for sex or worse to put food in their mouths. I've never heard of one Karen has refused to help. So forget what people say, they lie, and just want you to believe there is no one to help you - particularly if it's a trafficker telling you."

They fell silent. Chinwe watched everything that went on as she slowly got used to being on what was a very strange mode of transport to her. She also noticed no one would acknowledge anyone else. Each seemed to be in their own bubble, avoiding eye contact, which was working for her as nobody realised or was even bothered about who she was.

"Right, Euston's next, that's our stop," Harry muttered. "Stick with me and be prepared to run if the rail police see us doubling up through the barrier."

If anyone had seen them double up through the gate, no one bothered. Although to be fair the crowds who came off the train along with others created a huge bottleneck at the exit. So unless you were watching carefully, there would have been no time to prevent either of them leaving the station.

They made their way around the back of the station past the arches, where people had made their home. Some nodded to Harry, as if in recognition, but said nothing. A short distance further on they arrived at Frank's café, and went inside.

There were a few people seated, tucking into breakfast; a lady behind the small counter was spreading bread. She'd looked up when the door opened.

"Take a seat, loves, I'll be with you in a minute. Tea for both of you?"

"Sit down, Chinwe, I'll talk to her," Harry said quietly. Then he walked up to the counter. "Sorry, I don't have any money for breakfast. Is Frank around?"

She looked at him for a second. "Why would you want to talk to Frank?"

"The girl who's with me is called Chinwe. This is the

one Karen Harris is looking for and I know Frank has a way of contacting her. She's very scared and has run away from her minders, she needs help desperately."

"I'll fetch Frank. In the meantime, take a seat, tea is on us. Would you like a bacon butty each as well?"

"It would be appreciated, we've come across from the other side of London this morning and had nothing."

"That's fine. I'll bring them over."

Frank was in his flat above the shop. He had only just got up, after working until two in the morning, when the lady called him on the intercom. Dressing quickly, he came down into the café, walking over to Harry and Chinwe, both tucking into their bacon butties, and sat down with them.

"I'm Frank, Margrette tells me you're Chinwe? Is that correct?"

"Yes, sir. I was brought here by boat but managed to escape, not once but twice. At home, we are told if we are ever snatched by the gangs and escape, to ask for Karen Harris. She will bring us home. Do you know her?"

"I do, very well in fact, and you're correct, Karen will make sure you get back home, although she doesn't live in England, but France. But that isn't a problem, I will get in touch and she'll tell me what is to happen to you until she arrives."

Harry finished off his tea and stood. "I'll leave you now, Chinwe, good luck, love, and stay safe."

Chinwe stood and gave him a hug. "Thank you for all you've done for me, I'll never forget you, Harry."

"You're welcome. Take care of her, Frank, she's a very special and brave young lady. Thanks for the tea and sarny."

"You can be very sure we will. See Margrette before you

leave, she'll make you up a sandwich for your dinner later."

"Much appreciated, Frank."

Frank stood. "Come on, Chinwe, we need you out of the café and upstairs. Then I'll talk to Karen."

While Chinwe had a shower, Frank called Unit T on a number Karen had given him some years back, if he ever wanted to get in touch with her.

'Camp EU553 please select from the following options,' came a recorded voice.

Frank frowned, what was EU553? Why not just say Unit T? But no option suited apart from one that would take him through to the switchboard.

"May I help you?" a lady's voice answered.

"Yes, am I through to Unit T, if so I'd like to talk to Karen Harris?"

"Do you have an issued code number?" she asked.

"Just a moment. Karen wrote a number down for me along with the telephone number I've just dialled. It's ten digits, shall I read it out?"

"Yes, please."

Frank gave her the number and was told to hold. Minutes went by, then if it wasn't for music playing he would have thought he'd been disconnected.

"Sorry for the delay," the woman suddenly said. "I'm putting you through to Unit T intelligence. The person you want to talk to is not available. They will require you to give your full name, date of birth, social security number and current address."

"That's fine, but this is Unit T I'm talking to?"

"We are an EU military location, that is all I can tell you. I'll put you through."

It took another five minutes of giving his details to yet another person before Frank was finally talking to Stanley.

"Do you know how difficult it is to actually talk to someone, Stanley?"

"Sorry Frank, but we get a lot of calls, mostly nothing to do with us, just people wanting certain departments of the camp or reporters. It is a very large camp believe me. You were fortunate to have a code from Karen, otherwise you wouldn't have got beyond the switchboard. What can I do for you? Karen's not available at this moment. Although I hope to talk to her later today."

"I've got Chinwe at the café. She was brought in by a homeless man. Apparently she escaped from the traffickers and he found her wandering around the streets."

"Good god, that's a turn-up for the books. You've not called the police, have you?"

"No, she's insistent that only Karen will help her, no one else."

"That's fine, I need direction from Karen. In the meantime, Jasmin's in London, I'm calling her as we speak to come to the café and look after her."

"I know Jasmin, I'm comfortable with her. Is Sherry not around then?"

"No, I believe she's in Spain, and not due in London for a couple of days. But Sherry is no longer part of Unit T, she's LBNF and carries no armed protection, where Jasmin does."

"You believe Chinwe needs such protection?"

"I do, that girl, whether she knows it or not has very important and useful information. The traffickers know that and will go all out to find her. I don't want to risk you or anyone in the café so we'll get her out as quickly as we can. It's just a pity

Karen's not available."

"When you say not available, she's not ill is she?"

"No, it was Midnight's birthday earlier in the week, so they have gone off to Nice for the weekend. I think they must be on the beach, maybe in the water as the phone's just ringing out."

"No worries, so long as she's okay, I'll leave you to it, Stanley. It's good to talk to you at last. I've heard a lot about you."

"And I you, Frank. I'll be in touch and let you know when Jasmin will be with you. You may even get a call from Karen when I finally get hold of her."

Chapter 20

Eryk was with Fabian at his home sorting out the money from their various dealings. Fabian began a conversation with a man on his mobile and finally told him he'd see him right before cutting the call.

"Who was that?" Eryk asked.

"Eddie?"

"The Eddie, who lives on the streets?"

"Yes."

"What's he after, besides money?"

"He's just left Frank's café close to Euston. Apparently Chinwe is there. He saw her go through to the flat above with Frank as he entered the café. He recognised her from the photos Blackthorn circulated with the offer of a reward. He couldn't get hold of any of the Blackthorns so called me."

"I knew there was something odd with that Frank, always giving the kids an extra bit on their plates. Maybe he has a price that's not so obvious?"

Fabian wasn't so certain. "We'd have heard on the street by now if that was the case. After all, he'd be a potential client. But it's also a café Harris frequents and has done for years so she could well be backing him, which is why I always insist we steer clear of the place, drug-wise. I even heard that at times she'd stay overnight. The woman must be desperate to be fucked by him. There again, she was brought up in the back streets of Manchester and is probably not fussy who she goes with."

Eryk laughed. "If you're right, it's a sad person with money and looks, who reverts to being fucked by an older man."

They both sat for a while, glasses in hand, carrying on

counting out the day's takings.

It was Fabian who broke the silence. "Thinking about what Eddie said, and Frank knowing Harris, could Chinwe have made her way to his café to ask for his help in contacting her?"

"It's possible. There again, Chinwe's caused us and the Blackthorns a lot of problems. Why not snatch her back before Harris has time to collect?"

Fabian grinned. "I like your thinking, I'll speak to Ryker," he answered, at the same time pulling his phone out from his pocket, pressing buttons.

Ryker Blackthorn looked at the caller on his mobile, then answered. "You want me, Fabian?"

"Yes, the girl you're looking for is holed up at a café close to Euston. Do you want to go and get her, or should we?"

"Fuck her, she's a bloody nuisance. You collect and sell her for us."

"We'll not get top money now, she's too hot."

"No worries, we made something out of her anyway. See what you can get," he said, then cut the call.

Fabian then called another number, a man answered. "Simu, get Rica and a couple of extra lads and go to Frank's café at Euston. He's got Chinwe hidden in his flat above it. Take her to the farm - when we've finished with her, she'll wish she'd never made a break from Blackthorn and put us all in jeopardy."

"No problems, what about Frank?"

"Fire the shithole and leave him with a personal reminder to keep out of our business."

***

Jasmin arrived at Frank's and went up to the counter. "All right, Frank?"

"Yes, yourself?"

"I'm good, but I'm also starving, what's on the stove?"

Frank sighed. "Don't any of you girls eat? Potato pie and beetroot, grab a seat, I'll bring it over."

Jasmin lowered her voice. "The girl, is she upstairs?"

"Yes, she's fine, watching television."

Jasmin nodded and went to sit down, positioning herself so she could see anyone entering the café. She also pulled out her gun, slipping it inside the belt of her jeans.

Following dinner, Frank took her upstairs. As he'd told her, Chinwe was sitting watching television when they went in.

"Chinwe, this is Jasmin, she works with Karen and will look after you until Karen arrives. I'll leave you both to get to know each other and be back later. Any problems downstairs, Jasmin, I'll buzz the intercom twice." Then he left them alone.

"So what are you watching?" Jasmin asked, looking at the television screen.

"Everything really, we have nothing like this in our village. Of course we know about television and at the school they have one."

"You don't miss much, most is rubbish, I watch films on streaming channels. Anyway, let me explain a few things. I don't expect any trouble, but if there is, you go to the bedroom and lock yourself in. You only come out when I tell you - no matter what you hear, like gunshots or shouting."

"I understand, when will Karen be here?"

"I'm not sure, we're having trouble getting to talk to her. It happens sometimes when she's in meetings. This time she's with Midnight, her niece, on a weekend off and expects people to make their own decisions. Otherwise, they rely too much on her."

"Is that what's happening, everyone is waiting for her?"

"Probably, they're all a bit namby-pamby, although to be fair, most decisions are life and death. It takes a lot to make such decisions if you never have."

"And you have, or are you one of the namby-pamby group?"

Jasmin looked at her for a moment, before answering. "I'm not one of those, Chinwe. Like Karen, death follows me around."

"So what's your job? Then, you have a hint of an accent I know very well."

"Perhaps, after all I was born in Cape Town, South Africa. As for what I do, I work alongside Karen, at times help protect her and like now, help to protect the vulnerable."

Chinwe looked carefully at Jasmin as she spoke, inwardly shuddering. She could see it in her eyes, the coldness she'd seen so many times among the gangs who'd come to her village, raping and plundering. This girl was a professional killer, she had no doubt. Why would Karen have such people around? Was she wrong in her belief that Karen was their saviour, a good person, or was it all hype and Karen was just another killer, like Jasmin? She quickly discounted her doubts; after all, her mother had told her Karen was a good person and only she could bring her home.

***

With Chinwe not having much sleep the night before, she had gone to lie down in Frank's spare room - a room Karen had used often when she wanted to get away from the pressure of work. However, Fabian's assessment that there was something going on between Karen and Frank couldn't have been further from the truth. Their relationship, particularly when she first frequented his café over ten years ago, had been more father-daughter. He understood Karen, in fact far more than she ever suspected. He also respected the girl for what she'd given up personally, to help others abducted for sale into prostitution. In the early days it was obvious that the money she'd always put behind the counter to give the street children that little bit extra on their plates, often crippled her financially, when at the time she was struggling to keep her charity running. But no matter how much she struggled herself, she would always leave the money. Later, her rise to power as well as wealth could have overwhelmed Frank and his café, if he'd allowed her to assist in the way she'd offered. In fact, even now he would only accept up to a hundred pounds, and that in his view was far too much. Although, unknown to him, when his café came under threat from the landlord who wanted to demolish the block, she had stepped in and secured its future. Frank wasn't completely naïve, he had suspected something had happened in the background for the landlord to place any development on hold, but it was never talked about between them. Although he was relieved, if only for the sake of his customers, who were mostly street people, that the café survived.

Over the last months Frank had become very concerned over Karen's mental health. The pressure on her seven days a week was taking its toll. She looked tired and had begun to spend the odd night in his flat just to get away. He remembered the last night she had been in his flat. The girl was shaken with not only physical injuries, but mentally, following an operation that had taken a sinister turn, resulting in her being caught in an explosion when an aircraft was shot down. He knew she needed help and couldn't take much more. But yet again Karen seemed to pull herself back together and on the face of it, outwardly Karen gave the impression to be back to what he knew her to be. Although

Frank suspected this was all a front for a very troubled girl.

While Chinwe slept, Jasmin was sitting on the settee, drink in hand, watching television. As usual, her gun lay by her side - a Glock 19, a weapon used by plain clothes police officers, with a capacity of ten rounds. She also wore an ankle knife the same as Karen, hidden from sight by her jeans.

At that moment a buzzer used by staff to call Frank back downstairs when he wasn't working in the café, went twice. Arranged earlier as a warning, before Frank went down to the café, Jasmin was immediately alert. Grabbing her gun and giving it the usual check that all was well, she switched off the sound of the television by remote control, moved quickly to the door and listened.

She could hear shouting and the bottom door being forced open, with the noise of heavy feet coming up the stairs. Jasmin backed away sufficiently, so she could not be rushed without retaliating. Her gun was raised, held in two hands and directed towards the door. In her view, whoever was coming up the stairs had a death wish if they wanted to take her on.

The flimsy door to the flat gave way as two men, Simu and Rica, brandishing short iron crowbars, burst their way into the room.

"That is as far as you go, both of you throw your weapons away from you and put your hands above your heads." She hesitated a moment, changing her tone to one with more aggression, demanding, "Do it or I fire."

Simu had not been warned they'd be facing a gun by Fabian when he was told to collect a child. If he'd known, the operation would have been approached in a completely different manner, bringing guns as well. Even so, Simu, while a little shocked, wasn't going to have a young girl threaten him. Besides, he wasn't convinced it was a real gun, more like a replica she held, or if it was real, did she have the guts to use it?

"I don't think so, we've no argument with you, we want Chinwe, so stand aside or face the consequences," Simu threatened, at the same time moving further into the room, raising the arm holding the bar.

Jasmin allowed a hint of a smile to spread across her face, he needed to be taught a harsh lesson, taking on a contract killer. They never argued, they killed for a living. Even so, on this occasion when she fired without further warning, her aim at this stage was not to kill, but disable and she did that perfectly. The bullet ripped through the shoulder of the hand holding the iron bar.

Simu screamed in pain, dropping the bar. "You bastard, you'll pay for this," he spat at her.

"Such threats given by someone blubbering like a baby make me really scared," she mocked. "What is it, an assault on your pride, or a man thing that a girl can't have the upper hand? I wouldn't feel so inadequate if I were you, I've faced some of the most dangerous contract killers in Europe and I'm still here... they're not. But be warned, by not doing as I ask you will meet with more deadly retaliation. I kill for a living. How many are downstairs?"

"Enough to take you out even with your peashooter of a gun," Simu answered.

"You have a death wish then? I may have wasted one bullet as a warning shot, but be very certain, I'll not waste another. So how many and think carefully before you answer, or answer to the almighty."

"There's two," Rica cut in.

"Very sensible. Now hands in the air and go back down the stairs to the shop. Warn any others still inside there to drop their weapons. If they refuse I will take you both out first, followed by them, have no doubts. Now move."

They both turned and began to go down the stairs.

"There's only her, we can take her downstairs," Rica whispered.

"See you do then, she's already pissed me off," Simu whispered back.

The rumpus in the café had immediately emptied it of customers, with most taking advantage and getting out without paying. Others left cash on the tables. Frank had attempted to stop the men, but was now lying on the floor in a pool of blood.

Jasmin held back as they came down the stairs, not allowing either of them to feign a trip and be close enough to take her. She was far too experienced to fall for such a low-level trick.

As they reached the bottom Jasmin reiterated and expanded her instructions. "Tell the others to drop their weapons and stand facing the far wall, then both of you join them."

"Lads, we've got ourselves a gunman, or more a gun girl in pigtails," he mocked. "Move to the far wall after dropping your weapons," Simu warned as he came through the door, at the same time showing them his thumb stuck up, then suddenly pointing it down and jabbing.

They nodded and went to the far wall. However, one had drawn a knife, slipping it up the sleeve of his coat and out of sight.

Jasmin followed them out, keeping tight to the back wall, watching them. She took out her mobile and began pressing buttons. This was a direct line for a police response team if any of Unit T's operatives found themselves in trouble. When it was answered she gave her Unit T code and requested an armed response unit as well as an ambulance, giving the location. Then she cut the call.

"Let's all settle down and wait, shall we?" Jasmin told them.

"You're Unit T, I hardly think so, when did they revert to using contract killers?" Simu asked, after listening to her call.

"Since when did I mention I was a contract killer? I have only faced them. Because if I was acting as one you'd all be dead by now. I know of no contract killer who'd wing a person, unless it's to disarm, followed by a bullet in the head. As it is, all Unit T field operators will kill if cornered. If you want to try your luck and take me on, I'll gladly show you I'm well able to use a gun beyond winging," she mocked.

Simu said nothing, but glanced at the man to the far end of the row who just gave a hint of a nod to him. Suddenly Simu gripped his shoulder. "Fuck, fuck… god I shouldn't have moved," he cried out, then doubling up, dropped to the floor in feigned pain.

Jasmin smiled inwardly, but didn't allow this man's attempted distraction to take all her attention, immediately seeing one of the men in the café also drop to the floor, and at the same time spin round and raise his right arm, revealing the glint of steel from a knife he held in his hand.

She never hesitated - dropping down on one knee, reducing the hit area, with the gun gripped firmly in two hands, she fired, not once, but twice in succession, the first shot shattering the man's hand, the second his leg, sending him sprawling and like Simu, screaming in pain.

"I'm getting pissed off with you lot. Face the bloody wall

and don't move again, or the next one who doesn't understand such simple instructions will die," she demanded.

This time they did as she asked, without comment. Jasmin began taking stock of the café and the original struggle. Moving position, she knelt down beside Frank to check his pulse, but it was either very weak or there wasn't one. She knew he needed help, but guarding four, she could do nothing for him until assistance arrived.

Time went on and still no one came. Jasmin called Unit T's only direct contact number. After being answered she gave a code and was switched through to Stanley.

"You have a problem, Jasmin?" he asked.

She told him what had happened, finishing with, "I've called the UK police on the special number, but they're being slow in their response."

"Very strange. Leave it to me, I'll see what the problem is."

However, at that moment Jasmin saw the telltale flashing of blue lights through the window.

"Sorry, Stanley I might have pre-empted, help has arrived."

"That's okay, Jasmin, I'm still not in contact with Karen so have the police take Chinwe in for protection. Support for you by us would be a good two to three hours away. Karen wouldn't want you out on a limb for that time in view of what has happened."

"Will do, I'll call later."

A loudhailer burst into life. "This is the police, we are armed. Everyone come out, hands in the air. There is no escape."

"You heard them, start moving, one at a time," Jasmin demanded.

She watched as each left the café, then she followed.

As Jasmin came out someone among the armed police called out, “Drop the weapon, then lie face down on the ground, hands above your head.”

Jasmin knew this would be the norm, with not knowing who was who. A man ran over, dragged her arms around her back and handcuffed her, before standing her up. Another took her gun. Two ran into the café and in minutes were out with Chinwe, bundling her into a police car that had just drawn up.

“Excuse me, I’m Unit T. My ID is in my back pocket. There is also an injured man inside needing urgent medical help,” Jasmin told the policeman.

She never got an answer, apart from the ID being taken from her pocket and given to the officer in charge.

He walked over, handing back her ID after the handcuffs had been removed. “Sorry about that, first we secure and make sure the building is empty, then we sort out.”

“Understandable. I need to remain with Chinwe and our commander has requested her to be kept safely inside a police station until she arrives.”

“That’s not up to me, but we’ll arrange for you both to be taken to a police station and they will make all the arrangements.”

“What about my weapon?”

“He shook his head. I cannot give it you back. People have been injured, it’s now to be held as evidence. A receipt will be issued at the station. If you join Chinwe, we’ll get you both out of here.”

Chapter 21

Midnight ran over to Karen, who was lying on the beach reading. Aged nine, she had similar features to Karen, deep blue eyes, her hair straight but finishing halfway down her back and tall for her age. Then, unlike Karen, who had brown hair, Midnight's was blonde, but had been bleached virtually white from the sun, since she came to live with Karen in France. All in all she was a very pretty girl and although coming from a difficult hand-to-mouth life with her mother, Midnight fitted in well with the very different life she now had with Karen, since her mother had died from an inadvertent drug overdose.

"Look, Aunty, I've found a shell and you can hear the sound of the sea if you put it to your ear," she told her, pushing the shell into Karen's hand.

Karen had a listen, then smiled. "You're right. I remember when I was your age, we'd gone on a seaside holiday and I was looking in the pools left when the sea went out and I found a shell the same as you. Your grandfather asked me if I was taking it home, or leaving it for a sea creature to live in?"

Midnight looked genuinely surprised. "You mean it could be someone's little house?"

"Why not, something used to live in it to start with, so now they have gone, it's vacant."

She thought for a short time, staring down at the shell. "Did you take your shell home?"

"I'll not answer that, Midnight, only you must decide what to do with your own shell."

"We'll leave it here. Then, if we come back one day, I could see if anyone has moved in."

"Good idea, we shouldn't deprive a little creature of a home. Right, it's time we wandered back to the hotel, got cleaned up and went for lunch. Are you hungry? Mind you, that's a stupid question, you're always hungry, I don't know where you put it all."

Midnight grinned. "That's cos I'm still growing," she said, then ran off to replace the shell while Karen collected up their belongings, packing them in a bag. Finished, Karen stood watching her run back. She felt sad that her sister hadn't come to her earlier when she'd first fallen into financial problems. Her stubbornness in not asking for help had lost this little girl her mother, which was a tragedy. Midnight was very special and between them all, working as a family, they could have done so much. Now Midnight was stuck with her and with all that was going on in her life, she couldn't give Midnight the attention she deserved and needed to grow up, relying on a nanny to give her the family life she didn't have time to.

"What are you thinking about?" Midnight asked, looking at Karen.

Karen, lost in thought, hadn't seen her approach. "Nothing in particular, have we got everything?"

Midnight looked around, "Yes."

"Come on then – let's go."

As they walked back to the hotel, her mobile began to ring. Karen looked at the caller. It was Stanley and the third time he'd called. She pressed answer. "Hi, Stanley, do you need me?"

"At last, I was beginning to worry. I won't keep you on long, but Chinwe was brought to Frank's by a homeless man. Found her wandering the streets apparently. With her asking for you, he thought Frank's would be the best place to take her. I've sent Jasmin to protect her until you decide what you want us to do."

"Good thinking. Can you put documentation together. I want her out of the UK and back to our camp? She needs careful debriefing."

"I thought you would say that, so I'm ahead of you in sorting documentation, which would be needed anyway. Transport is due in London later tomorrow. I'll have it all in place by then. What about the UK police, wouldn't they need to be informed?"

"Yes, tomorrow. But let Hardy Melcher know. Tell him we will send a full report as soon as. Any word about Ryan, which I think the police would be more interested in?"

"Nothing, Karen."

"Okay, fine, I'll go to London early next week and see if we can move on with anything we get out of Chinwe. Keep me in the loop will you, but don't wait for my okay before you make any decisions, time could be of the essence now Chinwe's escaped once more."

"Will do. How are you enjoying your break with Midnight?"

"We're good. Spent all morning snorkelling, which is why you couldn't get me. I needed this break, Stanley. We're now on our way back to the hotel for lunch."

"Then you carry on and leave it all to me. I'll only call if we have problems. But I'm happy Jasmin is with Chinwe. She couldn't be in safer hands."

"She couldn't, talk to you later."

"We've not got to go home have we?" Midnight asked, after Karen cut the call.

"No, they're managing. Besides, we've got the theatre tonight, then tomorrow morning, if the weather is kind, we're going up in a balloon, and after that experience, as you keep growing, it's a spot of shopping in the afternoon. "

***

Midnight was in bed when Stanley called Karen again. After she answered, he told her what had happened at Frank's.

"That's bad, Stanley. It seems they are determined to keep Chinwe quiet. Have you got details of what police station she's at? I want Melcher to follow up and make sure she stays secure."

"Not as yet, but neither has Jasmin called us and her mobile is dead. The only report I've had is from the commander in charge of special operations."

"What about Frank, is he okay?"

"No, he's in intensive care. They are worried he won't come through."

"You'd better log me a flight plan to the UK for later tomorrow. Also contact Sherry, she'll want to know about Frank and she's due in London tomorrow anyway."

"You're taking Midnight with you to London?"

"Yes, she'll be fine and can return to camp on the service aircraft. Make sure Ariel is in London for when we arrive. Someone will have to stay with Midnight."

Ariel was Midnight's nanny for when she was back at Unit T and Karen was away, but would often accompany the two of them outside of the camp. She had been with them since Midnight came to live with Karen.

"Leave it all to me. I'll text you your flight time and call if there are further problems."

Chapter 22

Chinwe was sitting in the back of the police car, after being collected from Frank's with Jasmin. Now they were on their way to a police station.

"What happened?" Chinwe asked.

"It seems, Chinwe, certain parties are determined you don't get to talk to Karen. But they didn't expect you to be protected. But it's cool, I sorted them out."

"So it was gunshots I heard?"

"Yes. Did it worry you?"

She shook her head. "No, I've been hearing guns being fired since I was a baby. It's a way of life in our part of the country. Where are we going now?"

"The police station, there you will be kept securely until Karen arrives in the UK tomorrow."

They both fell silent, Chinwe looking out of the window, thinking of home and just how far away it seemed.

Why Jasmin did what she did in the next moment, was down to lightning-fast reactions when her sixth sense told her something wasn't right. Out of the corner of her eye as the police car crossed a road junction, she saw a large SUV with a bull bar on the front travelling at speed, heading directly for them - in her view the driver of their car had little or no chance of avoiding a collision. Immediately she grabbed Chinwe, dragging her away from the door as the car hit them on the side Chinwe was sitting on, with the car being shunted sideways before finally stopping dead when it was pushed into a lamppost. The impact threw Chinwe literally over Jasmin, knocking her head on the door pillar, before she passed out.

In seconds two other cars drew up, with the occupants getting out and forcing the back door of the police car open, before dragging Chinwe out. She was carried to one of the cars and thrown into the back. Jasmin was next, and put in the other car. Both cars sped away, leaving the two policemen dazed, one trapped and the other attempting to call for help on his radio.

***

The car Chinwe was inside had been travelling for nearly half an hour. While she'd been awake, she'd felt groggy and slightly disorientated from the blow to her head, not taking much notice of what was happening. But now she was wide awake and beginning to have concerns as to how far away this police station was.

"Where are we going?" she asked.

The passenger turned and looked at her. "Awake at last are we? Thought you'd escaped did you? Believe me kid, that is not going to happen, so just accept it and sit quietly. Otherwise, I'll make sure you do."

Chinwe felt very down. With escaping twice, she expected that this time her punishment would be severe, and was certain there would be no chance to escape again. Even with these thoughts, she was still considering it, although in her mind an attempt had to be made before they got her inside a building. If they did, it was certain they would watch her very carefully and not make the same mistakes.

Following another hour of travelling, the car slowed and turned into the drive of a detached house. Chinwe, as yet, had been unable to form an escape plan. She couldn't see how to overcome two people, who could well be expecting a struggle, and succeed.

The man in the passenger seat turned around to look at her. "Put your hands out, let's get you secure before you leave the car. We can't have you doing a runner can we?" he finished with a smirk on his face.

As he spoke, he put his hands between the two front seats, holding handcuffs, expecting her to just accept what he said. Chinwe suddenly saw a way of possible escape. She snatched the cuffs off him, dropped them to her feet and grabbed his hair, dragging his head between the two front seats towards her and pushing her thumbs into his eyes. This was something her mother had taught her to do if she was ever set upon, with the trick of not going central, but in at the top of the eye sockets, effectively squelching them on the weakest side, like pushing on the side of an egg. The man was screaming in pain when apart from his eyeballs virtually bursting from the pressure of her thumbs, her sharp nails, manicured by the girls the last time she was held, dug into the eyelids, tearing the thin skin open, making him bleed profusely and adding to his discomfort. Then, this position between the seats prevented him from using his hands to drag her hands off his face.

The driver, realising the man was in trouble, also turned to help except Chinwe, knowing the blood oozing around her fingers would temporarily blind the man, let go and dropped her hand into the car well, grabbing the handcuffs, determined to use them as a weapon. Seconds later the driver was hit in the face with the handcuffs. While he was still disorientated by the unexpected blow, and with the handcuffs now gripped in both Chinwe's hands, she dropped them over his head and around his neck, choking him as she pulled him back against the seat headrest with all her strength, determined to at least disable or even kill him.

Much as the man struggled in an attempt to pull the cuffs off to prevent her choking him, the small chain between the cuffs was directly on his windpipe and in seconds he became light-headed, before slumping unconscious.

Chinwe released her grip and reached down, grasping one of his arms, pulling it up so she could snap the handcuff on his wrist, snapping the other end onto the steering wheel. However, even though the man in the passenger seat was in pain and virtually blind, he pulled a gun from his pocket and was attempting to switch off the safety to turn the gun on her. Chinwe saw the gun, but couldn't reach it, so she grabbed the man's hair once more, dragged his head across and smashed it on the steering wheel. Time after time she hit his head on the wheel, trying to make him drop the gun. That was before the gun went off. The noise in the confines of the car was devastating. Chinwe released him, her ears ringing and disorientated, raised her hands to her head, at the same time choking from the cordite smoke in the air. The man in the passenger seat, with his head spinning from Chinwe's onslaught, had problems of his own - the gun he'd fired in panic, not realising where it was directed, had shot himself in the foot. His screams of pain kicked Chinwe into action, opening the car door she virtually fell out onto the road. Without even bothering about whether she'd injured herself, Chinwe was up and running. In her confused mind, the struggle, followed by the sound of a gun, took her back to Africa, to doing as she had done so often, run in panic from gunmen entering her village.

How far she ran Chinwe had no idea, she only stopped when the stitch in her side had become unbearable. The last time she had escaped was in the city, but this time everything looked very different. At first the road had houses set back behind garden gates, but soon that was gone and she was in the countryside. Although this was not countryside as she knew it, there was the constant rumbling sound of traffic, their headlights casting an eerie glow ahead of her. She walked slowly along the poorly lit road before coming to a bridge. Chinwe stood looking down onto a motorway, with headlights of vehicles going in either direction and not even a break. Never had she seen such a busy road and for a time remained captivated and bemused, before she moved on. She had also begun to feel at home, having reached a quieter road with woods on either side, and no streetlights. This was her sort of terrain, an area where she could settle and hide out, finding food, she hoped, in the many shrubs around. Turning off the road, Chinwe was soon deep in the woods. She sat down, leaning on a tree - only now giving herself time to think.

Her thoughts returned to the café and the girl who had arrived to supposedly look after her. She couldn't believe the girl had come from Karen. Then the trust began to disappear as soon as she opened her mouth, with the distinct South African accent. South Africa over the last few years had become particularly violent, and she had also heard from her oldest sister that there were many South Africans who, in search of easy money, had joined gangs that roamed the villages of the Sudan. They were never to be trusted, only there for the money, with no interest that they were destroying families and villages in their hunt for profit. No, she decided. The café couldn't be a part of Karen's operation, it was just a place where the gangs congregated and maybe even the street people, outwardly nice and helpful, had actually sold her back to the traffickers and she'd walked directly into their trap. This meant from now on she must avoid the people on the street, find her own way to where she could contact Karen to come for her. Where that was and who to trust she had no idea, but tonight it was time to sleep, tomorrow she would decide on how to move forward.

Chapter 23

Karen joined Sherry Malloy at the hospital, finding her in a waiting room. She gave Karen a hug.

"How did you know I was here?" Sherry asked.

"Stanley called before I left Nice. I've come directly from home after dropping Midnight off. Ariel's with her now. How's Frank?"

Sherry shook her head. "Not good, Karen. We could lose him. Stanley should never have left Chinwe with him."

"If it was just Frank I'd agree, but Jasmin had gone to Frank's to protect Chinwe. Jasmin had already taken on the four men who came for Chinwe and had control by the time the police arrived."

"So at least Chinwe is safe."

"I hope so, except we don't know where she and Jasmin are being held. I'm seeing the Chief Constable in an hour. Maybe I can get a better picture as to what's gone on."

Sherry frowned. "You're saying Jasmin hasn't contacted Stanley?"

"She hasn't and that's not like Jasmin."

"You'll sort it out. Is LBNF taking Chinwe?"

"No, I've a mind to take her to the camp and send her home from there."

"In that case, I'll remain here with Frank if that's okay?"

"I think you should, Sherry. We're all he has."

"We are. I've also not eaten and am not good at starving for hours like you seem to be able to do. Let's inform the nursing station we're going to the restaurant."

Soon they were sitting at a table in the restaurant.

Sherry was sipping her tea. "I know you've a lot on, but I've a problem in Tossa del Mar which needs your input."

Karen shrugged. "That's what I'm here for, Sherry, it's not your responsibility to sort problems beyond operational aspects, that's up to me. So what has happened?"

"We have at least one girl and maybe more, dealing. I think it's a cartel that's feeding them the drugs."

"Does Odette know?"

"Yes, it was her who told me. She's not sure what to do and with me coming to London and meeting you, she wanted you to be aware."

"Now I'm aware, you forget it, I'll sort these girls out."

Sherry frowned. "How do you manage to do everything, Karen? I'm really serious in asking the question because your responsibilities for Unit T as well as LBNF are far greater than what I have to handle, yet I'm struggling just with my bit."

"I'm surprised you've never asked this question before now, after all, you must know by now how large an operation LBNF is. Take these drug allegations, I've people who will move in and sort it for me. The girls won't know what hit them. You can't look after thousands of victims of trafficking without getting a few bad apples and believe me, over the years I've had my share. But they don't last long, they are out, and any others considering that route will think twice. You need to be ruthless believe me, or those types will walk all over you."

"I can understand that and agree wholeheartedly, the only way is to crack down hard. But what about collecting the rents, the maintenance of all the apartments and villas, apart from security and even down to the lettings, who controls that? I've never understood how things seem to get done, yet no one ever comes to me."

"They won't, those aspects are not part of your job. The complex managers have a number to call. Their calls go through to a central switchboard and requests are coordinated by a team working out of London in control of a million-pound-plus budget. Someone has to direct our maintenance teams as well as security."

"I suppose, now you point it out and with the number of properties you have, you'd need to have considerable resources to keep everything going. Yet you never bring these groups together, seeming to keep them well apart. Why is that?"

Karen gave an indifferent shrug. "It never began like that - take maintenance, at first it was one building service man working from home. Since then we've grown to the size we are now. Then, while policing the complexes in the high-risk areas is Unit T's domain, on the other side, I have to have private contractors on my payroll as well as in Corsica, to keep things secure. I've been fortunate having very good people surrounding me. It also keeps the press from tracking what I'm doing. They have no idea just how large the operation has become, otherwise they would never be away, trying to find a story. So it's best to keep them guessing with the belief it is all me."

Sherry fiddled with her cup. "So I'm a tiny cog in a multimillion pound operation?"

"Tiny yes, but a very important cog, Sherry, relieving me of the mundane day-to-day issues, so never pull yourself down. Your job is to look after the victims, not cloud the issue with the logistics of running the complexes. That's my responsibility. Hopefully when Midnight's old enough, she'll also come on board." Karen glanced at her watch. "Time I wasn't here. Keep in touch, I'll be back later."

Sherry watched her go. Deep down, she was a little put out. She believed they were friends and confided in each other. But on Karen's side, it seemed not, when not only did she run Unit T, but she also controlled a massive logistical operation and it would seem a private security operation unknown to anyone. She wandered back to the intensive care unit, still thinking about what Karen had told her. Then was she surprised? After all, she was a child of a prostitute and alcoholic, with an education that alongside Karen's, was abysmal. Yet Karen had given her an important and prestigious job and she never really knew why. Now she understood, her job was just a front, a position for a friend who stuck by her, with the real power operating in the shadows. An operation where at the drop of a hat, Karen could produce people to sort out the problem in Tossa del Mar. But to do that required planning and more importantly, money and Karen was not short of money. So were the papers not far off the mark with their outlandish claims that Karen was now very close to becoming a billionaire, with a fifty million a year income? Then, if they were, where was all this extra money coming from? The answer was beyond her. Never had she felt as small and insignificant as she did now.

Sherry was met by one of the nurses. "Frank's awake, Sherry. Would you like to talk to him?"

Sherry went into the single room to see Frank with machines surrounding him and the steady but reassuring bleep of the heart monitor. She sat down at his side and grasped his hand gently.

He opened his eyes. "Why it's Sherry, it's nice of you to come."

"I've just arrived. Karen's also been here but she's had to

go to New Scotland Yard, it seems there has been some mix-up with Jasmin and Chinwe. It's a bad business, Frank. Then, she told me over dinner in the hospital restaurant that when you leave here, you're going to France and staying in her house while you recuperate. No argument, you're going. She will take care of the café until you're better."

"Karen's a good friend. Sherry, I don't deserve her, but then, I've never seen the girl so stressed as she is now. I'd only be a nuisance. It's best I just go home."

"Oh come on, this is Karen, she's always stressed. And it's time you got a glimpse of her world for yourself - it's a world I thought I knew, but it seems not. Anyhow, France is her main home, with a housekeeper and security. Corsica, where you spent a couple of weeks on holiday, pales into insignificance compared to France. It's a stunning house, you'll love it. That's if you can put up with Midnight, who'll want you to do things with her all the time? She knackers me with her constant enthusiasm for life."

"Yes, I'd forgotten Midnight's there. It will be nice to see her again. So is Karen there most of the time?"

Sherry grinned. "Karen's the original Scarlet Pimpernel, even Unit T has no idea where she is at times. You'll see her for a couple of days, then without warning she's gone and maybe you'll not see her for a week. Believe me, you see more of her at the café than you will at her home. So you won't be a nuisance for her."

He reached out and gripped her hand. "Tell me, Sherry, why did you say 'it seems not' when you said you believed you knew Karen?"

She shrugged with indifference. "It was silly really, I'd never considered how everything, like repairs, policing of the complexes and all the other thousand and one things that go on in

LBNF get done. Then Karen casually mentioned another operation that runs alongside the charity, that I never even knew existed, yet it employs around a hundred people who look after every aspect of LBNF and her own properties. It makes sense something like that had to exist, I know, but to be with her for years and not know, shook me."

"Yes, she can be very deep, telling you what she wants you to know. But you shouldn't blame her, that's the military side of her coming out. Then with you also coming from the military, you should know you're only told what you need to know to do your part of a job and no more. I remember, a few years back, I had trouble with the taxman and my tiny savings pot. She shrugged it off, giving me a number to ring for an appointment with someone to sort it out for me. I found myself in a large modern building in the heart of London with plush offices. The man I saw resolved everything, but I've never received a bill to this day. Now, by what you've said, I think I went to a building Karen owns and all the people in it work for her. When I mentioned to her that I'd not received a bill, she brushed it off, telling me it was a friend doing her a favour and I owe nothing. Then another thing happened. I was given notice on the café, the landlord was going to knock the entire block down. All of a sudden it was all off and my rent never even went up. I always believed Karen had a hand in it, but I never found out if that was the case."

Sherry gave a weak smile. "It looks like both of us are beholden to her in lots of ways."

"I don't think beholden is the right word, Sherry. I think Karen has always tried to help people, be it a friend or someone in trouble and she doesn't like to flout such assistance in your face, just because she has the means and money to make things happen.

She has very little in her life beyond work, then knowing Karen, who's very astute, she probably writes off most of her assistance, when it's monetary that is, to tax."

Sherry laughed. "Now that's the Karen I love, thoughtful, but always, these days, the businesswoman."

Chapter 24

Karen, accompanied by Unit T's liaison for the UK government Sir Hardy Melcher, was in the office of the Commissioner of Police at New Scotland Yard. Coffee had been brought and following general pleasantries, they were all sitting around a table.

"I'll not beat around the bush, Commissioner," Karen began, "Unit T requires to know why there was such a significant delay for armed assistance as well as medics, for one of my field officers? She was faced with holding four violent men, as well as trying to help a seriously injured man. Furthermore, since her communication from the café waiting for assistance, we've had no word from her. It is essential we know which police station Chinwe and my field officer have been taken to."

The Commissioner looked at Karen, genuinely shocked. "You don't know? Yet I understood a report had been sent directly to Unit T."

Karen frowned. "Excuse me, know what?"

"The car bringing Chinwe and your field operative was in an accident. Apparently it was rammed by a vehicle, leaving two of my officers injured. Chinwe and your operator, according to witnesses, were bundled into two cars, which left the scene."

"You knew about this, Hardy?" Karen asked.

"I didn't, when was the report sent, Commissioner?"

"I'll check," he replied, at the same time lifting the telephone handset and talking to the operations room, then he replaced the receiver and looked at Karen. "It would appear I was misinformed. A report was sent to our Security Services MI6 and they were supposed to inform Unit T and yourself, Hardy. But from what you've told me they have not done so."

"I can assure you they haven't,"

"It would seem there has been a serious breakdown in communication," Karen cut in, obviously concerned. "But this raises another issue that could be part of the same problem, Commissioner. I understand that an instruction was added, that when Unit T make an assistance request to the police, it is to be passed on to your MI6, and should not be acted upon until sanctioned by them? We do not make a request for assistance lightly. There needs to be an immediate or imminent risk to life and it's done when our personnel cannot contain the situation. In view of this development, I cannot allow any of Unit T's personnel to be left in such a position. I've instructed all operations in the UK to be suspended, unless the UK government can give us a firm assurance that such changes will not add delays in obtaining assistance. Without such confirmation, we'll pull out of the UK permanently."

"That is not necessary, Colonel, I've already ordered the instruction to be removed and to refer anything else that alters our arrangements with Unit T to both my office and Sir Hardy's to be sanctioned. We will get to the bottom of this, you have my word."

"Very well, but I am required, as Unit T's commander, while the UK remains in the EU, to remind the UK government officially of their responsibilities and the consequences if this happens again."

"I understand completely and will also be making known the police force's stance on this variation in procedure."

"Wouldn't a request to alter agreed practice have come via my department, Commissioner? We are responsible for coordinating any Unit T operation in the UK with all departments, including the police and military?" Hardy asked.

“I agree, Hardy, normally it should have come from you, but a junior minister at the Home Office sanctioned the request, so my officers didn’t see a reason to seek further clarification from your department.”

“The junior minister, was it Mr Bennett?” Karen asked.

“It was, do you know Mr Bennett?”

“I don’t know him as such, I was summoned to a meeting with him a short time back.”

The commissioner frowned. “Why would he want a meeting with Unit T? He has no ministerial responsibility for anything you do in this country.”

“He wanted Unit T to drop the charges of human trafficking against Sir Richard Knight and his son Sir Robin Knight, as apparently they were working on behalf of MI6. If we agreed, the further charges of engaging contract killers to kill me and an Italian businessman would be transferred to the UK.”

“That would make a difference?” he asked.

Karen decided not to mention that the Italian businessman was in fact the leader of Circulo, in order not to complicate matters. “It would, Commissioner. The Directorate of Public Prosecutions would first consider the case under UK law. There was a suggestion by the minister the case was weak and would be dropped, mostly because it all hinged on a recorded confession, which would normally be dismissed in a UK court. I also attended a meeting at MI6 offices with a Max Hart and Charles Sutton, who reiterated the same request. The meeting with Mr Hart was somewhat thwarted when we refused to move our position, unless directed by the courts. Mr Hart and the minister made it plain to me and Unit T’s legal representative that they were not happy, actually accusing me of pursuing the prosecution through Unit

T because my charity and myself stood to make a considerable amount of money. While under EU law, it is true that proceeds of crime regarding human trafficking are paid over to LBNF, Unit T has never prosecuted with a view to extract money. We follow EU law as it is written."

The commissioner was staring down at a sheet of paper in front of him. Then he looked up at them, both watching him. "Your mention of Mr Hart struck a chord. I've just checked the report of the delay in our response and apparently the instruction came from a department headed by a Mr Hart. When my people talked to him about his delay in sanctioning, he insisted there had been a miscommunication, saying they just wanted to be informed and not to sanction any response. Apparently with the UK leaving the EU and Security Services possibly taking over the role of Unit T, he wanted to keep abreast of operations currently going on in the UK by yourselves. I'll be candid, I don't like what I'm hearing, Colonel. Not on your part, I hasten to add, but about what could on the face of it seem to be collusion between two government departments over having the Knights' charges dropped."

He fell silent for a moment, then sighed. "I will have to get advice as to the police's position on this. I will not have any of my people seem to be attempting to pervert the course of justice, particularly regarding a man who was allegedly involved in a conspiracy that saw a number of my colleagues killed. I assume such intimidation will not result in Unit T dropping the case?"

"I can assure you, as far as Unit T is concerned, only the EU Steering Committee can ask that I do that. Even then, they would need a very good reason as to why I should and their arguments must follow EU law. Can we move to Chinwe and my field operative. Do you have any leads?"

"We don't as yet. But we are currently reviewing CCTV in the area and I've a number of my officers working on statements from the public who witnessed the crash and what followed. Can you tell me why Chinwe could be so important to the traffickers - and why they have taken one of your field officers?"

"I need to consider that in view of what I've heard at this meeting. But an initial thought would be, for what she knows - or what they believe she knows."

"In what way?" the commissioner asked.

"Possible routes from Africa, as well as being able to describe her captors and how the criminal gang who took her operate. As for my field operative, if whoever has taken her has a distorted belief that pressure can be asserted on Unit T for an as yet unknown ransom, they will be very disappointed, it won't happen. We have lost operatives on high-risk operations many times, but Unit T will always pursue the perpetrators and they will pay dearly, I can assure you."

The commissioner frowned. "You seem to have written off your field operative?"

She shrugged. "Commissioner, we are constantly faced with some of the most dangerous criminals, both individually and when they are part of a cartel. Which is why our operations are based on military law and not police procedures. The continued silence of a field operative often points to a possible loss, not that we will stop looking. But our operative may have gone dark for another reason and most can handle themselves in difficult situations, particularly the one who has been taken. If she's not dead, they will need to be very careful in how they contain her. She is extremely dangerous cornered, which they will find to their cost."

"You often use such personnel?"

"No, the UK is not the normal area she operates in. It's just that she was the only person available on short notice to look after Chinwe, which apparently she did, taking prisoner four armed criminals on her own before she called for assistance."

"Very well, we should agree to work together. Perhaps, Hardy, you can sit in with our investigating officers and keep us both abreast of the situation?"

"I will, Commissioner."

"Thank you for your time, Commissioner, I need to move on, we have our own lines of enquiry to pursue," Karen told him, at the same time standing. They shook hands and she left, leaving the commissioner and Sir Hardy alone.

"Do you trust her, Hardy? I'm not getting good reports on how she's operating in the UK, leaving me with concerns."

"I do. But you must realise that apart from having a very difficult job, a number of your own colleagues in the lower ranks have been particularly obstructive, resenting her being here. They seem to forget she is military and as such, their operations are very different to those involving civilian policing. Having said that, at times Karen won't listen to reason, preferring to do her own thing. You can understand it from her point of view. She has hundreds of personnel under her control who risk their lives on a daily basis. Take the field operative who's missing. You could see Karen's attitude and her level of concern, there was none. Karen has written her off and in my view, that is scary, that she could be so complacent about the loss of a colleague. Although, if the girl that's missing is the one I believe her to be, it would be better if she is dead."

"I would certainly be upset at losing an officer in the line of duty, but why do you say she's better dead?"

"I'm given to understand Karen has some field operatives who are very violent and used in special situations. The girl she's lost is one such operative and will one day, if not now, die by the gun, But even she's nothing to what Karen's capable of. Karen's wealth makes her very powerful, particularly politically, with the backing of the public who see her as some sort of knight in shining armour, but the real Karen is not like the public's perception, of being kind, thoughtful, someone who looks after children and brings them home - she's ruthless, uncompromising, with a distorted view of what is right or wrong."

He sighed. "It's a mess, Hardy. I'm going to have to report to the Prime Minister, his secretary has already been in touch and pencilled in an appointment. He is not going to be happy. For reasons only known to himself, he likes Karen a great deal, and is working behind the scenes for Unit T to still have access into the UK after we leave the EU. I think it will happen, very much like we will still contribute to NATO."

"It is for the best. As Karen said, the criminals she pursues are extremely dangerous and we can't afford the free-for-all that would come to the UK, if she pulled out."

Chapter 25

Jasmin couldn't believe the lengths someone was going to capture Chinwe. But why her, she'd be no value to them? Jasmin was also very fortunate they hadn't searched her, believing the gun in her hand would be her only weapon. But like Karen, she carried an ankle knife and if given the chance she would use it. But first she needed to be released from the handcuffs.

The car Jasmin was in stopped within a quarter of a mile of the crash. She was dragged out, only to be pushed into the back of a waiting van. Even as she was being transferred, Jasmin could see a man ripping off the number plates of the car she'd arrived in, revealing a completely different number. Now she was certain this was a snatch, but to what end? Karen would not negotiate, she was on her own, although she knew Karen would never give up and would find the abductors, whether she survived or not.

They travelled on for around an hour, before the van slowed. Jasmin suspected, from the way the van was being thrown around, they must have turned onto an unmade road or track. Soon the van came to a halt, the engine cut. They had reached their destination, but where? Again Jasmin was dragged out and this time, marched through the open door of an otherwise blank wall into a back hallway. A door halfway down was open and Jasmin was taken through it, then down some stone steps opening out into a small area with three doors. One door was already open, revealing a small windowless room. This was the one she was taken into. The handcuffs were removed before she was pushed inside. The men slammed the door shut, then there was the distinct sound of a key being turned in the lock, along with a bolt being slid into place. Jasmin looked at the door. Their caution in using a bolt outside was understandable, the door's lock assembly was screwed to the inside, designed to prevent someone from gaining access once the lock was secured. However, if someone was inside without the addition of the bolt, all that would be needed was a screwdriver to remove the lock assembly and the door would open.

She looked around. The room was dimly lit by a single light bulb hanging on an old rusty hook fixed in the wall, The cable for the light left the room through a small triangle cut in the bottom corner of the door. There was nothing else there, so Jasmin sat on the floor, leaning against the far wall, enabling her to see who came in. She considered removing the knife from its sheath, but at this stage decided against it. She could well be facing a gun, maybe more than one person, so to reveal her only means of defence was not advisable, until she knew the extent of the threat.

***

Time went on, in fact, she'd been in the room virtually a day according to her watch, with not a sound coming from outside. She had also drifted off to sleep a few times before waking with a start, when she heard voices. The bolt of the door was slid open, followed by the sound of the lock turning over. Two men came inside. The larger of the two carried a short stubby cosh; he was wearing jeans and a jumper. The other man wore a suit. He closed and locked the door behind him, pocketed the key, then looked at her.

To Jasmin, locking the door was an obvious precaution, making any attempt to get out impossible, but in another way it was intimidating, in that they must have the intention to remain in the room for some time, rather than just feed her. Not that she could see anything like a bag or container that might have food.

"What do I call you?" the man in the suit asked.

"Jasmin - and you?"

"Vincent, and my associate Spooner."

Jasmin stifled a laugh, he looked like a Vincent. "I seem to have disturbed your night, Vincent, dressed as you are," she commented in a mocking sort of way.

"No, not at all, I've had a very pleasant afternoon, relaxing following an exceptional lunch. A little better than you've experienced, I assume?"

She gave him a withering look, preferring not to comment.

"Anyway," he continued. "I presume you'll be interested in knowing why you are here and more importantly, what will happen to you if certain actions don't follow?"

She shrugged. "Oh, I'm really excited to know. Can't you see me ready to jump for joy to learn my fate? Before you begin with this enlightening explanation, how about you allow me to eat and use the toilet, after leaving me here for hours with not even a bottle of water? Prisoners at least get fed."

He shook his head, allowing a smile to cross his face. "Maybe prisoners do get such luxuries, but you're not one, you're a hostage. Whether you get out of here alive depends if you are wanted by an interested party, if not, whether your boss, Harris, is going to cooperate. Your request for food is not going to happen. After all, this is not a hotel, so you can hardly expect to be fed, provided with a blanket or anything else to make your stay more comfortable. As for the toilet, you can squat in the corner for all I care."

Jasmin shrugged indifferently. "Then you're wasting your time, Karen doesn't negotiate. All field operatives know that. We're on our own. But believe this, if I'm dead or not, she will come for you. It's what she does and she will never give up. Then expect a bullet in the head - Karen won't give shit like you the opportunity to squirm your way out with fancy lawyers."

Vincent suddenly changed his stance and raised his hands to face-height, beginning a weak effeminate clap. "Oh, such brave words for a girl in the position you're in, don't you think, Spooner?" he virtually squeaked.

Jasmin stifled a laugh, the man was nothing like the threat of Spooner if his mannerisms were to be believed. She'd enjoy making him squirm.

However, Vincent carried on. "But oh so meaningless. Because if the interested party doesn't want you and Harris doesn't do as we request, it won't be a bullet in the head for you - you, girl, will starve to death. No one will come; no one will hear your screams for help. Plenty of time to understand what a shit your boss is, if she's prepared to let one of her own starve to death. It is not a nice death, so I'm led to believe. So before we leave you to contemplate your future, or not, I'll have the clothes, to add to your discomfort. Then I'll take your photo for our client, or maybe for Harris to see your dilemma, when we tell her just how cold your room gets at night, coupled with the complete lack of food and hygiene, for as long as it takes for her to come to your aid. With such problems on your side, maybe it will change her mind on this one occasion."

Jasmin came back at him with aggression in her voice. "If you have the belief I'm stripping so you can take a photo, you're one off. I strip for no man."

Vincent looked towards Spooner. "Do you hear that, Spooner, Jasmin's shy, with an aversion to being photographed naked? You should give her a sharp lesson to remind her it is us in charge here, not her, so she knows if she continues to refuse to strip, we'll have fun stripping her ourselves and maybe give her a going-away present - after all, it could well be her last shag."

Jasmin realised from the way Vincent had been talking earlier, there could be a distinct possibility she would never see either of them again? That is once they had their photo and the door slammed shut, particularly if this so called client of theirs rejected her, leaving only Karen. After all, even if Karen agreed to their demands, would they let her go free, or keep raising the bar squeezing more and more out of Karen? Jasmin knew, because of such a possibility, Karen would not enter into any negotiation, but go all out to find her, but time would not be on her side before she starved to death.. Either way, Jasmin had no intention of sitting around in this room naked and starving without putting up a fight. Vincent's naive idea she'd strip voluntarily gave her the opportunity to refuse and required Vincent to force her by using Spooner. She also considered if Vincent saw she was gaining the upper hand with Spooner, he was not the sort to assist and may even decide to leave the room and lock them both in, besides throw away the key. This mustn't happen, so her position as she took Spooner on must be such that it would be impossible for Vincent to leave. Since they'd entered the room, Jasmin had also weighed up the cosh Spooner held. This was not a weapon he should be using, unless it was the telescopic version, which she doubted. The cosh was far too short, requiring him to come very close for it to have any practical use. It may be good for hitting someone from behind, or even a defenceless woman, but a Unit T field operative, trained in close combat? He was in for a nasty shock if he'd not considered the possibility he'd be facing a dangerous and competent opponent with a very poor weapon to aid him.

Spooner also had the added disadvantage of taking on a

contract killer, who would never fight to disable - for them there could be only one result, killing their opponent, giving their quarry no chance of retaliating.

All these thoughts were flashing through Jasmin's mind as she weighed up Spooner. His height, his stance, his handling of the cosh and what hand he held it in, all made a difference. While she did this Jasmin began to back away, purposely moving around the room as if in retreat, but determined to push Vincent away from the fight area and thus the door, to remain safe and not become embroiled himself.

"There's nowhere to run, Jasmin, you must have noticed I locked the door and hold the key. So why not strip like a good little girl and Spooner here will leave you alone," Vincent mocked, while moving further into the room, out of the way of the inevitable oncoming fight, if she still refused to do as ordered.

Meanwhile, Spooner, waiting for Vincent to move out of Jasmin's way, had begun to lean slightly forward, passing his cosh from hand to hand with a huge grin across his face, ready to enjoy beating her up. "Time to face the music, kid," he mocked, with obvious confidence that she'd just fall apart. Then, without further delay he came directly at Jasmin, raising his hand to strike her with the cosh in his right hand - once close enough, that is.

It was all Jasmin could do not to laugh. His balance was wrong, his other hand flailing, she just sidestepped at the last moment, kicking the leg on her side from under him, sending him stumbling and crashing into the wall. But unlike any fair fight or film that would allow the attacker to stand up and resume for effect and excitement, Jasmin followed him down, drew the knife from its sheath and sliced the right shoulder in a disabling move. Spooner screamed in pain, dropping the cosh, as Jasmin pulled away slightly, positioning herself to take hold of his hair in one hand, to drag his head back – which then allowed her to draw the knife across his throat. Seconds later he was in his death throes and she turned her attention towards Vincent.

Vincent's mouth had dropped open; the speed of the girl in downing Spooner stunned him, leaving him in shock and fear for his own life, while staring at the ever-increasing blood pool surrounding Spooner. Never in his life had he seen someone die. Even now it was so quick he could hardly believe it had happened.

"Just you and me now, Vincent," Jasmin commented, at the same time wiping the bloodied knife on Spooner's clothes. "It was very remiss of the person you work for, not mentioning that you should be very careful around me. You see, I've been killing since I was eighteen, it's second nature and comes with no remorse on my part. Spooner was a threat, so he died, I don't take prisoners, particularly ones who are out to kill me. Then the gloves are off and it's every man or woman for themselves. Are you prepared to take me on and die, or do you intend to remain the little shit you are, hiding behind others to do your dirty work?"

"You've made your point. What do you want of me?"

"The key for a start, we can't have you making an attempt to leave. Not that you'd get far."

He pulled the key out of his pocket and held it out for her to take.

"Place it on the floor, then back away, facing the wall."

Jasmin collected the key, then went over to Spooner, checking his pockets and pulling out a mobile phone. She pressed the buttons, but it was locked. "You have a mobile?" she asked Vincent, standing up.

"I do."

"Then place it on the floor like the key and go back to the wall."

He looked at her as he placed the phone on the ground. "What are your intentions for me?" he asked, at the same time backing away to the wall.

"I've not decided. Why?"

He shrugged. "Why shouldn't I ask, after all, it is my future I'm asking about?"

"True, so who are you working for?"

"That I can't tell you. But you should leave Unit T, powerful people are closing in on Harris. She's on her way to a spectacular downfall and will take many with her."

"Our commander will weather it, have no doubt," Jasmin commented, at the same time trying the mobile. Again, like Spooner's phone, the mobile was locked. "What's the unlock code?"

"All the fours."

She pressed the buttons to satisfy herself that was correct, then opened the door before glancing back inside. "Hope you had a good meal earlier, if you want to shit use the corner," she said, then left the room, slamming the door shut and locking it before making her way cautiously up the cellar steps and into the hallway. At one end of the hall was a door, half open, which she assumed would lead outside. At the other end were two doors.

Holding her knife tightly, Jasmin silently moved down to the two doors. She very carefully opened the first to reveal a room obviously abandoned and damaged by vandalism. The room opposite, a kitchen, was similar. Confident there was no one else in the building, downstairs at least, Jasmin turned her attention outside. The area was deserted apart from one car parked a short distance away. Jasmin dialled Unit T, giving a special access code once connected.

"Jasmin, we were getting a little concerned not hearing from you, where are you?" Stanley asked, once the switchboard had put her through.

"God knows, Stanley, it looks like a derelict farm, can you get a fix on the mobile I'm calling on?"

"Will do, do you need assistance?"

"Not really, there is a car so I can get out of here. I've had to kill one man, but the other is contained and could give information. So you may prefer I stay until you talk to Karen. The place looks empty, but I still need to make doubly sure."

"Is Chinwe with you?"

"No, I've not seen her. Again, I'll need to do a thorough search to confirm that."

"Do nothing, Jasmin, till I check with Karen. But at the very least, she'll want to interview the man who's left. She'll also want you out of the building in case any others arrive before a Dark Angel unit can get to you. You should not be in a position to risk confrontation. You're alive, that's the most important thing. It would be good if you can take photos of the house and surrounding area. That will allow us to pinpoint your exact position, when added to the mobile's coordinates. Just hold a moment." He went silent, Jasmin waited and watched. "We have your approximate location. We've a Dark Angel unit around three quarters of an hour away. I'll mobilise it as we speak. Take photos, Jasmin, it'll save delays."

"Okay, I'll call if there are any developments."

Outside was a large concrete area, probably the foundations of a long gone barn or just a parking area for farm implements.

Already weeds were growing through. The edges were far more overgrown, with shrubs and long grass. Jasmin had no problem hiding in a position to see anyone approaching. While she waited, she sent the photos of the outside area to Stanley.

She'd silenced the mobile after settling down, leaving it on vibrate, and it now began to buzz.

"Hello," she asked quietly, believing it was Stanley or the officer in charge of the Dark Angel group heading to her.

"Who's that, where's Vincent?" a male voice asked.

Jasmin thought quickly, she needed a likely excuse as to why she was answering. "I'm Shelly, Vincent's tied up for the moment. Can I get him to call you?"

"What do you mean tied up; he's supposed to be at the farm."

"We are, well, I'm sitting in a car outside what looks like one and he's inside. Left his phone on the car seat. I can go and find him if you want?"

"No, you stay where you are. When he comes out of the house, tell him it's Don and to call me back."

"Has he your number? You're showing as withheld."

"Of course he knows it," he said, then cut the call.

Twenty minutes later the phone vibrated once more.

"Hello," Jasmin said again.

"Jasmin?"

"Yes, who's that?"

"Lieutenant Cropper, we're less than fifteen minutes away, are you okay?"

"I am. You have made fantastic time. I'm outside watching the entrance, but it's all quiet."

"That's good. Most of our journey has been on the

motorway so we've managed to average close to ninety all the way, with our blue lights flashing. Your location is on a B-road with no real turn-offs, apart from to a couple of villages. There would not be an alternative route if someone was travelling from where you are to London. We'll be on the B-road in minutes, then I intend to keep our second vehicle a distance behind us. We have the registration of the vehicle from your photos, so if someone you haven't seen decides to leave in it, don't prevent them, we'll block the road and pull it in."

"Thanks, I've only got my knife as a weapon."

"Defence only, Jasmin, no heroics, love."

"I promise."

"We're turning onto the B-road as I speak. They're stuffed now. Be with you very soon, but keep the line open, then you can update us in real-time."

The first Unit T vehicle came screaming up the track. With blue lights still flashing, five soldiers, all wearing combat gear and carrying M4 carbines, piled out of the vehicle, taking up defensive positions, even before it had come to a complete standstill. Minutes later the next one arrived, with more soldiers. Jasmin came from the undergrowth and waved. It would seem Stanley had gone for overkill and sent a complete unit, for one man, if you could call Vincent any sort of man. A soldier ran up to Jasmin, taking the key to the downstairs door off her, before ordering her to remain out of sight until they had secured the building. She did as he asked; it was up to Dark Angel to sort it out now.

Chapter 26

Karen arrived at the farm where Jasmin had been held an hour after Dark Angel secured the place. Only one Unit T vehicle remained, the other, carrying Jasmin and a number of soldiers, had returned to London.

Lieutenant Cropper saluted Karen when she climbed out of her vehicle.

"Where's the prisoner?" Karen asked.

"In the kitchen, Commander. We also have one dead. I have a short written report by Jasmin as to what transpired. She'll make a detailed report back at base." He handed the report to Karen, who read it through.

"Right," Karen said, at the same time handing back the report. "It's time he and I had a conversation."

She walked into the lounge, while the soldier guarding the prisoner left the room, pulling the door shut.

Vincent looked at who had entered. Immediately, although he'd never met Karen, he recognised her from the many photos often splashed across the media. Even so, he was surprised how feminine-looking and attractive she was. In the business she was in he'd expected her to be more of a hard-featured woman, reflecting the constant strain she must be under. But if she was under such stress she wasn't showing it.

"The name's Colonel Harris, commander of Unit T. It looks like you're in the shit, Vincent," Karen commented, taking a seat at the table opposite him. "Now we have you, you'll be abandoned by your partners. They'll not lift a finger to help, allowing you to be sent down for ten years for abduction, then with the addition of attempted murder in the charges, maybe more, unless you can convince the judge you never intended to kill the girl. Mind you, unlike most sentences, where you can earn fifty per cent off for good behaviour, that doesn't exist if you're prosecuted by Unit T, there is no remission. Believe me, it will break someone like you, every day being a living nightmare." Then she gave an indifferent shrug. "While you fester in prison, I, or rather LBNF, mandated by the EU to pursue any person convicted of abduction or trafficking offences, will instigate legal redress for the victims under proceeds of crime. That will put your family out on the street, if you have a family that is? Either way you lose everything."

He looked clearly shaken as she spelled out the ramifications of his involvement, but quickly pulled himself together to come back at her. "You have the belief I'll go to prison on my own, do you? I won't, I was told a dossier was being built about your often illegal activities and soon you'll be answering far more difficult questions than me. I'll be a hero helping to point the finger at you, not a criminal in prison."

Karen said nothing at first, pulling two snack bars from her pocket, offering him one. "I missed my dinner, having to come here, would you like one?" she asked.

He shook his head.

She pocketed one bar and began to eat the other slowly, before relaxing back on the chair. "You really believe your co-conspirators can take me down, do you?"

"They tell me they can," he answered confidently.

She shook her head slowly. "Sorry to disappoint, Vincent, they're winding you up, so you'll take all the blame. I can assure you it won't happen."

"You're saying that to save face."

"Am I? An interesting assumption on your part, but a very

long way from reality."

"Why?"

"Have you any idea just how many in the past have tried to take such a road? Believe me, a great many, some high up in governments, senior police officers, important persons in Security Services and even the judiciary, but you see, Vincent, it will come to nothing. Let me explain why to you in simple terms. Such people have no perception of the grey world I live in and the way it works. It's violent, and no one cares about anyone else. However, for those who dip their toes into this world, from the investor who likes the high returns on their money, or perhaps a person who wants a bag of weed, a trafficked girl or a child, someone in this grey underworld provides the service. The provider will also know that participant's name and maybe what position he or she holds. But what is less known by such participants, is that their name has a monetary value beyond the income received for whatever was provided. Drug dealers and providers of girls are always looking for clients, fraudsters looking for victims, and informers looking for income, so you can understand that such knowledge has a price. Informers looking for an extra few quid to cover their next fix, to informers making a business out of selling information, are always on the lookout for buyers of their information. For me, knowing what's happening and more importantly, the names of people using such services, is paramount to doing my job. Why should informers come to me? Because we at Unit T are the best and most reliable of payers, with no comeback for the informer. Those who attempt to pull me down are not the ordinary man in the street, who have the belief I'm one of the good guys, but the very ones with their toes in the water, who want me out so they can carry on their investments or depravities without constantly looking over their shoulder. Those sort of people also have the mistaken idea if I'm gone, the knowledge of their indiscretions also disappears. It's a naive belief, Unit T will always be there, no matter who leads it, and Unit T will have logged their name and what they are involved with into the database."

Karen hesitated for a moment to let her statement sink in. "Then, armed with perhaps a snippet, we watch and wait. Unit T is like the internet, information never goes away; it can only be built on, except this build-up of information can be devastating for the individual. You wouldn't believe what we know about all manner of people, but we choose to bide our time to let the person hang themselves, or we join up bits of information directing us to the ones who run, or finance the larger groups."

Vincent was no fool. Karen's explanation as to why any attempt to take her down would risk failure, in his view could be true, coupled with her wealth which would be a factor, giving her access to the best legal brains available to hide behind. Then, with her talk about using informers, it would seem she was at times turning a blind eye to what was going on, with a view to going for the people at the top. Was there a get-out clause for him here? He had to try, or the alternative, no matter what happened to her, was he faced years in prison.

"The way you're talking, informers play an important part in your operation and ones who have value could possibly earn special consideration?"

Karen smiled inwardly to herself. How many times over the years had she sat down under the same circumstances, watching criminals squirm as they had the reality of their situation spelled out to them? Of course, this was a tactic that often got results. People like Vincent were two a penny, low-grade in the pecking order. And as he suggested, she could ignore a criminal act if it took her further towards the real perpetrators, but Vincent made a living doing jobs for such people, he would soon trip up and if his usefulness had come to an end she would pull away and allow the authorities to put him behind bars. Their eyes met. "If you believe you have a value, anything is possible."

"I certainly have value. So with that in mind, what has happened here could be made to go away, as far as I'm concerned?"

"It could."

"I see, but with me not being a trusting person over what people say off-the-cuff, so to speak, do you have such power? After all, you're not alone, with soldiers knowing, and then, there's the girl, who may be a little pissed off if I walk away. Would they not object?"

Karen gave an indifferent shrug. "We're military - that means we take orders from those above us. We don't question, because if we do, in times of conflict, how can you send people to their deaths if everyone questions right or wrong? As a soldier you just accept what is being done is the correct way. Often it's because the officer giving the order has that little bit more knowledge about the operation than you. As for the girl, she's one of my field operators. Her part in the operation is finished and she's moved on and believe me, she has no interest in what happens to you. Although, there are occasions when she may be called back. One being if Unit T prosecutes, then she'd become a material witness." Karen hesitated for a moment to make an important point. "The second would be if this operation expanded and required her unique skills, similar to what you've already witnessed."

"So she's more than just a field operative?"

"You'd better believe it. In fact, out of all my field

operatives, she was the last one you should have snatched."

Vincent shuddered inwardly; he had heard that Karen had professional killers on her books. Was Jasmin one, particularly when she'd claimed she'd been killing since the age of eighteen and in particular, given the way she dispatched Spooner so coldly? "So if I agree, you will keep me out of this?"

"Of course, work for me as an informer and you walk out of here. You may ask, how am I going to ensure that? My report can just state our field officer was brought here by one person and a fight ensued, resulting in his death. I can't see you running down to the police station and giving another version that would see you in prison. After all, if I was questioned later, I'd claim you must have been hiding and we didn't find you. You can be sure the girl who was here will claim the same, as well as my troops."

"Yes, I've heard you often make your own rules up as you go along."

"Not rules, Vincent, variations as to what really happened, but only if it moves me forward. Even so, it's a bloody good job I can, don't you think? So what's it to be - prison or freedom? I'll leave you for a short time to think about it. But while you consider my offer, if you believe you can spin me fairy tales, think again. Whatever you say must match up with what we already know. I always cross- reference and you'd be surprised what information we already have, so we'll know immediately if what you are telling us doesn't add up. Also, I don't have the time to be messed about so you can be sure if I believe you are doing that, you will find we can be just as bad as the people you work for."

"You mean you'll send your thugs after me?"

Karen gave a hint of a smile, standing at the same time. "Too messy, and the health service has far better things to do than patch up informers who receive gentle reminders. In our case, I suggest you don't make too long a commitment as to your future. If you understand my meaning?" Then she left the room.

Vincent remained seated. She had him and he knew it. But what was he getting into? He'd made a living doing the bidding of the rich. He was of course very aware just how dangerous it was to take on Unit T, particularly their commander, but if things had gone his way it would stand him in good stead for more work to come his way.

Shortly Karen returned and stood at the door, looking towards him. "Well, are you in, or out?"

"I'm in."

"Very well." Then she pulled a mobile from her jeans pocket, showing it to him. Vincent recognised it as his phone, and the one Jasmin had taken away.

"For a start, while you were locked in the cellar a man called Don rang. My operative answered, calling herself Shelly and told him she was sitting in the car waiting for you to come out of the building. She wanted to know if she should fetch you, but he said no. He wants you to call him. Who is he?"

"Don Wang, he's the man who passed me this job."

Karen frowned. "He must have some very good contacts, after all, my operative had already called for police assistance and she and Chinwe were on their way to the local station, when they were hit deliberately and both of them were taken. How did he manage to get people in position to do that? Then, was his information coming from the police themselves?"

Vincent shrugged. "That I can't tell you as I don't know. But have you ever heard of the Blackthorns, a family into drugs that also provide prostitutes, some trafficked and some underage?"

"I have," she answered, but didn't elaborate as to what she was doing about them.

"I suspected you would. Don called me to say the Blackthorns, who I've dealt with in the past, had told him one of their girls called Chinwe had escaped and was now holed up in a café. People had been sent to get her out and I was to collect Chinwe off them. Apparently the Blackthorns had had enough of her. This was the second time she'd escaped and they didn't want her back. Don had purchased her cheap from a trafficker. I don't know who that was. My part was to secure Chinwe while he made arrangements for her to leave the country. He called a little later and told me plans had changed. His contacts in the police and MI6 had become involved, after your operative captured the men who went for her. However, Don had been able to delay the police going to the café while he set up a means of taking Chinwe back. How he did that and how your girl ended up here I've no idea. But all of a sudden Chinwe was on her way out of the country, and the field operative dumped here. Don then told me your girl could well be the one a criminal cartel was looking for. If it was, they'd pay a great deal of money for her. I was to come here, take a photo so he could send it to the cartel. The photo of her had to be naked, to indicate a birth mark that would identify her. I asked what mark they were looking for, but he didn't know. I think the cartel didn't tell him where it was on the body or what it looked like in case he painted it on. If it wasn't the girl, nothing was lost, he had Chinwe and would barter your operative with you. I was to leave her in the cellar. I'm not sure who was going to feed her, but I understood no one was."

"Charming man, isn't he? But why is Chinwe so important that people are going to such lengths to get her back?"

"Who knows what a girl sees as she's taken from place to place, besides, she'd be able to describe minders as well as clients to the authorities. Your mistake was to leave her relatively unprotected. After all, a café, come on - I thought Unit T were better than that."

Karen gave an indifferent shrug. "For us she was just another girl to be taken home, if I'd suspected even the police couldn't be trusted, she'd not have remained there. Under normal circumstances, a field operative would have been sufficient to protect her. As it is, it's time to call Don and tell him you have the photo and arrange a meeting. If he asks about the girl who answered, she was someone you'd met at a pub or whatever and had no idea why you were at the farm. She was just waiting for you to come out and take her home. Which is why you are late calling back, she never passed the message on."

He smiled. "You have it all planned, don't you? Is this how you operate?"

"This isn't planning, I'm here in response to one of my operatives being in trouble and building a way out for you. When we plan you'd never see us coming until it was too late. But before you call this Don, Chinwe - have you an idea where she'd have been taken?"

Vincent thought for a moment. "If she's leaving the country, Don would want her in Liverpool. There's a halfway house girls are kept between Liverpool and London, somewhere outside Birmingham. I can try to get you an address, but I'll need to talk to people who may know."

"Very well, one step at a time, call Don."

Vincent took the mobile and called the number.

"Where the fuck have you been. I told your woman to call

me soon as?" Don demanded.

"She's a fucking wanker, Don. Got back to the car after taking the photos and she'd taken a couple of mollys. High as a fucking kite she was. She's only just come round and told me about your call. I'll give her a good thrashing later to teach her a lesson, she's useless anyway."

"You do that."

"I will, what about the girl, she's had nothing to eat or drink?"

"Forget her, if she is the girl they want I'll know in a few hours, then we'll feed her and move her on, otherwise if Harris won't deal, she's of no value, so it's one less piece of shit fucking our operations up."

"If that's what you want. When are we meeting for the payment? I'll give you the photos then."

Don gave a forced laugh. "Don't trust me to pay you, so you're holding back the photos?"

"It's business for us, Don. We do a job and get paid."

"When are you back in London?"

"I'm already here."

"Then we'll meet in the car park of the M25 service station at South Mimms in two hours. Don't bring Spooner, just yourself. You can pay him later."

"I'll be there," he said, then cut the call.

"You did well, it was convincing," Karen told him.

"Maybe, what about the photos?"

"I'll have them downloaded onto your mobile, so you can pass them across to him. It won't be her, for reasons you don't need to know."

Vincent grinned. "So your operatives are shy at taking

their clothes off and you need a stripper? I would think in their line of work, it's the norm, even for you in the past I suspect?"

Karen gave an indifferent shrug. "One of the hazards of being a female operating in what is ostensibly a man's world. If it served a purpose why not, but in this case it would serve none, apart from identifying one of my operatives to a cartel, which I don't intend happening."

"Then I'd better get off, it's a good hour's drive with no traffic, and he thinks I'm in London."

"You do that, we'll be in touch."

Karen watched him drive away and called her surveillance team, giving them the location where Vincent was to meet Don. Then she called Stanley. "Are we tracking?" she asked.

"We are, both the car and the mobile are online. Do you think we've lost Chinwe?"

"If I was them, she'd be dead by now. But this is traffickers; they believe they can control anyone. Many have learnt the hard way with me, that that's not the case, but it hasn't stopped some from trying. So there's a good chance she's still alive. As it is, Stanley, she's now become superfluous in this game; we are after bigger fish, ones who can go as far as keeping tabs on police operations and maybe even manipulating the Security Services of the country."

"I think you're correct. It'll be interesting to see who this Don Wang contacts."

"It will. We'll talk later, after their meeting. I'm going to drop in on Frank, then go home."

Chapter 27

Don Wang, originally from Hong Kong, turned his car down the long drive of a large country house in Kent. He was a small man, with round wire-rimmed glasses. Already he had collected the photos from Vincent and paid him off. Now he was meeting a consortium of businessmen he worked with. A number of vehicles were already parked in a large gravel area outside the front of the house.

Don walked up to the front door and pressed the bell. In seconds the door was opened by a tall man wearing a pinstripe suit, with greying hair and coming up to the age of fifty.

"Ah, Don, at last, we were getting a little worried you'd not be here for the meeting." The man who welcomed him was Julian Sharp. He worked in the city and owned this house.

"Apologies, Julian. My contact was insistent he was paid for the job, before he'd hand over the photos. It's understandable, he'd made a journey to the farm and that was not part of our original plan."

"It's worth it if the girl taken with Chinwe is indeed the one wanted by Circulo. They are offering big money and it's a fifty-fifty share between you and me."

"And no one else is involved?"

"No, they believe we've just pulled Chinwe to protect our routes."

"No problems - let us go through to the lounge."

Inside the large lounge a number of men were standing around, holding wine glasses and talking between themselves.

"Let me see the photos?" Julian asked.

Julian looked at the shots that had been transferred to

Don's mobile phone.

"Is it the girl the cartel's looking for?" Don wanted to know.

Julian sighed. "Bart, have you a minute?" he called, somewhat concerned after looking at the photos.

Bart, a man in his forties, came over.

"Didn't you know the contract killer Jasmin Dlamini, who worked with Nick?"

He smiled. "No one ever knew that one. But I did meet her once at Circulo, why do you ask?"

"Nothing concrete, but Don's obtained this photo off someone holding her and claiming she's the girl Circulo's looking for. What are your thoughts?"

Bart looked at the photo. "If it is, she's shrunk and changed her hair colour and style. So no, she's not the Dlamini I met."

"Thanks, Bart."

After he wandered off, Julian turned to Don. "You're absolutely certain this was the Unit T girl at the farm?"

"I have to presume so. I never saw her; she was taken directly to the farm? But while we knew the girl was a Unit T field operative, why did you suspect her to be the one wanted by a cartel?"

"A contact inside Unit T told me that a girl called Jasmin Wright had been directed to Frank's café in order to look after Chinwe. Her ID taken at the café confirmed this. Her real name is Jasmin Dlamini but she uses the name Wright in Unit T. It is known that Dlamini, a South African, is now working alongside Harris - our contact confirmed some time back that it was Harris who brought her into Unit T and she received training from Dark Angel's experts. Her reports from the trainers showed a very competent girl, well used to being around guns, with an extraordinary ability in marksmanship before she even arrived. Harris does not have idiots alongside her. Such a girl must achieve Harris' level in capabilities and the ability to operate alone when taking on extremely violent and vicious opponents. Dlamini is such a girl and very like Harris - a cold-blooded killer of the worst kind. And so she should be, after all, Dlamini was working freelance with a male contract killer, mainly for Circulo, before he was killed. You had to be good to work for Circulo. When we got word that an armed response team was to be dispatched to the café to assist a girl holding four armed men at bay, I knew it could only be Dlamini. I gave Circulo's boss Ale a call. He desperately wanted that girl, she killed their previous leader and as their new leader, he'd pledged to find and execute the assassin in front of the heads of the many groups that make up the cartel. But if Vincent was at the farm it raises a concern in my mind. Did they underestimate just who they had, and couldn't hold her? If that was the case and she gained the upper hand and Vincent is still alive, has he been compromised, and might he now be working as an informer for Harris? That, Don, puts not only you at risk, but everyone in this room, if Harris is on to us."

"Shit, if you're right, I've brought her directly here."

"You have, so we need to make appropriate arrangements. If any of the group are approached by Unit T they must all have the same covering story. As for Vincent, don't give him any inkling we are onto him, then maybe we can pass him misinformation to feed back to Harris."

"Good thinking. Shall we get on with our meeting?"

Julian turned to the room. "Gentlemen, please, it is time to begin the meeting, shall we all go through?"

Soon everyone was sitting around a large table in the dining room.

"As you all know," Julian began. "Unit T has turned its huge resources towards our clients operations in the UK because of the escape of a girl called Chinwe. If that wasn't enough, even though she was re-captured the Blackthorn group, who purchased her, also allowed her to escape. Now we face yet another problem with that girl. I won't go into details as to how, but no sooner was she re-captured she's escaped again."

"Are people searching for her?" one asked.

"They are, but this time the thinking on what to do with her has changed. While originally she was heading to Algeria and a brothel that she could not escape from, that is not now going to happen. When Chinwe's found, she will be eliminated. Unfortunately, her escapes have caused a great deal of disruption to people we finance, requiring them to move operations. While Fabian Nowak is not responsible for Chinwe's initial escape, both he and his partner Eryk Kowalski, along with the Blackthorns, pose a real financial risk to us."

"Why is that?" another in the room asked.

"We believe, but it is not certain, Karen Harris is on to them. This is why it's important to find Chinwe. Information from her, particularly descriptions and in the Blackthorns' case, about how they are operating, may accelerate Harris's investigation. Then, if Harris can make a link between them and us, she'll hit us hard and we all stand to lose our liberty and assets, like the Knights are risking at present. Although we're still hopeful we can get the Knights' charges thrown out for them, it's not easy while Harris is calling the shots. Associates of ours, who have been working to exert influence with people who hopefully could change Harris's mind, have reported back disturbing news. Harris will not change her stance, hiding behind the legal arguments among other things. I understand instructions have now been passed down from the inner circle to eliminate any routes that might come back to us - that includes Nowak, Kowalski and the Blackthorns, as well as certain people attempting to get the Knights off the trafficking charges. I cannot disagree with their concerns; the risks of giving Harris any route to us are too high."

"But what of our investment in the farms decarbing cannabis, run by Kowalski and Nowak?" Gavin, one of the men in the room, commented. "It's now coming to fruition."

"No problems, Gavin, we have people who will take over. You didn't think for one moment we'd rely on two criminals to run such a lucrative enterprise? They were good as fall guys, but beyond that are worthless."

"Regarding the Knights. Can you not work with Harris; give her something concrete to get her teeth into. She's no fool, like everyone believes, and if she can see value, even if it means dropping the trafficking case against the Knights, she could bite?" Gavin asked.

Others in the room mumbled agreement, leaving Julian to answer.

"You are correct, Harris has turned out to be very astute and as you say, no fool. But you may have something there, Gavin. What do you think, Bart, do we really need to keep the contact with the Sinaloa cartel, now we've a far more lucrative product courtesy of the decarbing operation?"

"We don't and I've argued for some time that they are dragging us back into hard drug operations for profits no better than we will achieve in decarbing. Then, there is a difference for our couriers between being caught with class A drugs and cannabis."

"Then we must vote to request that the inner circle allows us to make contact with Harris to offer her the chance of a lifetime," Julian told them.

"May I make an addition to the proposal to the inner circle?" Bart cut in.

"Of course, Bart, what's on your mind?" Julian asked.

"I suggest we include the boy, Ryan, if he's still alive. Harris is after both him and Chinwe and even if she takes your carrot, she won't stop until she knows the fate of the children, or if they are dead, has sought out the perpetrators."

Julian nodded his head up and down slowly. "That is good thinking and if Harris can get the white kid, she won't waste much time looking for the killers of a black girl from Africa. Shall we now vote, unless anyone else has a suggestion to further strengthen our negotiations with Harris?"

Nothing else was added and everyone raised their hand, before they carried on with other more mundane business, breaking up around two hours later after a round of drinks and more socialising. It was Julian's job now to put the recommendations forward to the people who sat in the inner circle.

Chapter 28

Karen returned to her London apartment, made herself a drink and flopped down in a chair deep in thought. After Vincent's meeting with Don, Don was followed to a country house. Surveillance had managed to obtain all the car registrations of vehicles parked outside it and sent them to Unit T's intelligence unit, who had found the names of each vehicle owner. Then, as visitors left the house, photos of each were added to the intelligence. What initially surprised Karen was that no person they identified leaving the house had come up in Unit T's database. These were all new names. But in the business she was in, not knowing names was good, meaning these people may not be users of a trafficker or pimp's services, but part of the finance arm of the industry. This could possibly be the break she'd always dreamed of. That was, to get at the money men. The men in grey, who lived in the shadows, using others to do their dirty work while they got rich. She couldn't help smiling to herself; a simple deal with Vincent had moved them forward in leaps and bounds, bringing them closer to such men. Yet in her view it was about time she had a little luck, which was now being brought about by one little girl who just wanted to go home, and who could well become the catalyst for bringing down the entire trafficking and drug money laundering operation.

Jasmin came out from her bedroom after a shower. "That's better, at least I feel clean following my time in that shithole I was put in," she commented, flopping down on a settee. "Have you been to see Frank?"

Karen shook her head. "Not yet, I'll go tomorrow. Midnight has been waiting for you to finish so we can all go out for dinner. We then need to talk, Jasmin, a new chapter is opening and to shake it up a little I'll want your skills."

"Sounds good and I look forward to it. As it is, did you have a good weekend?"

"Yes, Midnight's growing up fast and is pretty astute, you can't put one over on her."

"Sherry's said the same thing a few times. Maybe a miniature Karen in the making perhaps?"

"God, I hope not. I'd not wish my life on my worst enemy, let alone my family."

"Good point, another Karen let loose on the world; I don't think anyone would cope. But changing the subject, have you signed your side of the purchase contract of our new home yet?"

"Done and dusted, even paid for. Mind you to be fair, I had a few quid that came my way and drifting around which needed a home."

Jasmin laughed. "A few quid, I assume you mean a few million quid. I suppose now I'd better raid my piggy bank and give you my bit. So where's this money come from that needed a home?"

"Barbados. I had a house there as well, rented to some film star. He decided he wanted it and made an offer." Karen shrugged with indifference. "It wasn't really my house as such, I inherited it when the Sextons died. So it meant nothing emotionally, apart from as rental income."

Jasmin shook her head. "You're unbelievable, what else do you own that you have little interest in?"

Karen sighed. "I wish I knew, every day something seems to turn up I knew nothing about, or have just forgotten. Last week it was a warehouse in Calais. Seems the Sextons used it as a bonding warehouse. The bloody thing's full of pallets loaded with boxes of who knows what. I only found out when customs wanted documentation."

"So, how long have the boxes been there?"

"No idea, I've left it to the legal lot in LBNF to sort out who owns what is inside the warehouse and get shut. Then I'll see if I can sell, or maybe lease it out."

"Are they capable, the ones at LBNF?"

"My legal lot are. Most of their work is creating documentation for victims of trafficking that need repatriation, so a few boxes in a warehouse will be child's play, believe me. Anyway, now you're ready, will you give Midnight and Ariel a shout? I'm starving."

***

The following morning Karen woke up to find a text on her mobile, but not from anyone she knew. She read it.

'We should meet; I've information that has a great deal of value to you. Text back yes, place and time later today.'

Karen wasn't one to jump at such a text, although when she was younger she probably would have. So she was cautious in her reply.

'You want a meeting. No problem once I know who you are and what it's in relation to.'

Karen had finished breakfast when a reply to her text came back.

'Julian Sharp. Regarding Sinaloa and Ryan. We meet alone, no recording devices otherwise it's off.'

The name rang a bell and Karen looked down the list of names provided by Stanley of those at the house Don had gone to, finding it to be the registered owner of the house. She smiled to herself, they were in a panic, she was certain. She did have one concern. How was Sharp able to obtain her Unit T mobile number? It pointed to someone inside Unit T passing it across to him. Stanley must look into the possibility of yet another informer. Even so, she texted back accepting his conditions, asking for a time and location, then she called Stanley.

"Morning, Stanley."

"Good morning, Karen, I understand Midnight and Ariel are not returning in your aircraft, but on the service aircraft leaving tonight. Are you not coming back to the camp?"

"Not just yet. I might have a lead on Ryan; I want to follow it up. But I've called because I need information on one of the men from surveillance last night. A Julian Sharp, it's urgent Stanley. I want to know everything about him."

"There's a particular reason?"

"Yes, he's texted me and wants to meet. Talks about information on Sinaloa and also Ryan."

"In that case, you use Jasmin as your direct protection, Karen, and we keep the Dark Angel team currently in the UK close by. Sinaloa are not a cartel you mess about with. You know that."

"I will, you can be certain. I really do need to know about him by seven tonight. I also want you to look into how he got this number. We could have another informer close to you. In the meantime, I'm off to see Frank."

"Very well, we'll do what we can. I'll talk to you before you meet. Any chance of a recording device?"

"He's insisting not, but I'm thinking about that. I don't want to wreck the meeting when a child is involved."

"Understandable. You get off to see Frank, while we find more on Sharp. I'll also look into how your number was obtained."

***

"Well, aren't you going to say hello?" Karen asked.

Frank opened his eyes and smiled. "Why, if it's not my favourite girl."

Karen bent over the bed and gave Frank a hug. "It's good to see you awake, Frank, last time I was here, it wasn't looking good."

"Apparently so. But a tiny knock on the head won't keep me down; I'm tough as old boots. Then Sherry tells me I can't return to my café for a while, what's that all about, Karen? It's my livelihood."

"I've people who will keep the café going. As for you, look at it as protection, until we round up the perpetrators. Besides, you said you wanted a holiday, so you've got one."

"I did, but even with a hit to the head, I seem to remember I'd been promised sun, beach and plenty of pretty girls. I've certainly got the only girls I'm more than happy to spend my holiday with, and being the south of France the sun, but no beach."

"Maybe not a beach, but we've a swimming pool, heated, never gets crowded, and a forest of a few hundred acres, what more do you want? Oh, a housekeeper as well, so you don't even need to cook. Besides, among your girls is a nine-year-old going on sixteen, who'll drag you everywhere and drive you completely mad. Well, she does me anyway. So no arguments you're going and that's the end of that conversation."

Frank could see the military commander side coming out in Karen. This was a girl no longer used to having her decisions questioned. You were with her, or not, there were no half measures. "Okay, but will you be there?"

Karen shrugged. "Who knows, I'll certainly be there at times, I do run Unit T and work backs up if I'm away too long. But

I've still got a little boy and girl to locate yet and I'm not finding that very easy. Anyway, I understand you can leave hospital later today, providing you have someone at home, with it being a head injury. That's fine for me, our transport is due to leave Gatwick at seven tonight for the camp. Midnight, Ariel and Sherry will also be on board, so a Unit T vehicle will collect you just after five."

"It would seem you have it all worked out. What about my clothes?"

Karen pointed to a suitcase. "All done, you just be ready to leave. I'm tied up so you'll not see me again today. Now I have to go, I've left Midnight with Ariel and Jasmin, shopping. God knows what she'll buy if I'm not there. And I've another pressing engagement I need to prep for."

As she turned to leave after giving him another hug, he called after her. "Thanks, Karen. I know you have a lot on your plate, but I appreciate your taking time out for me."

She turned and smiled. "You're very welcome, it's what friends are for, I'll see you soon." Then she walked away.

He lay back on the bed. In all the years he had known her, he'd never been able to unravel the real Karen hiding within this very complex and often secretive girl. In fact the more he got to know her, the less he seemed to know who she really was. She was a girl who at times seemed strong and resilient, but the next moment she was in a state of depression, which had become more prevalent over the last year or so. And then, she'd taken to staying at his flat, only for a night before she would move on, as if she wanted to hide away from the world she lived in. But now he was going to stay at her house in France, the house that, according to Sherry, out of all her homes, was distinctly Karen, where she was her most relaxed. "Yes," he muttered, "maybe finally I will understand just how the real Karen ticks and what drives her, often to and beyond the limits of human endurance."

Chapter 29

"Julian Sharp, works for a Nigerian bank in the city as a broker, Karen," Stanley began, when he called her an hour before the meeting. "He has a team of twenty and is tipped for the top job in their investment arm. He collected bonuses of around two hundred thousand last year and it's expected he'll top that comfortably this year. The house that surveillance followed Don Wang to is owned by Sharp. It was inherited from his parents who died in a car crash some years back. He also rents an apartment in the same area as you at Canary Wharf and has an interest in a thirty-metre cruiser based at St Katharine's Dock marina. His partner, a Preston Wrangler, is twenty years his junior. Wrangler likes fast cars, had a few brushes with the law and was fined a number of times for drinking offences, followed by skirmishes. He's a hot-headed lad well into the London scene, likes gambling, but interestingly, in the nightclubs he prefers the pretty girls, particularly if they or their daddy are rich. Overall, it seems a strange relationship, with Sharp not being with Wrangler when he's in the clubs."

"It does, but with Sharp in the investment arm of a foreign bank, he could be well placed to control finances and investment of the not-so-legal type."

"Correct, and looking into the affairs of others coming out of that house, they too have accounts at the same bank. We could well be onto something."

"Maybe, but it's not going to be easy to make any links on the banking side. Let me have a list of the men present and what you know about them. If any of them look vulnerable, an unofficial visit for a quiet word in their ear could reap rewards."

"I'll leave that to you, Karen, that is your expertise. But

you are correct; we have to break into the group to get anywhere."

"Well, we have a start and already they have shown their hand by having someone wanting to meet me, and mentioning a cartel as well as an underage girl. That is stupidity on their part, if they believe I'm going to walk away with whatever they want to throw me. I'm not and I'll hound them until I wring out their true involvement. Thinking about the boat Sharp has a share in, do you think it could be used in drug or people smuggling?"

"Oh, come on, Karen, that's got to be wishful thinking on your part. Why is that, do you fancy the boat under proceeds of crime?"

Karen laughed. "You've seen through me. It's my fixation over boats isn't it?"

"Well, you did inherit a shipping company; and don't you still have a share of it? If so, use one of their boats."

"Unfortunately, yes, like ten per cent. I've tried to offload it a few times, but without any success. Then I may like boats, but cargo ships and oil tankers, they're not exactly something to go cruising on. Anyway, send me everything you have and I'll spend some time reading it, before I meet him."

***

Julian Sharp had suggested dinner at a top-class restaurant in the Strand by the side of the Savoy Hotel. Karen was happy with that - in her view, the more public the better and when she turned up to eat at such a high-class restaurant it would be very public. Just after the arranged time of the meeting, Karen's Unit T car pulled up outside, with the doorman coming forward to open the door. She thanked him and walked into the restaurant. How Julian had managed a booking at such short notice she had no idea and really didn't care, except it was interesting to know what sort of influence he had, which in her view exceeded his status in the city, unless he'd used her name as his guest; then, they could well have been accommodating.

The head waiter approached. "Lady Harris, welcome to our restaurant. Your dining partner is waiting in the bar, if I may take your coat."

Karen thanked him, then walked through, immediately recognising Julian sitting at a small table, from photos provided by Stanley. He stood as soon as she approached.

He came over to her, offering his hand, which she took. For her it was a soft, namby-pamby shake, not a man's firm grip. "Lady Harris or would you prefer, Colonel? Thank you for accepting my invitation, may I order you a drink?"

"I'm not one for formality, Mr Sharp; Karen is perfectly acceptable to me. As it is, it was an intriguing invitation." Then she looked at the wine waiter hovering, waiting for her order. "May I have a vodka and tonic, no ice? The vodka from a fresh sealed bottle and bring the tonic bottle to me still sealed, please."

"Of course, Lady Harris," he said, then walked away.

"You must call me Julian," he insisted after the waiter left. "Shall we sit down?"

Julian was assessing just how to approach her while she sat down. Then, while he wasn't one for women, the press, who were forever talking about her, were correct in one way, she was a very attractive woman. Her clothes were not pretentious but smart and suited her, and the obviously expensive diamond ring, like the Rolex watch she was wearing, helped to create the impression of someone at ease with themselves and very wealthy, without thrusting it in your face.

"I'm not one for wasting time on personal introductions,

Julian, I already know a great deal about you, where you work, who you live with and that you had a meeting last night with a Don Wang. This is a man of interest to Unit T. Bad move on his part. Pointing Unit T directly to others, including you, who may be part of a conspiracy within the definition of abduction or human trafficking, is not to be advised. We never forget."

Julian said nothing for a moment when Karen's drink was brought.

"Then let us not beat around the bush, Karen, you followed Don to my house. That in my view makes the contact he met, compromised?" he came back at her, after the waiter had gone.

Karen shrugged with indifference. "Going up against one of my top girls in a complacent manner, can only have one outcome in combat. You lose."

He sipped his own drink, looking all the time at her. "Particularly if the girl was a Jasmin Dlamini, I assume?"

A hint of a smile crossed her face as she twisted open the top of a bottle of tonic water. "Particularly," she said, then poured a little tonic into her glass.

"You operate with some very unstable, dangerous people, Karen. Dlamini has been known to turn on the hand that feeds her, with no allegiance or remorse."

"It's the world I live in, Julian, and I assure you I've had my share of traitors. When it happens, I'm more than capable of retaliating with deadly force, which you can see when you consider I'm still here where most of them are not. That also goes for the ones who decide to target me; they will find I can be just as unpredictable as you suggest Jasmin might be."

'Yes,' he thought to himself. 'I can see it in your face, the coldness of the eyes, often found in contract killers who enjoy killing. It isn't people like Dlamini traffickers should be frightened of, but you.'

Menus were brought; Karen just glanced at hers, while the waiter went through their specials for the night. She looked up at him, handing back the menu. "Sorry, they are not for me. Can you do prawn cocktail followed by steak and chips, maybe peas if you have any, the steak well done?"

"Of course Lady Harris, if that is your preference. Would you like a sauce with the steak?"

"No thank you, English mustard only."

Julian didn't comment, ordering his own selections from the menu. He had heard she could be difficult in restaurants, often sending food back and having top chefs pulling their hair out in anger, but that was their problem, not his.

After the waiter left, she didn't dwell on her food decisions, but decided to go in hard rather than skirt around the surface. "You and most of your visitors last night are involved in finance as well as now linked with Don Wang. I hope for all your sakes it doesn't go as far as money laundering for the cartels, or the financing of human trafficking operations, Julian? If so, I will come for you, have no doubts and the last thing you want is me knocking on your door, or that of your associates. We are not the police and are far more dangerous, for the ones who believe they can take us on. Then, ten years in prison, coming out with nothing, is not something someone like you would relish, believe me. Many have taken their own lives rather than face that future, such is their fear."

"Those are a lot of assumptions, Karen, when I asked for a meeting in order to help you."

"I receive many offers of help, but always ask myself what is in it for the one who's offering. Most times it's out of self-preservation and very rarely public-spirited. Some attempt to turn me away from their own indiscretions, or have a price coupled with their generous offer. What is your price, or are you the rarity that has a public-spirited approach?"

"Sorry to disappoint, I'm not the rarity as you hoped. My price? You forget about last night. Take out all references to us on your database. In return we will give you the European operation of the Sinaloa cartel and throw in Ryan. Is that not a good deal for you?"

Karen didn't have to answer immediately, as the waiter came over to say their table was ready. This suited her, she needed to think and dinner was a useful diversion.

Dinner was good, the chef providing everything she'd asked for, conversation reverting to general talk. After she declined a sweet, they were sitting with coffee and brandy. It was time to move on to why she was here.

"Returning to our original discussion, Julian. If I agree to your offer, why would you believe I'd go away?"

"You're astute, sharp, and know your business inside out. But more importantly, you are honourable and if you agree a deal, you keep your word." Then he gave an indifferent shrug. "Mind you, we have our sources who would know if you'd done as agreed or if you didn't."

"You are correct, I do keep my word, it's the only way to operate, if you're fighting a war in the underbelly of society. There, the rules of engagement mean very little, it's live or die, there is no in-between. But I have my limits in cooperation, particularly where children are involved. They are vulnerable and as such, I won't compromise. That means, Julian, if you know anything about Chinwe, or Ryan, I want that information even if we deal or not. If I don't get it and either, or both, dies, you will see another side of me - that is not to be advised and no, I don't need the likes of Dlamini to do what has to be done."

He picked up his glass, rolling the brandy around inside it before taking a sip, then looked directly at her. "Very laudable, with such a statement referring to yourself as a saviour for the children. Both of us know that's not the reality of your thinking. It's for public consumption. You are the last one who would compromise an operation to save a child. You ask me how I know, believe me, I know a great deal about you, as you think you know about me. It is also the likes of me and others with a vested interest in the underbelly of society you claim to be fighting, who have prevented certain cartels from placing a gun to your head. Why? Because like you, I assume, to know your opponent, and their ways, is far better than learning the ways of a replacement, just for the sake of being bloody-minded. I can assure you, one call and you would not leave this restaurant alive. It's been like that for some years, while we allow you to nibble at the tips, make your money to keep LBNF alive and enjoy the backing of the public, get too close to the real power behind the industry and such protection goes out of the window. No one, not even the Queen of England or the Prime Minister would survive if such compromises were not practised. I advise you to take the deal, have your day to see the European arm of Sinaloa fall and return Ryan to his parents, then we revert back to an equilibrium. And while you think about that, accept the fact Richard Knight was working for the MI6. Of course, his son Robin, caught with his pants down fucking a minor, is a different kettle of fish, you can destroy him if you desire, we have no allegiance to fools."

For someone to threaten her so blatantly, besides dictating

what she should or should not do inwardly annoyed her. Karen wasn't someone who would cower down in fear, although she was realistic that at least because of a serious error, on Don Wang's part, the real power that ran the criminal gangs - although she didn't believe this to be Julian - risked being exposed. She needed time to decide on a course of action and in particular, just how extensive this group's operations were, or was it just a fraction of something far larger? She delayed any reply by picking up her coffee cup and taking a sip, replacing it slowly to the saucer, then she looked at him watching her. Maybe on his side he was trying to read her body language.

"I will have to think about what you've said tonight. Although I'm a little confused as to why you would throw the Sinaloa cartel into the mix. You know they are a particularly violent group who would not sit down and take it and would never give up looking for the person who turned them in. Perhaps you believe they are so powerful worldwide, they would send their people from their strongholds in South America to extract retribution? Leaving me in the firing line and you lily-white?"

He smiled. "For us to go our own ways, a fall guy has to be of high value. After all, to go away, you'd hardly consider a deal for a local pimp running a couple of girls, would you?"

"No, but by the same ruling I'll have to consider if even Sinaloa is sufficient."

"You'll get no more, Karen Harris, believe me. But your choice now is how much do you really want to rock the boat? Maybe a few years back when you had nothing, you'd have a go, but circumstances change. You have the world at your feet, a little girl to bring up and substantial assets that will ensure a comfortable future for both of you. Do you really want to risk all that, after all, you've already given fifteen years of your life? Surely it is someone else's turn, while you take a back seat, maybe even retire and mess about with LBNF."

Karen finished her brandy, after pressing her watch winder to tell the driver of her car she was ready to leave - then she stood, him following suit.

"I've enjoyed tonight, Julian, thank you for dinner. I will be in touch. But to redress the balance somewhat, a simple signal from me, or even an attempt on my life, and you also would not leave this restaurant alive, particularly with the one behind the trigger being someone who would not hesitate."

He smiled. "I had expected nothing less of you, Karen. In fact, if you'd not made arrangements I'd have been very disappointed. Send my regards to Jasmin, tell her next time she won't be as lucky."

Karen shook her head slightly. "I think I'll refrain from passing on such a message, Julian. You never throw the gauntlet down to a contract killer, even less one who has been at it since she was eighteen. Despite any pressure I could exert, she would ignore me, take it as a personal threat and come for you. I could safely predict you'd never see this time next week." Then Karen walked away.

Julian followed, but stopped at the reception, watching Karen's car draw up just as she left the building. Tonight he'd pushed her as much as he dared. Karen was unpredictable and showed no fear, with his threats just brushed aside. Had he done enough to wet her appetite, by giving her the opportunity to go after a particularly vicious cartel, or would she backpedal and do nothing? And then, her open admission she was indeed using the services of Jasmin Dlamini, and it wasn't just rumours, meant there were two particularly dangerous and experienced killers to take on. Maybe it was prudent to recommend to his superiors that they should engage people equally experienced as backup?

Chapter 30

The following morning, Karen returned to Unit T. She had called ahead and had Stanley form a working group of senior team leaders. When she came off her aircraft, a vehicle was waiting to whisk her to the intelligence building, not to her own office on the camp.

"Good flight?" Stanley asked when she came into his office.

She just shrugged. "Same as normal. Have you a list of the team leaders and their teams for me to see?"

He handed her a file. Stanley could tell she wasn't interested in any small talk, just wanting to get down to work.

"Coffee while you go through the file, Karen?"

"No thank you," she replied, continuing to look down the list, then back to Stanley. "These four team leaders, are they completely trustworthy - and the ones who work with them?"

"They are, I'd stake my job on it."

"Never go that far, Stanley. We've had too many bad apples to be completely certain. And money talks, no matter how much you earn. Even so, from now on, each and every one of them will be subjected to the most stringent observations in every part of their life. We have an informer, high up, passing on information. I want you to find that person. In the meantime, get the team leaders together and bring them to my house. All meetings concerning what I'm about to say to them and yourself are to be conducted in my private high-security rooms, not here."

Never had Karen gone as far as using her security area at home for meetings like this. Stanley suspected something serious had happened last night, although she'd mentioned nothing when they'd talked this morning before her flight back to Unit T.

He glanced at his watch. "Ten o'clock, okay?"

"That's fine; I'm going on ahead for a quick shower and change of clothes."

***

The high-security area inside Karen's house, introduced when the building was rebuilt after the original château was destroyed by missiles, consisted of a steel door leading into a passage. Off this passage were three rooms. A large windowless meeting room able to accommodate ten people, Karen's office and a room where she had a safe. Inside the safe was her slush fund, used to pay informers, along with a considerable amount of cash, gold and diamonds that Karen had accumulated during her many covert operations. Some of which had been in the safe for years, yet slowly she was reducing the hoard by funding many private operations that did not go through Unit T. Stanley knew she had such operations, but wasn't interested in finding out more, or how they were funded. This was the way Karen worked and it brought results, particularly if such an operation was not following the terms of reference for Unit T or their rules of engagement. For Karen, this was not the only location where she kept undocumented funds. She also had safe deposit boxes in a number of banks across Europe, again containing substantial funds. Another but important aspect of the meeting room was that it was radio-silent. No signal could get in or out. Even so, mobiles could not be taken inside and each person would be scanned for metal and electronic equipment in their possession, including watches and similar.

At home, Maria, her housekeeper, was surprised to see Karen come through to the kitchen, she had no idea she was back on the base.

"Good morning, Lady Harris, have you had breakfast?" she asked.

"Only coffee and a biscuit on the aircraft. I've a meeting here at ten; can you make me a slice of toast along with a coffee pot for when I'm down from showering? Who else is at home?"

"Your guest, Frank, he had breakfast with Midnight and Sherry at eight, but went back to his room to lie down. Midnight's at school and Sherry's in meetings at the camp. It's Ariel's day off and she's gone to the town. Sherry will bring Midnight home after school."

"Then I'll have lunch with Frank at one o'clock by the pool, with dinner at seven as usual. Midnight should join us tonight, so only let her have a biscuit with her drink when she's back from school."

Just before ten, Karen went through to her secure meeting room carrying a mug of coffee. Soon all the others joined her and the doors were closed. In the room were an investigative accountant, Samuel Mecon, an internet hacker and programmer, Brad Clivinger, Stanley for intelligence and Lieutenant Chris Farrer for the military side.

"Today, gentlemen, we begin a new investigation. This is the one, I believe, that will lead us to the money men. The ones in grey suits we've always known to exist but have never been able to track down. You talk to no one, not even your partner, as to who our targets are. With what has transpired over the last two days, I'm certain that yet again, there's a high-level informer feeding back information to this group, so you must suspect everyone, no matter how trivial your suspicions, because that person could well be the informer. Be on your guard, watch everyone in your cell and report anything suspicious directly back to me, or Stanley.

This brief must never be discussed at the camp, all meetings are to be held in this room. Before I begin, I will tell you what transpired in London, leading me to a meeting with a man named Julian Sharp. I recorded a conversation I had with him over dinner, you can hear it, then we'll discuss the next stage. Some parts of the conversation I've had to blank out, it is extremely sensitive and only concerns our field operatives." Karen had in fact taken out any reference to Jasmin that pointed to her being a freelance contract killer, including her final threat to Julian. While most in the room knew how important Jasmin was in the field, working alongside Karen, it was prudent that her life before she joined Unit T remained confidential.

For the next hour Karen told them about her meeting with Vincent and the surveillance work that included following Don to the house, before they listened to the recording she'd made over dinner with Julian. Now it had finished.

"This is where we're at. Forget the threats to me, that's par for the course, and then, I was told not to record the conversation, but he was in cuckoo land if he thought I'd not. It's what we do and we won't be dictated to. The link to the Knights, and the ability to produce Ryan, points to either a gigantic wind-up on his side, or he has that ability. I believe he and his group do have the ways and means to deliver the child, it wouldn't make sense to make offers and not be able to deliver. As for the Sinaloa cartel, that's something I need to think about very carefully. Personally, I believe their involvement in the human trafficking of girls in the EU must be very small, otherwise I would have heard about it, if only by rumours among our field operatives and informers. I haven't, and in my view Sinaloa are more involved in the import and distribution of Class A drugs, which is not part of our remit.

Even so, I will look into the possibility they have gone into trafficking, although I suspect once we infiltrate that group, I'll become a prime target for the rest of my life and it will be no holds barred. But I won't lie down and die that easily, I'll hit them with everything I can muster - both with Unit T, our covert operators, and others not known directly by our intelligence networks but sitting covertly inside the major criminal groups. It's a resource which can be brought into play at the drop of a hat and sound the death knell for many of the largest cartels operating in Europe."

She hesitated by taking a drink of her coffee. Stanley was listening carefully, this was the first time Karen had ever admitted what he had suspected for a long time. She had effectively built a private army with the huge financial resources at her disposal, and it seemed it was ready for the day when the risk to her life was so great, the only way she could go was to retaliate. This army, he considered, would be far more deadly than any official army that she could call upon, since it was already deeply entrenched in the cartels, well-armed and well-trained, ready for the day when she gave the order. If it was there, why hadn't it been activated sooner? Had she held back, waiting for the money men to complete the jigsaw, knowing that to do so may bring the entire human trafficking billion pound industry to its knees and even rock governments? In his mind this was scary stuff and he prayed she knew what she was doing, but then, did Karen ever really know what she was doing? He was brought out of his thoughts when she carried on.

"Your prime objectives are to follow the money, the people on the list, and build from that. We hack, we record, we look into every aspect of their lives, financial and private, for anything, no matter how small and insignificant, so we can build a picture. Because taking out the money men, along with the actions of my covert operators inside the cartels, chaos will follow and our Dark Angel forces will be there to sweep up, both officially and from inside the cartels themselves. I have waited and prepared Unit T for this break, alongside others, ever since I became commander. Now it's finally coming and I won't let go until every one of them is behind bars or dead. In the meantime, I've a mind to agree to his terms, let him believe he's won and that I'll no longer be a threat. How very wrong he would be, I'll always be a threat, even more so when someone threatens my life - then it's no holds barred, as he'll find to his cost. Questions?"

"As we find information, how will we act on it?" Samuel asked.

"You never act alone. It is imperative you report back to this group and we all know the steps being taken. Mess it up and they will go to ground. If necessary, I'll move in covert operators to follow up leads, while you move on. The covert operators on their part will be constantly passing everything they find back to me or Stanley, and then us all. Keep coordinating as closely as possible, similar to past operations, then a complete picture as to who's who in this group is bound to emerge. While every one of you are experts in your fields, if you must use the specialist teams you lead, use them for general research and nothing specific that could indicate just what we are doing. With your help and my covert operators, Unit T will know who and what to target."

"What is my role, Commander?" Lieutenant Farrer asked.

"Your job is to work between the covert operation and Dark Angel. Each step will at times require us to search officially as well as make arrests. That has to be legal and put in place as a cover for the covert operation going on in the background. By the book, Lieutenant, always by the book. A good instance is the Knights - they are still wriggling on the end of the hook, but even with all their contacts, and some of those risking conspiracy charges to help them out, the Knights cannot find a way to escape the inevitable justice. Although to be fair, with the intervention of Julian Sharp, as their trump card, I may well end up dropping trafficking charges against the father. But I'll only do that if it has value and we're certain we can get him on different charges."

"You're walking a very tight rope this time, Karen," Stanley commented.

"Maybe, but I have only two choices. Walk away, or take them on. You all know me, have I ever walked away from a fight?"

"No," they all agreed.

"So I fight, even if this is the last thing I'll do as commander, I'll go, knowing I never turned away when the going got tough. Now it's time you all went to work. I'll leave you to discuss strategy and come up with a plan. Being here, I'd only interfere and cut in. Better without me. Besides, I'm knackered; I've been up since five. My days seem to get longer and longer."

After Karen left, Stanley took charge. "I don't think we're going to find it as easy as Karen hopes. These men have survived, I suspect for a number of years, with tentacles well-entrenched across the industry. Having said that, Karen has got us names we've never had before and the use of covert operators, and don't forget her informers, who don't work directly for Unit T. On my part I'll dig deep and I will find the Unit T informer, then we either take him or her down or use them to pass on misinformation. The most important part of this operation is to keep Karen safe. They will target her as we dig deeper, you can be sure of that, and you know Karen, she'll just brush the risks aside as usual. So, Lieutenant, apart from working alongside Dark Angel, your soldiers stick to her like glue to neutralise any threat to her life, wherever it comes from."

"I will, Stanley. She's not easy to protect and she'll hate me before this is over, but I'll keep her safe."

He smiled. "I have a feeling the pressure on us will push us all to the limit. But the reality is, this is why we came to Unit T, to make a difference. Karen won't let up, you all know that and she'll expect a steady stream of information coming from us so she can pass instructions on to her own resources, allowing them to know what to look for and target."

***

Karen, after changing into her bikini and slipping on a beach coat, came out on to the extensive patio surrounding the swimming pool. Frank was on one of the loungers reading a book. The table was set out for two, ready for lunch.

"Hi," she said, removing the coat and flopping down on a lounger by the side of him.

Frank looked up and smiled. "Hi to you as well. I was really surprised when Maria set the table for two, with both Midnight and Sherry being at the camp. Then she told me you had arrived and were to join me for lunch."

"Around here it's normal; I flit in and out all the time. I could well be gone again tomorrow."

"You should step back sometimes to take a breath, Karen."

"I'd like to, but when lives, particularly children's lives are at risk, to delay is not an option."

"Understandable. Changing the subject, I have to say, I thought your home in Corsica was fantastic, but this is something else. My room, or rather guest suite, is larger than my own flat and the house, from what I've seen is stunning. You should be proud of yourself to achieve what you have, Karen."

She sighed. "I suppose, but it's been costly, not so much moneywise, more a pretty crap lifestyle. Then the new house, it's not like what was here, I had a fantastic château. That was before it was blown up with a couple of missiles. Although it did give me the opportunity to have what I always wanted built. Would you believe it's now protected the same as the camp, with not only soldiers patrolling the forest and guarding the entrance, but surface-to-air missiles. How many private houses on the planet have that sort of protection?"

He grinned. "You've got me there, now I really do feel safe, but a little apprehensive perhaps, when there is a perceived need for such protection. So what else have you hidden?"

"Nothing really military, but the château had a cellar, most of it dark and dingy, I suppose for wines. I turned it into an entertainment area, with a fitness and games room, along with a squash court, besides a cinema room for whiling the time away during the winters around here," Karen grinned. "Sherry and I tend to lounge in the recliners eating popcorn watching some weepy, tears running down our faces. But I've not used any of the facilities apart from the pool for some time. These days I'm never here you see, often it's only a few hours, before I'm gone again."

Then she stood. "Although today at least I'm going to have a swim," she said, walking off towards the far end of the pool. "This, Frank, is what living in the South of France is all about," she called out, at the same time climbing up the steps of quite a high diving board. The next moment she took a short run and launched herself into the air, brought her knees up, forming herself into a ball to spin once, before straightening up and hitting the water with hardly a splash.

He watched as she glided effortlessly along, length after length, mostly below the surface.

Soon she came up close to his lounger. "As soon as you're better I want you swimming at my side, are you game?"

"I can swim, but I'm not a fish and you, girl, make it look so easy. I'd be left in your wake."

"It's just practise, ten years ago I'd have knocked three minutes off my usual twenty lengths compared to what I do now," she replied, at the same time climbing out of the water.

"Maybe, but look at yourself. Not an ounce of fat, a body built for speed, particularly when swimming. Where I've eaten far too many of my café dinners."

"Yes, well," she answered, at the same time rubbing her hair with a towel. "If you'd had your way I'd be in your café every day eating the meals. Then gone would be the waif-like figure and no man would look at me twice."

"You shouldn't pull yourself down, Karen. You're a very attractive young woman, but beyond that you're intelligent, articulate and great fun to be with. Believe me; a few extra pounds could never take that away."

Karen stopped to look at him. "I may be many of those things, except I'm not that good a catch, Frank, most of my boyfriends are dead because of their association with me, while other potentials, as soon as they realise who I am, run like scared rabbits." She gave a shrug of indifference. "It's understandable - who wants someone who was raped and has been forced into prostitution many times, added to the fact I kill for a living. Even I wouldn't want me and that's saying something. Anyway, I'll change, then lunch and we can have a conversation far more in keeping with a beautiful day alongside a sparkling blue pool."

He shook his head slowly, at the same time watching her return to the house. It made him sad to hear what little self-esteem she had, with so many outstanding achievements both personally and professionally. The girl should be proud, not pull herself down.

Chapter 31

"Frank, Maria tells me Aunty is here?" Midnight shouted as she hurtled through the house doors onto the patio. "Where is she?"

"She told me she'd be in the house office for an hour or so."

"Oh, the secret room," Midnight replied, a little deflated, and flopped down on a lounger.

He smiled. "Secret room - that sounds intriguing."

Midnight scrunched her nose. "Not really, I'm banned from going in, well, not just me, but everyone is banned, so I've no idea what's in there. I think Aunty made that rule to keep out of the way of me when I'm annoying her."

"Why should she do that, I thought you both got on really well?"

"We do, but Aunty complains I'm too demanding and always want to do things. Aren't all kids?"

"Yes, I suppose they are. So have you had a good day?" he asked changing the subject.

"It was all right, but we've lots of tests next week, so it's all the boring revision now. I'm eating with you tonight, normally I'd have my dinner in the kitchen, but with Aunty home Maria said I was to join everyone. Dinner's really posh, so I've got to wear a dress, no jeans or shorts, but it's cool, I got a new dress for my birthday. Would you like to go on a bike ride in the forest? I got a bike as well, but haven't really used it yet. I can't go on my own and Ariel's not here, so you can use her bike. We can only be out half an hour, then I've homework and I need time to get ready for dinner."

He smiled. "You've got yourself a really full day then. As

for riding, I'm still a little groggy for riding, Midnight, but I'll go with you, although I'll walk if you don't mind?"

"Great, I'll fetch my helmet."

***

Following dinner, with Midnight in bed, Karen, Sherry and Frank were sitting out on the patio, drinks in hand. Karen had changed her departure for the following day after Brad had requested a meeting in the morning.

"I must say the silence here is overpowering for someone who lives in a city. It really is a fantastic location, Karen," Frank commented, at the same time sipping his drink.

"Yes, it is noticeable. You know I once very nearly sold it, well it was sold, but I changed my mind. Those were dark days, don't you agree, Sherry?"

"Times I prefer to forget, Karen. Even so, it had its moments and we all came back stronger."

"You did, yet it was the beginnings of disaster after disaster for me. Even my attempt to get married ended up as a farce. Did I ever tell you I was seconds away from crashing my aircraft?"

Sherry frowned. "No - how?"

"I was tired, frustrated with everything going wrong at the time and had to be in Paris for my wedding and the engines failed just as I began my run to take off. My ever-so-loving fiancé wasn't interested, accusing me of doing everything not to get married the next day. I ended up driving to Paris after every other mode of transport would have made me late, a nightmare in itself. I wouldn't have minded, after all most was of my own making, except the Sexton aircraft was available and could have collected me. He never volunteered that, preferred to mess about with a prostitute rather than help me."

Sherry grinned. "But you got your own back on the Sexton family big-time?"

Karen smiled. "I suppose, and I did get Corsica. Well, a villa I found they didn't own, but rented. I had to buy the bloody place. Even so it turned out a better deal than I ever imagined."

"How's that, Karen? Although I agree it's a fantastic place to holiday," Frank asked.

"When I met the sales agent after purchasing the place, on the set of keys he gave me were safe keys. I never knew about a safe being there. Turned out it was in the wine cellar and bulging with share certificates, cash and gold - others in the Sexton family as well as their solicitors knew about the certificates and safe, but hadn't told me? Probably never thought I'd ever go to Corsica, besides actually buy it. The Sexton family solicitor had arranged for Sexton's secretary to go there and take an inventory, and I suppose rifle through the safe, but I told him not to bother, I'd already people there and they'd do that. He wasn't happy, I can tell you. You remember, don't you Sherry?"

"I do – we were sitting cross-legged in the lounge counting all the money stuffed in the safe. It was fun and like finding a pirate's treasure."

"I can see that sticking in their craw, with you walking away with not only the shipping empire, but the hidden assets," Frank commented.

"Believe me it did and I'll tell you this, if I'd not had money, they'd have walked all over me. But they were up against someone who was a multimillionaire in their own right, with people on the payroll who could crush them."

"So what is the future?" Frank asked.

She said nothing at first, Sherry emptied the wine bottle

between them and Frank watched Karen carefully, well aware she was thinking of how to answer.

Finally, after taking a sip of her wine, she looked out across the pool to the forest beyond. "I'm tired, Frank; I can no longer face making the life-and-death decisions that come with the job. But I have a mission, which I can't tell you about because of the sensitive nature, except it will be the pinnacle of my career. Then I'll step down, maybe remain here for a time, but probably live in Corsica."

"Will you give up LBNF as well?" Sherry asked.

"To a degree, after all, you're looking after the day-to-day work. Maybe Midnight will want to help out when she is old enough."

"Good decision, Karen," Frank added. "I've seen the change in you over the last year or so and I must admit I've been worried. In your job, one small mistake can have massive implications for those who rely on you. It takes a great deal to admit that you are at the end of the road."

She shrugged indifferently. "I suppose, but I've known it for some time. Anyway, Frank, forget me. We need to bring you back to health, you should be thinking about calling it a day. You've spent long enough in front of a cooker, till the early hours seven days a week. So what have you in mind for your future?"

He looked around nonchalantly. "Here would be nice. After all, Karen, you will need a manager to keep the place smart once the Unit T protection and staff leave. Then, Sherry here can't live in this enormous house all on her own."

"Good point, Frank, I'd be homeless if you sell, Karen. Best we look after it for you till Midnight joins Unit T and needs a place to live."

"God, that's all I need, is a rebellion. Are you sure you don't want me to throw in London and Brussels at the same time, for your shopping expeditions?"

"Excuse me… you have a place in Brussels?" Sherry asked.

"Sort of, it's a fifty-fifty with Jasmin. She needed to live somewhere and I wanted out of the hotels in Brussels. It's nothing really. It's not your sort of place," Karen answered, playing it down.

Sherry leant back, glass in hand, looking at her. "Don't believe her, Frank. This is Karen, who calls her London apartment nothing. Come clean or we'll throw you in the pool, Karen."

"Okay, it's similar to here, but set in fewer acres. Like I said, Jasmin owns half so she's looking after it. Anyway, I'm fetching a brandy, anyone else want one?"

They all did so she wandered back into the house.

Sherry shook her head slowly. "She's out of control, Frank. Ask her to marry you and bring her back to earth."

He smiled. "Somehow I don't believe I'm going to become a significant aspect of Karen's life. Apart from which she needs someone more her age to grow old with. As it is, it's about time you had a boyfriend. Look at me if you want an example of too much work and no play."

Sherry laughed. "We're all just as bad as each other."

"What's that about?" Karen asked, coming out of the house carrying three glasses on a tray.

"A real life, Karen, something we are all short of at this moment," Sherry answered.

"Hmm, you may be, but I'm more than happy with mine thank you."

They both looked at her, then fell about laughing.

***

Karen was with Stanley and Brad in her meeting room.

"You wanted to see me, Brad?" she asked.

"Yes, I've already pulled out some interesting aspects on most of the names, in particular Julian Sharp, which I think you should be aware of, particularly if you're continuing dialogue with him. While he has received payments into his account in the six figures over recent years, he's in serious debt. Looking at his bank accounts, his payments - of rent and rates for a London apartment, and on a mortgage for the house, with general house expenses - are in line with his income, it's his credit card balances that are very high. Most, if not all the problem seems to stem from debts racked up on a second card under the name of Preston Wrangler, from charges in casinos and nightclubs around the London area. The man is bleeding him dry. Another aspect is the end-of-year tax payments. They don't match what's going through the bank so he's risking an investigation. Looking at the other men at Sharp's house, most are investors, with no salaried income, but they receive substantial payments into their bank accounts and make similar payments out. I'm awaiting tax return information on those people, but it's looking like they are either fantastically lucky investors, or they are working with insider information."

"How much is going through on average, if it's taken altogether?" Karen asked.

"Between the ones I've actually accessed, around forty million."

Karen sat quietly in thought for a minute. "It's a lot, but not nearly enough funding for the trafficker industry. But a good start, Brad. Dig deeper, follow the money trail and let's see where it's not only going but where it's coming from. Then the company names you link, go into their accounts. The picture is building and now we're in, it's only a matter of time before the pieces fit together."

"You give me the impression, Karen, you're thinking there are far more investors, in fact hundreds, all laundering a small amount to spread the risk?" Stanley asked.

"I'm leaning that way. I know the industry, the money I'm looking for is in the hundreds of millions, if you consider Circulo's estimated wealth is measured in billions, Sinaloa's perhaps triple that figure and with all the groups I've hit in the past, none have been worth under a hundred million. It's a massive business, Stanley, awash with cash and all of them attempting to launder it back to being legitimate. But Julian Smart interests me. He could well be a kink, because of his debts. Whether it can give us a way in, I need to think about, in the meantime, keep at it Brad. Can you leave us now?"

He thanked her and left.

"The informer, Stanley, where are you at?"

"Nothing as yet, except I'm down to around twenty who would have access to your private mobile number. While the number you use for informers and covert operators, which is the second SIM in your mobile, is well known, like I say the other isn't. I believe Sharp made a grave error in using that number, directing our interest to those who know it."

"You think it would be prudent to change it, with you keeping the old number in intelligence so you can track any calls to it and redirect, as if it's still the same?"

"I do, we need a direct number for us to contact you, Karen. It must remain that way."

"Very well, can you sort it? I'll personally give it to Jasmin and Sherry. No one else. All others that you think should have the number must go through you, but only on a need-to-know. That will give you control."

Chapter 32

Chinwe was sitting down, leaning against a tree, watching the sun rise. The night had been cold, but nothing like how cold it could be at night back home, so she wasn't bothered. Already she had shaped leaves to collect the early morning dew, a practice done at home. But the berries on the shrubs and the mushrooms she'd found growing, she kept well away from. Although inviting, they were unfamiliar and could well be poisonous. Her thoughts drifted back to the café. She was now more than ever convinced that Karen didn't really know she was at the café and she'd been set up to be taken by the traffickers. Now it was time to consider how to contact Karen. For her the police were an obvious choice, but it must be a large police station where there were lots of policemen around; after all, she had to trust someone and most police in her country were not corrupt, so it had to be the same in the UK. Then, while she felt relatively safe in the countryside, since she was very capable of surviving for a time off the land, Chinwe suspected if she followed the busy road, it must lead to a city, where there would be more opportunities to find a police station. With this in mind, she headed back to the road. Being morning, she considered the busy side of the road would be people heading into the city to work and that must be the direction she should take. Chinwe was correct, except she would be heading into Birmingham and not London as she believed.

However, Chinwe had not gone much more than a hundred yards when she heard the distinct sound of dogs barking. Not one, but at least two. She also recognised the way they barked, the tone and the direction they were approaching from. These were tracker dogs and she was certain they were looking for her. Chinwe began sprinting over a field, unfortunately away from the main road. At the far end she climbed a low fence and went across another field towards a minor road. More than once she stopped to listen. The dogs were on to her, following at a slower pace, yes, but relentless in their pursuit. She knew there would be no escape without some sort of barrier to break her scent, be it a river or even a lake, but there was nothing. On the other side of the road was a wood, not dense, but ideal as a place to hide if it weren't for the dogs. She turned left at the road, heading away from where she had come, sprinting at an easy pace. There was no panic, all that would do was waste time and Chinwe was very used to being chased back home. She knew you got further away from people who were older and not as fit, at a steady run, and it was something she could keep up for quite a distance without losing breath. However, every time she heard the sound of a vehicle, she'd leave the road, crouching down out of sight until it passed. While she hid, she'd listen for the dogs. They were still there and once arriving at the road, the searchers would know she was on it, if the dogs turned to follow. They could even call for a vehicle to attempt to catch her up. She was all too aware, if there was no alternative route to take, they would catch her. The area was open fields and it would be difficult not to be seen, even at a distance.

It was at that moment Chinwe came across a road going off to the right, with a sign at the beginning reading 'Private Road', followed by the word 'Marina'. She could also see a reflection of water. Chinwe didn't hesitate, she ran down the short road and directly into the water. She had expected it to be deep, but she was virtually standing on the bottom, her head and shoulders still out of the water. Even so, she struck out and soon found herself swimming among a large number of strange-looking boats, in rows, very narrow with windows on each side. Some seemed occupied as even at this time of the morning, smoke was coming out of tiny chimneys on a few boat roofs and one or two people were walking with dogs along the path next to the water. How no one saw her was more down to luck than her attempts to not splash as she carried on swimming, reaching a narrow entrance and passing yet more of these strange boats, but these ones were tied to the bank, where the others stuck out in lines with walkways from the bank between them. Shortly she pulled herself up on the bank, where quite a dense line of shrubs bordered the edge. She found a way into the shrubs out of sight of anyone walking on the opposite side of the water. What Chinwe didn't know was that the boats were narrow boats, berthed in a marina on a canal just outside the town of Tamworth. After removing her trainers, she slipped her jeans off, squeezing them out as best she could, before putting them back on, followed by her jumper. All she could hope now was she'd done enough to put the dogs off her trail. She knew they would take the searchers to the water, but this side of the water had no footpath beyond the few boats tied up, so she hoped they'd believe she crossed the water to a path at the far side. The water hadn't been pleasant to swim in. It was dirty and now her clothes were wet and smelt of oil, but at least she was safe for the moment.

Chapter 33

Hardy Melcher had been asked to join a meeting chaired by Chief Inspector Davis at New Scotland Yard. The meeting was in full swing when he arrived.

"Ah, Hardy," the inspector welcomed him when he came into the room. "Collect yourself a coffee, then please join us. You know everyone in the room apart from Charles Sutton from MI6."

Charles nodded to Hardy as he sat down.

"I assume because I'm here, Inspector, this meeting involves Unit T?" he asked.

"It does, Hardy. In fact, by what I'm hearing about Unit T, and in particular their commander, they are working against us."

"I cannot believe that. I've known Karen for some time and I've also spoken to my predecessor, Sir Peter on a number of occasions, who had worked with her since she was made commander. He, like me, accepts Karen can be evasive at times, due to the sensitivity of her work. She's under enormous pressure, with operations, not only in the UK but across Europe. But she doesn't work against us."

"Well, it seems she has this time, Hardy. I'm in charge of the investigation to find the killer, or killers, of Constables Clifford and Smart earlier this week and it seems Unit T probably knows all about it, and could in actual fact direct us to the perpetrators. But it seems they have no intention of passing us any information. It is not good enough, Hardy. Families are destroyed, colleagues in shock."

"And you know this because?"

"CCTV, Hardy. Unit T vehicles were in the area. While there was no CCTV outside the building where the policemen were killed, we can place Unit T close by at the estimated time of the murder."

"I will talk to Karen, of course. But their vehicles could have been in the area for a completely different operation and as I understand from press reporting, the policemen were killed inside a building, not on the street. So how would Unit T know who killed who and why, unless they were actually there? If they were present, I can assure you they would not have stood by and allowed two unarmed officers to be killed. That is not the Unit T I know, when you consider all the personnel out in the field are well-armed, and trained to retaliate to aggression with devastating force."

"How can you give us that assurance?" Charles cut in. "MI6 know a great deal about Harris and her operations. None has included involving the UK police. They believe they can ride roughshod over our laws and Harris is the worst one for doing that. We should summon her and have her explain, if she can."

"I demand that you withdraw that veiled accusation immediately. I won't sit in a meeting and have someone, no matter who they are, insinuate that an EU military commander would ever be party to the murder of British policemen, or in fact anyone working for Unit T," Hardy came back at him.

Charles said nothing.

The inspector running the meeting added his thoughts. "I agree with Hardy, in fact, I'll go as far as to say we all want the comments withdrawn from the records of the meeting and an apology, or you are out of here and I will make a complaint to the Director General of MI6."

Charles glared at Hardy, the obvious mistrust between them very apparent. "Very well, I apologise, although my intention was to highlight the breakdown of communication between Unit T and our regular police force, not to suggest anyone would stand by, or participate in the murder of the two policemen."

"Can we now carry on with the business in hand?" the inspector cut in. "We really do need help on the killings, Hardy. The press is having a field day, claiming we can't even solve murders of our own. Can you talk to Karen and at least find out what her people were doing in that area and if like you say, it was for something completely different, do they have any footage from their dash cams that could assist the investigation?"

Hardy nodded. "That I can do, without raising her hackles. It is not unreasonable to think that they might, without knowing, have vital footage that could help your investigation."

"Crap, there's no such thing as 'without knowing' with that lot. Harris will know all right. You should kick her arse; tell her non-cooperation will certainly ensure she's thrown out of the UK when we leave the EU," Charles persisted.

"I've told you once, Charles, refrain from your inane comments, they are not constructive, otherwise you can leave the meeting," the inspector told him curtly. "Hardy, please talk to Karen."

"I'll call her now, if that's convenient? Although she is extremely difficult to get hold of at times, but Stanley, her head of intelligence, will be able to get in touch and ask if she'll call me back."

"Please do that, will you?"

Hardy stood to leave the room, but yet again Charles intervened. "Why not in front of us all, Hardy? We all want to hear the lies coming out of her mouth. Without you preparing her."

If looks could kill, Charles would be dead by the way

Hardy looked at him. But this time he didn't rise to the constant negativity coming from Charles. Although he hoped Karen would be amenable to helping them out and back his confident claim that she would. "Very well, is that okay with you Inspector?"

"It is. Can you also place the call on speakerphone?"

Hardy dialled the number he had. He waited, then looked around the room. "The call's diverted, so I won't get to speak to Karen directly, it will be put through to the switchboard and then the Unit T intelligence unit."

He was right, but soon he was connected to Stanley.

"Hardy, I'm sorry, Karen isn't on site at this moment and can't be contacted. Can I help?"

"Do you keep records of the movements of all Unit T vehicles, Stanley?"

"When you say movements, we would normally only know their location as a live feed. Although when Dark Angel units are involved, we do keep meticulous records, more for evidence-gathering. Why do you ask?"

Hardy went on to tell him about the CCTV and the post codes of interest to them along with a date. "If you have any dash cam footage, Stanley, we'd appreciate copies," he finished.

"Give me a minute, Hardy, while I check what operations were live in the UK at that time and if dash cam footage is available. Normally it's automatically wiped each day, unless for some reason we want a record."

The phone went dead, then began playing music. Hardy looked around the room. "That doesn't give me any indication of non-cooperation."

"You've got nothing yet," Charles cut in. "Then it's bloody convenient that it gets wiped."

"We do the same, Charles, dash cam footage is only kept a short time, unless like Unit T it is required for evidence," the Inspector told him.

Stanley was back before Charles could comment further.

"Sorry about the delay, Hardy. With Karen not being available I've just checked with Captain Foster, who takes overall control of the military side of Unit T when Karen is off-site. He can see no problem in providing you with what we have. On the day in question you're in luck, at least one of our surveillance vehicles was in the area of interest and following a Ryker Blackthorn, a low-grade trafficker. Because it's a live investigation, we have kept the footage of his movements for evidence. He was suspected of holding five girls from Asia and using them as prostitutes. Unfortunately, they lost sight of his vehicle in the side streets and were cruising the area, trying to pick him up again. They did, and assumed he had been parked up out of general sight, within the same area, but we cannot confirm that, or where he was parked. If you give me the time slots you're interested in, I'll have the footage sent over."

"I appreciate that, Stanley, I'll email them. Many thanks and take care."

"And you, Hardy." The call was cut by Unit T.

"As I said earlier, I cannot see any indication of non-cooperation, Inspector. I'll have the video files forwarded to your office as soon as. I must go now, I've an appointment in five minutes with the Commissioner," Hardy said with obvious satisfaction.

"Thank you for your assistance, Hardy."

After he left, Charles was still not happy. "It's too pat, Inspector. I think the man Hardy spoke to at the intelligence unit did talk to Harris, and a story was concocted. A low-grade officer would not have the authority to pass across confidential surveillance tapes. I know in our service that would not happen and Unit T is even more secretive as to what they are doing. Then, I've never even heard of this Blackthorn guy and believe me, we would have if he was trafficking."

"For a start, we don't know the set-up at Unit T. When their commander is not available, it could well be a joint decision between two people of authority, the same as our police force. Then you may not know the man, Charles, but we do. Although our interest with the Blackthorns is about drug dealing, particularly class A, not human trafficking. I'm happy with the outcome and await the recordings with interest."

***

Charles returned to the MI5 building, then an hour later went through to Max's office.

"Any issues?" Max asked.

"You mean apart from Harris crawling out of another difficult situation?"

"It's to be expected, she's a past master at it."

"Melcher also put his oar in, backing her as usual. I think it's time Melcher was moved on. Mind you, if Unit T is booted out, he's not got a job."

"We wish, but it won't happen, I'm told confidentially our own Director General is backpedalling, pushed on by the PM."

"God, that's all we need, to have her around still. It also makes it more imperative that Richard Knight is confirmed as working for us."

"That is not going well. I've spoken to Richard and he's afraid she'll deliberately open a can of worms with him in the middle. Circulo will not be interested if he was, or wasn't working for us. They will want to distance themselves, as any criminal group would. Maybe even raise a contract to get shut of both the father and son, which in their mind would close the door on the problem."

"So what happens now?"

"I've an appointment to see the Director General, to explain the risks for the service and the Knights and to ask him to talk to the PM. If he can convince the PM to intervene, then Harris will back away."

"You think she will?"

"Yes, even Harris has to accept a request from the top."

Chapter 34

Charles was correct in his assumption; the release of information would need to be sanctioned by Karen herself, particularly with the operation having been conducted by covert personnel. Contrary to what Stanley told them, Karen was around when Hardy called, however Midnight, overjoyed she was still at home, had convinced Karen to go on a bike ride in the forest before lunch, with Karen leaving for London later. The forest was not good for mobile communication, which is why the call was diverted, although Stanley had managed to talk to her and taken instructions.

***

Karen had returned to London the same day, arriving late evening. Decisions had been made during meetings with Stanley and her legal team - much against her will, Richard Knight was to be let off the hook, by accepting that he was working with the British Security Services MI6 on a covert mission. The problem in doing this was that the added charge of him hiring two contract killers to kill her and the current leader of Circulo would now rest with the UK to pursue. From what she understood, with her evidence hanging on a covert recording, the case could well get thrown out by the Directorate of Public Prosecutions. But she was cool with that - his day would come, she was certain, particularly if he was also mixed up with Julian Sharp.

The following day, alone in her apartment, with a coffee at her side from a machine in the kitchen, she called Julian.

"Karen, I was expecting you to call yesterday," he said as soon as he answered.

"I have operations running across Europe, Julian, as well as not being in the UK. Now I'm back, we should meet."

"Only if you're on board with my suggestions?"

"I am."

"Very sensible, we will meet again for dinner. This time, perhaps, I should strive to educate your palette in dining, beyond the pub food you seem to live on."

"Whatever, but I don't eat most foods associated with so-called fine dining and often send it back. In fact, it doesn't make me popular as a diner in most of London's top restaurants; a pub would be better as far as I'm concerned."

"Maybe, but pub food is not my idea of going out for dinner. I understand you frequent the Mandarin Oriental in Paris? In fact, I'm told that is the only hotel you use in Paris. I will book us dinner at the London Mandarin; I assume their cuisine is to your liking?"

"You are correct; in fact, the Mandarin group accommodate me without any issues. Shall we say eight o'clock?"

"Eight it is." He cut the call.

Karen leaned back in her chair. It would seem he'd been taking an unhealthy interest in her, going so far as to know the hotel she used in Paris. What more personal information was he party to in her life?

***

Arriving dead on eight, Karen was shown to the bar, where Julian was waiting.

"That's what I like to see in a woman, promptness," he commented after she sat down and had given her drinks order. "We have a private room for dining and our meeting, Karen. I trust you have no issue with that?"

She sighed inwardly, annoyed at the way he was talking down to her, giving her no real say. Outwardly she gave a hint of a smile, if he believed he could control her, so be it. "No problem, it is prudent to avoid the possibility of being overheard, considering what needs to be discussed."

"It is. I also trust that you have no recording device on your person and your mobile will be switched off?"

His words took her back some years to when a trafficker suspected she had a recording device. He'd insisted she strip, checking all her clothing before he'd talk to her. At that time she was convinced it was more to belittle her, rather than an interest in what she carried. These days, that would never happen. People must take her word, or she walked away. Although in this case, even if she gave her word, it would mean nothing. Their conversation was far too important to rely on memory as to what was being said. Then, the recording system she carried was very sophisticated and used embedded sub miniature microphones in her clothing, transmitting to her mobile even if it was off and with the main battery removed. The recording device ran from another battery deep inside the mobile. This was expensive equipment, but essential for not missing anything an informer, or in this case a criminal, imparted to her.

"The same with you, I assume? Both mobiles on the table, batteries out and if you have an electronic watch, the same?"

"I don't wear tack," he came back at her, obviously indignant over the suggestion. "I've a Rolex and I notice you have a different Rolex on tonight. One of their limited editions. I would take a bet that cost a great deal of money?"

Karen smiled inwardly. In her view, such a comment would only come from someone who was still climbing the social ladder, besides their thinking that by wearing and pointing out expensive designer accessories, it made them look far more wealthy and important than they really were. It seemed to her that such comments made him unlikely to be the leader of this group. That person would almost certainly be wealthy, not virtually bankrupt, and as such, would never comment on something as trivial as the value of a watch worn by a multimillionaire. It also added to her suspicion that Julian was a cog, although perhaps an essential one, in the group being able to move money. Yet how could he seemingly pretend to speak as the group's leader, unless the real leader wanted it to look that way?

She gave an indifferent shrug. "It's a watch, they tell the time and that's it. What the watch cost I can't remember. I bought it because I like the style."

In fact, Julian's assumption as to the watch being rare and expensive couldn't have been more accurate, but not in the way he believed. It was rare, because it was not the original watch movement which would be found inside. Rolex had removed it for safe-keeping and replaced it with an electronic alternative that was capable of operating the signal system when pressing the watch winder.

The waiter approached to tell them dinner was ready to be served, at the same time collecting their glasses. They followed him into a private dining room that could seat at least ten people in comfort; however, the table had only been laid for two diners. They were left to settle down.

"I've been thinking, how is it my dinner is ready, when I've not even ordered yet?"

"Because I suggested to the head waiter, after telling him you were my guest, it would be prudent to speak to his counterpart at the Paris Oriental to find your preferences. I chose your meal from that list. It also turns out, talking to a waiter of another restaurant at lunchtime, you were not wrong in chefs not liking you, as you're well-known for rejecting what's put in front of you. Do you enjoy upsetting top chefs, because you can?"

"'I've a military background and am used to eating basic but wholesome food. Then my home is next to the camp where I employ a housekeeper, who knows what I enjoy. I may have lunch in the camp, but very rarely do I eat in the officers' dining room at night, and even the odd times I do, the chef knows my preferences. I'll not eat anything undercooked, dressed fancy or that comes in such a tiny portion that I have to stop off for a burger afterwards. Call me awkward, difficult to please, so be it, I couldn't care less what people think of me. Anyway, what have you ordered?"

He shrugged. "For you, soup - tomato, followed by rack of lamb. You can't get much more basic than that."

"That's fine, shall we sit down?"

Dinner in lots of ways was strained. Neither of them had anything in common, they were more just putting up with each other. Even conversations on various topics of the day fell apart. Karen had little idea of what went on in the UK on a day-to-day basis. She rarely watched the news, or followed the finance trends, where for Julian, that was his forte.

"You're a strange woman, showing little knowledge of finance for someone with substantial assets. Who handles your investments?" Julian asked, after her obvious lack of knowledge came out in conversation on up-to-date news stories and in particular, ones about finance and investments.

"I do it myself, I don't need help. Mind you, gambling with investments is not me, I hold quite a number of shareholdings in various companies and for the last year or so, I've never even bothered to see if they are up or down, that's how interested I am."

The shares Karen held were not her own selected investments, but those of the share certificates she had found in the safe in Corsica, all owned by the Sextons and inherited by her on their death.

"You should let me look after them and advise you on how to make real money."

She looked at him for a moment. "Somehow, I don't believe you and I are on the same wavelength. You see, when I say quite a number of shares, the total value, a year or so back, was close to twenty million. I don't think handing over my hard-earned money to a clerk working in a bank equates as a trustworthy investment opportunity." Karen deliberately downgraded his position to watch his reaction, it was time to pull this man down to the level he really was, a criminal.

His face darkened. "What do you mean by clerk? I'm a senior investment manager handling volumes of money on a weekly basis far in excess of your combined assets."

"Then it's a pity you don't take the same care of your own finances, after all, like you have looked into my private affairs, I have yours, and they are decidedly shaky. So were all the people at your house clients, or creditors wanting their money?" she mocked.

Julian was beginning to realise how smart Karen was, pulling him down and placing him in the position of having to defend himself. He tried to brush her accusations off. "I don't mix business with pleasure, particularly with clients. The other night involved friends, we meet on a regular basis to play cards, perhaps include a little wager or two, no more. As for my own liquidity, I live according to my income, I don't walk around like someone pretending to be a pauper, who has hundreds of millions of pounds in the bank because she's incapable of investing properly."

Karen didn't reply at first, sipping the remains of her coffee, noting the supercilious attitude now written all over his face. It was time to up the pressure. "You will find, Julian, beyond having somewhere to live and food on the table, there is very little else money can buy. Oh, you can claim it gives you exotic holidays, the ability to shop in overpriced shops selling designer products, or basic food dressed up with fancy names and high prices in restaurants, all produced and sold by clever advertising to the social-climbing idiots who believe people will look at them in awe for their purchases. They don't, the very wealthy and the poorer ones in the community only see them as fools attempting to be people they are not. However, if you want a larger bedroom in a posh hotel, or to have people run around at your beck and call, that's all well and good, but such indulgences are incidentals and you soon tire of them. In my case, I have more than sufficient for my simple life and don't have the need to accumulate more. Where you are currently being bled dry by Wrangler, twenty years your junior, who by all reports prefers pretty girls to a middle-aged man. Then I assume to keep up this high-flying pretence you have a high-pressure job, which demands success to earn a decent return? So who is the fool around here, it certainly isn't me? Then let's look at your so-called card buddies, that's a load of shit. I can only assume you and the rest of your 'card playing buddies' are up to your eyes in something that could see you all spending the next ten years in prison. So what you have to offer me had better be good and I mean good. Otherwise, I walk away and look further into you and your buddies' seedy pasts. As it is, rather than waste my time here, I've things to do tonight, so now we've finished dinner, phones on the table and batteries out please. It's time we got on with the real reason I'm here."

Julian pulled his phone out of his pocket. He was concerned by her remarks. What did she know about him and what was she prepared to forget, if anything? He was starting to think it had been a bad idea, talking directly to her. After both phones were on the table it was Julian who began.

"First of all, are you in agreement to pull back from Sir Richard Knight and accept he was working with MI6?"

"That's possible, but not his son. Rape a trafficked girl under sixteen and you go down. I cannot ignore that and neither would the authorities."

"As I said to you last time we met, Robin Knight was a fool, I won't ask you not to pursue such a man. My second condition is you remove all information held by Unit T on the abduction of one of your covert operators and you tailing Don Wang to my home, along with deleting the names of my other guests that night?"

"Again, based on what information you're offering, we will do that. It will be as if none of them ever existed as far as the Unit T database is concerned." Karen smiled inwardly - 'but not mine,' she said to herself.

"Very well, you want to know about the Sinaloa cartel?"

"Of course."

"At regular intervals they ship three tons of class A drugs from South America to Europe. In fact the next shipment is due to arrive in two weeks. Two tons destined for Europe and one ton for the UK. The system they use to distribute is inside fish. The ship bringing the drugs from South America drops drums four miles offshore. Three small fishing boats pick up the drums and inside them are ready-packaged plastic tubes of heroin, the perfect size for insertion into fish. The boats land the fish, the truck picks the catch up and it goes off to a warehouse for distribution. The operation is slick, fast and efficient. You will get all the details of when it's to happen and where the distribution warehouse is located."

Karen gave a sigh. "Sinaloa's methods sound a very clever way to move drugs about, Julian, but they can ship twenty-ton loads for all I care, and even if I know how and when, I'll still do nothing."

He seemed a little taken aback. "You are joking? You represent the EU, the police; I don't believe you'll turn your back on such an operation. Think how many lives three tons would ruin?"

Karen shrugged. "I'm not man's saviour, if someone wants to pump drugs into themselves, let them. It's one less idiot in the world. Talk to the police, the Customs and Excise of the countries involved, I'll not do a thing. Unless they are also carrying trafficked girls - then I will look into it. If they aren't and it's just drugs, I'll walk away."

He said nothing, so Karen decided to elaborate.

"You really don't understand the politics do you, Julian? You see, the authorities despise us, believe we should never have been formed and it was made even worse by me taking over. It is so bad that if the police intercepted the drugs and found girls with them, they'd not tell us; in fact, they would probably kick the girls out on the street and say nothing."

He frowned. "Why would they do that?"

"It's about something you know a great deal about - money. A trafficking offence automatically kicks in a proceeds of crime claim. The criminals' assets all go to Unit T and what's left to LBNF. The police, the country, get nothing. They can't get their heads around the fact that we work in all EU countries and if we didn't receive funds through the proceeds of crime we'd be knocking on each country's door for more money. So you and I are at an impasse with Sinaloa out of the mix. This is an exchange of information, what else have you got that you wish to barter?"

"Ryan?"

Karen acted indifferent. "Only one child, hardly worth an exchange for Richard Knight. If it was about groups that are holding a number of girls, then yes, but one, come on, I'd not put in resources to pull one out."

"You are unbelievable, what do you do all day, twiddle your thumbs?"

"We go after cartels, organised crime syndicates and similar. I bring out hundreds of victims."

"Then it all boils down to money? Is that how you got so rich?"

"Hardly," she came back at him. "I made my money from two bad decisions about men. Mind you, both weren't short of money and both died, leaving their fortunes to me. It's pretty normal; women often end up with all the money. As for Unit T, we don't have unlimited resources - I have ongoing, over a hundred live operations involving trafficked persons, of all ages. To mount any operation costs at least a hundred thousand, even more if multiple Dark Angel units are needed. That doesn't include the shipping of men and equipment across Europe. You're a money man, what would you do with limited resources? Spend a hundred thousand, or even more, for one child, or keep it to take twenty out, maybe fifty? I think, like me, you'd not look at one child as good value. They'd need to be part of a group, then it'd be worth it, providing we got the trafficker as well as their assets."

Karen was deliberately being hard, acting unconcerned. If Julian wanted her out of his hair, for her to walk away and supposedly forget he existed and let one of the Knights off the hook, that would cost him dearly.

"I need to talk to people. The Sinaloa cartel, yes, the kid, yes, but if you won't take either, that's a different ball game."

"Very well, I've one more night in the UK, then I'm in Brussels for four days, followed by appointments at the LBNF complexes in Spain. I should be free by the end of next week, with luck."

"You'd leave the kid in the hands of traffickers, because you've no time?" he asked, aghast at her seeming indifference.

"You seem shocked, not that I can see why, after all, I suspect it's people like you who perpetuate human trafficking and put them there to start with. As it is, I've been in the same situation the kid is in. Taken to an auction, stood in front of the buyers. Inspected like some animal while they make their bids. After that, put to work seven days a week, to line the successful buyer's pockets. So yes, I know what's happening to the child. As for Ryan, by you offering him, you have knowledge that he is still alive and making money for the trafficker. If that is the case, he will be looked after. He'll probably have been raped multiple times, I can't stop that, only collect and take him home. With or without your help I will eventually find both Ryan and Chinwe as well as many more. So if there is nothing else, thank you for dinner, and I'll get off. When you've sorted out your end call me, but don't leave it too long. The clock is ticking and every day we will find out more about what you're all up to. Then there will be a tipping point when it's too late, because we'll be coming for you."

***

Karen was sitting in the back of her car after leaving Julian. She knew her approach was a risk, particularly for Ryan, but what could she do? He'd look at her as being weak if she just took the child. It had to look a good deal on both sides for him to be convinced she'd walk away. Then there was no mention of Chinwe. Why was that, didn't they have any idea where she was. Or was she dead?

She called Stanley.

"Hi Karen, it's a late call, what are you up to?"

"Sorry, Stanley, I didn't realise the time and you must be at home. I've just left Julian. When you listen to the conversation tomorrow you'll understand. In the meantime, we do have trackers on his phone as well as the numbers he's calling, don't we?"

"We do, anything in particular you want us to listen to?"

"No, wait until you listen to our conversation, but be sure your people are on the ball tonight, log everything and miss nothing. I'll talk to you sometime tomorrow."

"You can be sure of that, Karen, and don't bother about the time, if you're working so are we. Besides, I'd been watching a pretty awful movie and am glad to have an excuse to switch it off. So was dinner good?"

"Yes, if you consider I had no say in the order, Julian took it on himself to decide what I ate. Bloody cheek."

"Dangerous to do that with you, you normally send it all back."

Karen laughed. "God, does everyone know my eating habits?"

"I suspect the whole of Europe does, Karen, well, at least the chefs. I'll talk to you tomorrow, have a good night."

"And you."

Karen came into her apartment, Jasmin was sitting cross-legged on the floor, leaning on the settee, television on and a half empty bowl of popcorn by her side.

"Hi, want some?" she asked, pushing the bowl towards Karen, who'd flopped down in an easy chair.

"Not for the moment, I've just eaten. Did you listen in to the conversation?"

"I did - it'll be interesting to know who he's going to talk to."

"Yes, there are times being a fly on the wall could be really useful. Did you think I took the right tack?"

"The only one I could see. Although your stance could be the death knell for Ryan."

Karen sighed. "We can't save every child. Then it's hard being in charge, Jasmin. Every decision I have to make these days is life and death."

"True. On another topic, I listened to the news tonight; the police are still baffled about their two officers who were killed."

"They may be telling the press that, but they must have some idea."

"Possibly, but don't you think you should have a quiet word with Hardy Melcher as to who was there so he can pass it on to the police. Maybe it will show he has some value. After all, he has quite a job in defending you all the time."

Karen shook her head. "Not advisable, they already know we were in the area and believed we could be holding back vital information. I'm not going to admit it, just let them see the dash cam footage that will take us out of any involvement and it will have to remain that way. I suspect Eryk Kowalski had a hand in taking Chinwe and Ryan. If that's the case, Julian could still come back with a deal, which may involve throwing him along with his partner Fabian to the wolves. Then we'll get a number of victims out, rather than just Ryan and maybe Chinwe."

"Perhaps. After all, we've dried up on surveillance so there's no route there any more. Although we know where the two from Sinaloa are holding out. Should we carry on watching them, or call it a day now it's only leading to a drug bust?"

"I wish I knew. It's all very messy. I've also not heard a murmur from Charlie, so he could be another victim."

Jasmin nodded agreement. "Do you think if we lean on Fabian or Eryk, one would break, if only to save his own skin?"

"Possibly, except they both have a lot to lose and as such, we'd struggle to frighten either of them like you did with the Jones's, or me with Vincent. Better the minder called Mark that you told me Chinwe mentioned. We'd break him for certain."

"There's a great many Marks in the world, Karen, but give me a route to him, and yes he'd break."

"Maybe, but I've had enough tonight. I think I will have some popcorn and you can tell me what the movies about."

Chapter 35

The following day, Julian entered the office of a director of the bank he worked for. A man in his late sixties, short, with a huge belly from over-indulgence, his name was Madelhari Richter. He had houses both in the UK and Dubai, but rarely came to London. He was also part of the consortium doing financing and money laundering for organised crime groups, including the cartels.

"Well, has the idiot agreed?" Madelhari asked.

Julian shook his head. "We fell foul of Unit T's terms of engagement. She won't touch drugs, no matter how large. Something about it earns them no money, whereas with trafficking they get all the assets. It's a strange setup, because they are actually in competition with the authorities in all EU countries, for money from the proceeds of crime orders, so she won't help them, neither will they help her."

He leaned back in his chair, looking at Julian. "I've heard this before from an associate of mine, about her walking away from a huge drug bust, but I didn't believe it. After all, the woman is very aware how drugs impact on human trafficking, and drugs often go hand in hand with it. So could this be just talk and she's holding out for a better deal, to include a substantial personal financial return, for giving up the Knights?"

"I can't see it, Harris has got so much money, she's no idea what to spend it on, apart from the charity. She even told me she'd close to twenty million in shares and had never looked at them for years. That's a lot of money in anyone's book, but it seems not for her. So we've nothing to barter with apart from the larger criminal groups who shift substantial funds through the accounts. She won't be happy with one kid for the Knights, in fact when

I suggested the child, she shrugged, saying she wouldn't spend close to a hundred thousand on an operation just for one child, and has effectively written him off."

"It's good to understand her mentality, always know your adversary, Julian, that's a strength."

"Maybe, but in Harris's case, she's out on her own, I can't see we'd ever understand how she ticks. The only part of her make-up that I can see has substance is she keeps to her word, so I still believe a deal can be brokered to have her walk away from us."

"Now I know the situation, Julian, leave it to me. I'll look at what has value and what doesn't. There's sure to be a package that will satisfy her, after all, she's only after money, the same as us all."

"Very well, but we really need to move fast. Every day she'll be collating information and will soon have built a picture of sufficient size that she won't want to let go."

After Julian left the office, Madelhari leaned back in his chair, deep in thought. Whatever happened, all possible routes to himself had to be broken. The group was too important. Also, he wasn't that naive as to believe that whatever agreement Karen had made with Julian, she'd go away - he knew she wouldn't. It was common knowledge among the cartels that Karen wanted the money men and Julian would not get in her way, he was certain. Julian's cell, and particularly Don, had been lax in allowing her in. Now that avenue had to be closed but before it happened, there was one last deal that Julian must make with Karen for everything to look as if he was running the show and she had her money man.

Chapter 36

Two days after Jasmin and Chinwe had been captured and Chinwe's subsequent escape, Kevin Story and his brother Rodney were on their way to Tamworth. With Chinwe getting away for the third time, both Fabian and Ryker had decided to cut their losses, so a contract had been raised to eliminate her once and for all. The Story brothers had no issues with killing a child, the value of the contract was exactly the same as for an adult.

Very soon they arrived at a house used to hold traffickers' victims, destined for the northern cities including Scotland.

Outwardly the house looked like every other on the street. Built just after the Second World War, it was commonly known as two bedrooms and a box. However, while most of the street was semis, this one was detached, being in a position where there was no space to build another semi, although a small extension had been built. The house was run by a woman from Romania, called Amalia Dinescu. Aged forty-two, she'd spent her early years on the streets and was well able to look after the girls waiting to be moved up north. She could also be sadistic in her methods, having experienced it while she worked the streets and knowing how effective it could be with ones giving them difficulty.

Kevin, a well-built man with a machete scar down his left arm, which often gave him pain, even after six years, knocked on the door. It was quickly opened by Amalia.

"Fabian sent us," he said.

"Come in," she answered.

Once inside and with the door shut, Kevin looked at her. "Has Chinwe been found? We've come to collect her," he drawled.

"No. We've given up searching as such; just let it be

known among the homeless and druggies that there's five hundred in their hand for information about where she is. With that sort of money, most would sell their own families. She'll turn up, you'll see. There's nowhere else for her to go."

"What efforts did you make to find her?" Kevin asked.

"My two minders, Patar and Grigore, spent two days looking. Grigore even got his mate who has two ex-police dogs to help out. They tracked her to a marina, but the girl must have jumped into the canal and swum for a distance. The dogs lost the scent and couldn't pick it up again. So while we had her general location, it was virtually impossible to keep searching inside the marina without raising the suspicions of people on the boats. They were confined to searching along the opposite bank along the towpath and among the shrubs to the side. There was no sign of her, then the other bank, beyond the marina, there are fields with little places to hide in. It wasn't easy, early-morning runners kept asking what they were doing, so rather than tell them to fuck off and mind their own business, Patar said they were after rabbits. It seemed to satisfy the runners. If she's hiding in a boat, or even if someone's taken her in at the marina or a local house, we've no idea. But there's been nothing in the news of a girl found wandering. So she's still out there."

Kevin pulled a printed card out of his pocket, with just a mobile phone number on it. "Give me the postcode of the marina, we'll go and look around. If you hear anything as to where she is, don't send your minders, call me. Understand?"

She shrugged. "You're welcome to her, but don't bring her here. We've got three girls due later today, so with what's already here and them, there's no room."

Kevin gave a hint of a smile. "She'll not be coming here,

that's for certain."

Once in the car, Rodney looked at Kevin, who had Googled the marina and was looking at the layout. "What's the plan?"

"We go to the marina, tell them we're interested in buying a boat and want to look around. Also, it will give us an idea which boats are for sale and their position. All the time we're there, we'll try to suss out if it's possible she could be living on a boat for any length of time without being seen or picked up on any CCTV they have. By the looks of it, there are loads of boats and she could be on any one of them. We can hardly search them all without someone calling the police."

"I agree. Personally, I think we're fucked, until she shows herself, or we get a call off Amalia."

"Maybe, maybe not. There's a pub close by which apparently serves food. Being by the side of the canal, it's likely to be frequented by boaters as well as some from the marina. We'll have a drink there and ask around. The girl has to eat and just maybe, she's been seen scrounging food, even if they sent her packing. That could well indicate she's still in the area, maybe holed up in the marina. If that's the case we hang around until she emerges."

***

Chinwe was cold, even after squeezing most of the water out, they'd remained damp, adding to her discomfort. From her position, she had been able to watch three people searching for her on the other bank where there was a towpath. She knew it was them, as one was urging his dogs into the dense shrubs running along the path; the other two had sticks and were prodding the shrubs. Soon, she decided, they would come to her side and the dogs would pick up her scent once more. She had to move on, but where?

Once the searchers were well down the towpath and out of sight, Chinwe emerged, standing on the edge of the canal. A few boats were tied up in front of her. Beyond the boats the path ended and the area opened out to fields, with a notice saying 'Private land - no mooring beyond this point'. This worried her, there was nowhere to hide if she went that way, but to remain here meant she was trapped. There again, why didn't they check this side first, it would seem logical, rather than go to the other bank? Unless that is, this side was private and it would be more difficult without people asking what they were doing? Chinwe walked slowly, but cautiously past the moored boats, coming out into a larger area of water where lots of boats were all tied up, but not flat to the banking like the ones she'd passed, they all stuck out into the water with walkways between each. She also noticed a few boats had smoke coming out of small chimneys on the roofs, but most seemed deserted. Returning to those tied up close to the bank, Chinwe selected one that was covered in leaf debris from the trees, it was obvious no one had been to it for some time. Climbing aboard, she found no lock on the cabin door, just a slither of wood jammed in the loop of the staple holding the hasp closed. She pulled it out, opened the small door and went inside. Like the outside it was a mess. To her it looked as if whoever owned it was in the process of painting, with tins of varnish on a small table along with various brushes. Everything else, like towels and cushions, was piled on a narrow settee. There were also pans on a small cooker and plates in racks above an equally small sink. For Chinwe this was ideal. She wasn't bothered about the mess, this was somewhere to hide and keep warm. Above the entrance door, to make it easier to get inside the cabin, Chinwe found the top would slide back. Utilising this she closed the entrance door and after sliding the top open she leaned over and pushed back in the piece of wood she'd taken out. Then she slid the top closed, bolting it and the door inside. She hoped anyone passing would not notice someone was on the boat. Going further inside, the bedroom was relatively clean, and there was a mattress on the bed with blankets folded up on top. Inside the drawers were clothes, all male, but at least they were clean and dry. Quickly she changed into a pair of trousers and a jumper. Both far too big, but it allowed her to hang up her own wet clothing to dry. Checking all the curtains were closed so no-one could look inside, she lay on the bed and soon fell asleep. The last two days had been stressful and although very hungry, she really did need to rest.

***

Chinwe awoke with a start, at first confused as to where she was, then it all came flooding back. She lay for a short time listening for any sound. There was nothing apart from what sounded like music and voices, but they were very weak and had to be some distance away. Standing, she checked her clothes, which were still slightly damp, but wearable. Pulling a curtain open slightly, she looked out. It was close to dusk. Chinwe was surprised; she couldn't have been asleep all day, could she? Either way, she was hungry and needed to find food. But a check in all the cupboards revealed only a half-empty jar of coffee, tea bags and sugar. There was no water that she could find, even the little tap over the sink did nothing when she turned it on. Chinwe did not know that for the water to run, the power on the boat had to be switched on. Because of this, there was no option, she had to go out and find food from somewhere. Quickly dressing, she left the boat, keeping close to the bushes and heading into the marina. On the far side of the water, she could see where the music was coming from. A building some distance away was all lit up, with tables outside and people moving around.

At that moment a man came off a boat a short distance ahead of her. He was carrying a black plastic bag. Chinwe followed, keeping well out of sight. He stopped at a row of rubbish containers, threw the bag in one and began walking back. He in fact passed her, with only feet between them, but Chinwe knew how to hide, and how not to be seen, and soon the man was back on his boat. Making her way to the bins, she looked inside. Everything was in black bags. In the next bin were empty tins, plastic bottles and such. Chinwe took out a large lemonade bottle. Further along she found a double tap used to fill the water tanks of the boats and quickly washed out the bottle, filling it with water. After taking a drink, she refilled it and hid it. She had the intention of looking around before collecting the bottle on her return to the boat.

It was now dark enough for Chinwe to feel a little safer and venture further into the marina. The lighting was poor, with only the odd low-level light to see by. An elderly couple walked past, with a 'good evening' acknowledgement. Chinwe answered with a simple 'hi'. She didn't stop to engage in any sort of conversation. Following the path around, and crossing a bridge taking her to the other bank, she eventually came to the large building that she had seen lit up. Chinwe had never seen such a building, with powerful up-lighters illuminating the frontage, and coloured lights surrounding a large area behind the building. She remained in the shadows watching. What interested her was seeing, in the area lit by coloured lights, a number of people sitting on benches at wooden tables, drinks in front of them. Some were also eating. A girl kept coming out from inside the building with drinks and food. Then she'd collect any empty glasses and plates lying around and go back inside. She, like Chinwe, was wearing jeans and a dark jumper, her hair tied back. Chinwe noticed the girl wasn't methodical in keeping tables clean, she'd just grab a few obviously empty glasses and plates to take back when she came out with more food. Most diners never engaged with her, in fact, in Chinwe's view she was ignored.

Close to where Chinwe was watching, a party of four got up to leave. Much of the food brought out had just been picked at by the two women in the party, leaving bowls in the centre of the table still half-full. Chinwe took her chance. As soon as they began to walk away, she moved quickly, emptying two bowls of chips into one bowl, along with some salad and chicken wings, before walking away. Now she was back in the shadows watching. The same as when the girl took the plates away, no one on the other tables even noticed or commented when she took the food. Although it was fortunate she took it when she did, when seconds later the serving girl came out with drinks, delivered them and collected up the empty plates and glasses from the table Chinwe had been to. Moving further away, Chinwe began eating. The food was not what she was used to, her diet had been based around broths with plenty of vegetables; only very occasionally would she have fowl and even rarer, meat, but when you're hungry, everything tastes good. She also couldn't understand why people would leave food, as if they had no sense of value. Never had she seen so much discarded. Shortly she wandered back to the boat, after collecting her water. While this way of survival would suffice for the moment, she had to find a means of contacting Karen. How she was going to do that, she'd no idea, but to go home it had to be done.

Chapter 37

Vincent, now working with Karen, was concerned that Karen could renege on their deal if he didn't at least give her something beyond Don. One piece of information he'd promised, was the location outside Birmingham where girls would be taken. Asking around among friends in the same game, he'd been able to find the address where Chinwe could have been taken on her way to Liverpool, where she was to be placed on a ship and leave the UK. Vincent called Karen, passing on an address in Tamworth, and suggesting that even if she wasn't there, it might still be housing other victims of human trafficking being moved around the country.

Jasmin had already left the UK and was on her way to Brussels. She had the decorators in their new house and she wanted to make sure they were doing as she wanted. Karen was still in London, along with a Dark Angel unit commanded by Lieutenant Cropper, who had been ordered to remain there to look after Karen on the instructions of Stanley.

With no real leads as to what had happened to Chinwe and Vincent's information coming so late after Chinwe was snatched, Karen knew the idea of her still being in Tamworth was a long shot. But with nothing else going on, she decided they may as well take a ride out. After all, if it didn't work out, it was nonetheless an opportunity to break a supply route for girls trafficked into the UK who were being sent north.

Sitting in the back of her vehicle with the table down, Karen was working through the mundane work that went with being the commander of Unit T when her mobile began to ring. She looked at the caller, it was a diversion from her original number. The caller was Julian Sharp.

"Julian, have you sorted out a deal to allow me to walk away?" she asked.

"Decisions have been made. We will give you the Knights along with Max Hart and Charles Sutton of MI6, and the minister, Carl Wright. We have recordings of conversations, documentary evidence, photos of them together, all pointing to collusion. This will certainly stuff them completely. They have no way out, Karen, and a big bonus for you will be their assets. We'll also throw in the boy, Ryan Selby. How's that for a deal?"

Karen had gone cold inside. If this was on the level, it could wipe out her problems with the UK authorities completely and net both Unit T along with her charity millions, besides giving compensation to both herself and a great many victims caught up in the actions of the contract killers the Knights had engaged when an aircraft was shot down. Not that she needed the money, it was more the principle.

"I'll take the deal, providing the documents of collusion place human trafficking violations at the fore."

"So it is just the money you're after?"

"Not at all," she lied. "I've told you, I'm governed by Unit T's terms of reference. If there are no trafficking violations, it's down to the authorities of the country where the crimes took place. So you may as well take your evidence to the UK police, we could do nothing."

"In that case you're in luck, we're only passing you trafficking violations."

"Then we deal."

"Very well, I'll send you a location for a meeting tomorrow night. Come alone."

"No, Julian, I won't be alone. You won't see them, but

a Dark Angel unit will be with me. Their standing orders are to protect at all costs, and costs means costs. I might end up being the sacrificial lamb, but you can guarantee no one will escape justice. They will either be dead, or in custody. A Dark Angel unit should not be underestimated, their firepower is unforgiving, with snipers that can kill at a thousand yards. So if there are any ideas this is to be a trap to get me alone, think again and don't send a location."

"Very well, but keep your trigger-happy lot under control. I intend to come out alive after I've given you the dossier."

"Don't we all. But life is cheap in the grey world of human trafficking, Julian. I look forward to our meeting," she said, then cut the call. She knew Stanley would have recorded the conversation and he wouldn't be happy about her meeting Julian once more. Particularly her being alone, even if Dark Angel were close by. He'd want Jasmin at her side.

Karen carried on with working through her paperwork.

***

Time moved on, Karen had already put her papers back in the bag and was gazing out of the window, when Lieutenant Cropper, sitting next to the driver, slid the soundproof glass between her and the front of the vehicle open.

"Five minutes, Commander," he called back.

Karen opened a small cupboard below her seat and took out her handgun, checked it quickly and pushed it in the holster on her belt. She also fastened up the bulletproof jacket over her combat uniform. Such clothing was mandatory when it was a Dark Angel operation and even Karen wasn't exempt. Finally, she also checked her ankle knife was secure. Not that she visualised using it, but this was just habit, to ensure her last means of defence was in place.

The vehicle came to a halt followed by the one behind. Immediately soldiers were out of the vehicles and quickly positioned themselves around the target house. Karen followed them out, slipping on a balaclava followed by her helmet and pulling the visor down. She watched the lieutenant along with another soldier approach the door and ring the bell, before they stood back a short distance. In the hand of the other soldier was what the local police call 'the big red key' or enforcer. Such a device was more than capable of opening most doors, with a three-ton impact from something only 58cm long and weighing 16 kilos.

Amalia pulled open the door, saw who it was and tried to slam it back shut. But she was too late, the lieutenant had quickly moved forward, slamming his full weight against the door, sending her stumbling back. Dropping the enforcer, the other soldier followed the lieutenant inside. In seconds she was secure. Immediately other soldiers moved in, quickly searching the small house.

After a few minutes Karen went inside the house too, leaving her helmet with a soldier guarding the entrance.

"Three girls upstairs, Commander. None of them speak English. The only other person in the house is the woman who opened the door, a Romanian named Amalia Dinescu, that's according to a passport found upstairs on top of a dressing table."

"Good work Lieutenant, I will talk to the woman. Does she speak English?"

"She does, but is saying very little. The room the three girls were found in has bars on the windows and two bolts securing the door. On that basis, we have to assume at this point they were being held against their will. We are taking photos and securing the evidence for forensics."

Amalia was in the lounge, the soldier guarding her left the room when Karen entered.

She looked at Karen. "So you're the famous Karen Harris then? Where were you when I was trafficked, sunning yourself on the beach, if you can believe the papers these days?"

"Probably, after all everyone needs a break at times, there again, it seems you've moved to the other side, so rather than me pull you out, you go down for ten years. I hope you think it was worth it, particularly as the ones who pay you to look after the girls, will be the ones on the beach sunning themselves, drinks in their hands."

She smiled. "I understand, this is the soft sell bit, maybe I get a reduced sentence by ratting on the people who gave me a roof over my head - dignity and money in my pocket."

"Sorry to disappoint, we don't reduce sentences. It's the law, caught trafficking and it's ten years mandatory, no exceptions. There again, by what you're saying, you were once a victim. You could still be that, held here under duress, that's if I was able to arrest the ones that were holding you here."

Amalia gave a hint of a smile. "You're a sneaky fucker aren't you?"

"More of a realist, Amalia. You see I've been there, the same as you, and know what it's like. I also understand the pressure on you doing what you do now, in exchange for being raped day after day and why you accepted this life. I can give you the chance to walk away, make a new life. Not like this of course, because we now know about you and will be watching, so you'd have to work for a living. But that's far better than worrying who's at the door every time the bell rings and losing your freedom, coming out an old woman with no prospects and who no one wants."

"I don't believe you were ever in my position. It's all talk and I'll still go down."

"That is where you're wrong. Besides what the public read about my early abduction and escape, in the course of my fight against traffickers I've been taken, sold many times and put to work in brothels that were living hells. I'm offering you a chance to get out, in exchange for help in taking down the real perpetrators who lived on the fat using victims like you and I. Why am I giving you this chance? Because people like you are two a penny, we can pull those in every day, to be replaced by others. The only way to stop it is to take down the ones at the top. You will be helping victims rather than perpetuating the crime. I'll give you ten minutes to choose your future, Amalia. Help me, or rot in prison. There are no other options." Karen stood, but looked back at her. "It's time they paid for what they put you through in your early years, Amalia." Then Karen left the room. She knew it would finally come down to self-preservation with people like Vincent and her. She would have no allegiance to the ones above her, ruling by fear. But such fears, instilled in her as a prostitute, to always do as you're told or expect a good beating, were difficult to forget and would weigh heavily on her decision. Karen was relying on her wanting out and realising only she could offer her that choice.

After the ten minutes Karen was back in the room. "Well, what's it to be? I can't remain here any longer; I have far too much work on."

"You win; I'll help in any way I can to convict the ones who pushed me as a child many years ago into prostitution. After all it is right what you say, they won't be interested in me now I've been caught."

"They won't, that is a fact, Amalia. When we document

this raid, we will highlight you were here the same as the girls under duress and your life threatened. When you are released, go to LBNF in London. They will assist you in getting settled. My people will debrief you, but a word of warning, don't take them for idiots. They know a great deal as to what is going on, so your information must coincide with what we know to be facts, otherwise we cannot help you."

"I understand, I just want out."

"I'd like to know one thing before I move on. The girl Chinwe, where is she?"

"The people I worked for would also like to know? She never got to this house, in fact escaped as they tried to bring her in. One of the men who brought her was injured, with his gun going off in the struggle. You should get his name from the local hospital. He was there all night, before they let him leave. Chinwe was tracked to a marina. It was impossible to search without raising suspicions. They even sent people from London to look for her. I had the impression there was no intention of taking her back, I think they were there to kill her, but she was never found. She's really keeping a low profile and believe me, if she'd been on the street we'd have known. My feeling is she's still in the marina, maybe being hidden by the residents or on an empty boat. I presume you, unlike the men who came from London, would have the power to search the place?"

"I have that power. What is the address?"

***

Leaving two soldiers in the house, Karen headed to the marina with the remainder. By car it wasn't that far away, so after fifteen minutes travelling they were turning onto the private road leading down to the main reception.

Karen, still in combat gear and armed, but not wearing her helmet, walked into the reception. The girl looking after the shop and reception just stared at her aghast.

"Colonel Harris, commander of Unit T. We have a warrant to search the marina. Is your manager or the owner on site?"

"Err, yes, Mr Ellis, he's the owner. I'll fetch him." She left through a back door. Karen spent the time looking at the boats-for-sale board while she waited.

A small but wiry man wearing overalls came through from the back. "I believe you want to search our boatyard?" he asked.

"We do, I have information that a young African girl could be hiding out here. I need to satisfy myself that is not the case."

"Then you are more than welcome to look around. But first, may I see your identification?"

Karen handed him the search warrant and showed her ID card.

He gasped, seeing the name. "You, you are Karen Harris?"

"That is correct."

"Oh my god, my wife is in awe of what you do and follows the reports of your work ardently. After your search, would you do me the honour in joining us for refreshments, which also includes your troops?"

"I'd be happy to. But first, how many boats are often left unattended for long periods?"

"Probably around fifty per cent, but there are not many someone could stay in without one of our regulars noticing. They are all very alive to the possibility of break-ins. Besides," he lowered his voice, "the nosy ones who seem to know more of what's going on than even us, would be shouting from the rooftops."

Karen smiled. "Possibly, but this girl has shown herself to be more than capable of remaining hidden, even in a city - if she doesn't want you to see her, you won't. Perhaps you can show me on the map, locations where someone may be able to hide out without being noticed?"

He pointed them out and asked if she wanted him with her, but Karen declined, asking him to temporarily close the main gates while they searched and prevent anyone from entering the marina.

As Karen left the office his wife ran through from the back. "Is it true, Bob, Unit T is here?" she gasped.

"It's true love, but not just Unit T, would you believe, Karen Harris herself. She even accepted my invitation to have refreshments with us."

"So who's she looking for?"

"Some African girl."

Her mouth dropped. "It isn't the missing African, Chinwe is it? If it is, we need photos. This is so cool, the most famous soldier in the world is here at our marina and a little girl the entire country's looking for. The local and national papers will be falling over themselves for an exclusive. It will put us on the map like we've never been."

"Don't go overboard yet, love. Let's hope she does find who she's looking for, then like you say, the papers will go wild."

Karen, along with the soldiers, began a methodical search. She, like the other soldiers, had replaced her balaclava and helmet, bringing down the bulletproof visor. While they believed, if Chinwe was here, she'd be on her own, they couldn't take that chance. She could well be held against her will and they may be facing a gunman.

As they progressed, and even with most empty boats well secured and locked up, not one was discounted, with windows and hatches checked for disturbance.

The couple who had seen Chinwe on the first night she was there, when they were coming back from a morning walk, were prevented by Bob from entering the marina.

"What's going on, Bob," the man asked.

"Unit T is here, they are looking for a young girl. We all have to keep out the way."

"Was the one they are looking for coloured?"

"Yes, why do you ask?"

"We saw a coloured girl a few days back. She was coming from the direction of those boats moored beyond the marina."

"Of course, it's a logical place where she'd hide. I'd better tell Karen."

He ran back into the marina, but was stopped by a soldier. Bob told him what the man had said.

The soldier called Karen by radio, giving her a possible location.

***

Soldiers surrounded the three boats moored away from the marina. This area would have been included in their search but they hadn't got this far as yet. One soldier moved cautiously closer, looking at each boat. While none of them were in regular use, the middle boat, although it was covered in leaves and looked as if it had not been used for some time, there were footprints in the mud between the gravel path and the side of the boat, as well as disturbed leaves around the entrance door. It was also the only boat that didn't have a padlock on the door. He reported his findings back by radio to the lieutenant and was ordered to check it out, while other troops moved up in support. The soldier climbed aboard, pulling out the wood put in place of a padlock keeping the staple closed, but the door didn't move when he attempted to open it. The door was locked from inside.

He knocked on the door. "Whoever is inside, come out and show yourself," he demanded in an authoritative voice. "We intend no harm, but there is no escape." Then with the area around the cabin entrance quite small on this narrowboat, he stepped off it to allow whoever was inside to come out.

Chinwe was hiding inside when she heard the sounds of crunching gravel. This could only mean someone was on the path that ran alongside the canal and past the boats. With no time to get out, she prayed they were not coming to work on this boat. However, when it suddenly rocked as someone stepped onboard, she knew that must be the reason they were here, and kicked herself for remaining inside during the daytime, rather than hiding in the undergrowth.

Her battle for freedom over the last days had been the worst time she'd ever experienced. She had been existing mainly on water and what scraps she could pinch from the pub. But this was midweek and the pub had been quiet. Also, diners were leaving very little on their plates. She had taken to rummaging through the bins in the hope of finding something she could eat, but found nothing that was edible. Chinwe had finally accepted she could no longer cope, and made up her mind that if she still found there was no food she could take from the pub, she'd hand herself in and hope they would call the police. Now it was too late. It had all been for nothing, she was cornered and the searchers had found her. However, peeping out of the window through a crack in the curtain, she could see the men were all dressed in black, with visors down and carrying guns. Such attire terrified her, taking her back to the time when men like these would come to her village in the night, raping and killing, coupled with the sounds of their laughter. Such memories would never leave her. But who were these men? Had the traffickers engaged mercenaries? But what could she do? She'd no weapons besides a stick, and what good would that be against a gun?

"I'm coming out," Chinwe shouted as she unbolted the door and came out, the stick still in her hand.

Immediately she was recognised. "Please, step off the boat, placing the stick on the ground, Chinwe. Is anyone else on the boat?" Lieutenant Cropper asked.

She shook her head, before jumping off the boat onto land and laying the stick on the ground as she was told, before putting her hands up.

A soldier went back on board, going directly into the cabin. He was out in seconds. "The boat's clear, Lieutenant."

"You can put your hands down, Chinwe. We just needed to be certain there was only you inside the cabin," Lieutenant Cropper told her.

As he spoke they parted to allow a soldier who had been behind them to come forward. It was Karen.

"I believe you're looking for me, Chinwe?" Karen asked her, at the same time handing her M4 carbine to a soldier standing at her side, before removing her helmet and handing him that as well.

Chinwe stood watching as Karen finally removed her balaclava, shaking her head to allow her hair to drop. Her heart was thumping, her body shaking as everything she knew about Karen, particularly the blue eyes, was confirmed in the person standing in front of her. “You... you are Karen Harris?” she gasped, hardly daring to believe after all she’d been through that Karen had come for her.

“Of course, but didn’t you ask for me to find you and take you home?” Karen answered with a smile.

“Yes,” she replied meekly.

“Then what are you waiting for, aren’t you going to give me a hug?” Karen asked, holding her arms out.

Chinwe didn’t hesitate any longer, but quickly came over to Karen flinging her arms around her, tears streaming down her face, such was her relief that no matter what people had told her, that Karen wouldn’t be interested in someone who was a nobody, she was actually here.

“My mother kept saying to me if I was ever taken, never to stop believing you would come and find me. I never stopped believing, in fact, every child in Africa knows only Karen Harris would not give up on us and bring us home.”

“It’s nice of you to have such faith in me, but you must understand, Chinwe, I cannot do it all alone. There are over two thousand others behind me. Every one dedicated to finding children like you and making sure they go home.”

She stood back a little and looked Karen directly in her eyes. “Maybe. But you came for me yourself. I feel so humble you would waste your precious time for a nobody like me, and I can never hope to repay you, but you will always be welcome in our family’s house. We have very little, but it is all yours.”

Karen smiled. “You are not a nobody, Chinwe, never believe that about yourself. Every child can make a difference in this world and soon you will embark on such a journey. As for your offer, it is very generous of you, but you see, I never went into this for personal gain. I want nothing for helping a child taken from her home, but you will find my help does not end there. I have hundreds, no, thousands of children who have been in the same position as you and many are given the chance to join my education program. Those children are supported through school, university anywhere in the world, to become doctors, nurses, social workers, engineers and given many other opportunities that will help your people, your village. Your journey has just begun, Chinwe, all I ask, whatever you decide to do, is make your family proud."

"While I've been hiding on this boat, I have had time to think long and hard as to why I wanted to return home, beyond wanting to be with my family. After all most if not all my life, it has been hard, very hard, besides being surrounded by violence of one type or other. I even considered asking if I could join you in your cause, but now I know I must go back. Our country needs, even more, citizens who can tell the world about ourselves, and not just tackle issues like poverty, or violence. I have learned, including from my older sister, that this is the way people from outside our continent talk about us. We have so much more to offer, our culture is rich and my nation is hungry for change."

"If that is what you believe, then that is what you must strive for, Chinwe - perhaps being a reporter is your path. With my help, you will have all the tools to achieve what you want. Now it's time we left, are you hungry?"

She nodded her head up and down. "Starving."

"Good, so am I. The owner of this marina has prepared a little food for us. Later tonight we'll go out for dinner in London's West End. Would you like that?"

Chinwe's eyes were as big as saucers. Karen wanted to

take her out. "Yes, please."

Karen turned to the Lieutenant. standing by her. "They must have a shower block here and we need to find Chinwe clean clothes, Lieutenant. We can't take her back looking like she does."

He saluted. "I'll sort it out, Commander."

Chinwe walked at Karen's side towards the main offices of the marina. "What happened to Ryan, has he gone home?"

"We're still looking, Chinwe. But I think very soon he will also be free."

Bob came up to them. "One of your soldiers has requested the use of our shower block. That is no problem and our daughter is the same size as Chinwe, we'll sort her some clean clothes to wear with pleasure."

"Thank you, but you did mention refreshments, besides which we have a very hungry young lady with us now."

"Of course, please follow me; my wife has it all prepared."

Chapter 38

Chinwe followed Karen into her apartment, and stopped in complete amazement. “Is this your home? It’s beautiful,” she gasped.

Karen laughed. “One of them, but I’m only here for around three days a month, my main home’s in France. Normally you would move on to one of my complexes in Spain, run by LBNF. But if you’d prefer, you can come with me to France and meet Midnight, my niece. We can do all the paperwork to get you repatriated at the Unit T camp next door.”

“I’d like to stay with you, please?”

“Then it’s France. You can act as a co-pilot for me.”

“You have an aeroplane?” she ask wide eyed.

“Yep, I fly, where everyone else uses cars. It’s very useful, with constantly moving from country to country. Anyway, while you watch television I’ll get changed and then we’ll go shopping for clothes more suitable for you, before we go out for dinner later. Which reminds me, I’d better give them a call to make sure we’ve a table.”

She looked at Karen shyly. “You don’t have to spend money on me, these clothes are fine, really, and we can eat in. Jeans are very valuable in our country. New or second-hand, it makes no difference, I’ll always treasure them.”

“Sit down, Chinwe and let me explain a few things.”

She sat down.

“For a start, when you are with me, you will be eating out. Mainly because I’m pretty bad at cooking apart from ready meals, and believe me they are not recommended for any sort of balanced diet. The places I eat you need a dress, then staying at my home in

France you'll need underwear, suitable clothing, shoes, swimming costume, the lot. So no arguments, we get you a new wardrobe. There is also another thing that has happened which will affect you for years to come."

"What?" she asked, confused.

"Your plight, because you mentioned my name, hit the headlines in so many countries across the world - people wanted to help you. A Just Giving site was set up by LBNF on your behalf. Donations have been coming in from all over the world, with a current balance of over thirty-five thousand pounds, and it's still going up. All that money is yours, Chinwe, to spend as you like. If you want I, or rather LBNF, will look after it for you and make sure you're never cheated until you come of age. It won't affect the help LBNF will give you, or the funding of your education. We will still do that."

"Why would strangers want to give me money? I have nothing to offer and could never pay them back."

"There are a lot of good people in the world, Chinwe, not all are bad. All will be more than happy you've been found and they have played a tiny part by contributing towards your future. No one would want, or expect you to pay them back. Then I believe with your help we could locate the people who snatched you. If that is the case, you will be entitled to compensation. LBNF will see you get what is coming to you. Anyway, rather than go out in combat clothing, when I've changed into something more suitable, we can hit the shops."

Chapter 39

The Director General of MI6 had requested that Max Hart and Charles Sutton attend a meeting in the boardroom. Now they were on their way there.

"Wonder what he wants?" Max commented.

"Whatever it is, it's bloody inconvenient. I wanted to get away early today, Meg's got her pilates class tonight and I'm on babysitting duty."

Going into the boardroom, Max was surprised to see the MP Carl Wright.

"Carl, why are you here?"

He shrugged. "I've no idea, all hush-hush I think. The PM's office asked if I'd attend."

Moments later the Director General came into the room. "Gentlemen, please take a seat. I understand the people joining us have arrived and are being signed in."

"What is the meeting about, Sir, I really need to get off tonight?" Charles asked.

"I'm not sure myself; I was only asked if I could attend. Ah, here are our guests."

Sir Hardy Melcher and Karen entered the room.

"I should have bloody known, what the fuck does she want now?" Max said quietly to Charles.

"Probably whinging to the PM and wants an apology," Charles came back.

"In her fucking dreams."

"Colonel Harris, perhaps you can enlighten us as to why you have requested this meeting?" the Director General asked.

"Yes, Sir, I have here three warrants of arrest. For Mr Hart,

Mr Sutton and Mr Wright. The charges are conspiracy to pervert the course of justice regarding charges already lodged against Sir Richard Knight and Sir Robin Knight. Sir Hardy has looked at the charges and the evidence against these men; he is in agreement with the warrants. With the charges relating to human trafficking, Unit T will handle the cases."

"Have you gone completely mad?" Max blurted out. "If anyone should be charged, it's you, by the way you go on. We live in a democracy, not a dictatorship run by the likes of people such as you."

She looked at him. "If I were you, I'd keep that mouth of yours shut, otherwise I'm out of here and the next time you'll see me is when you're behind bars. You are all facing a mandatory ten years without remission as well as the loss of all your assets. You should all have no doubts that with the evidence we hold, convictions are assured."

"These are very serious charges, Colonel, but I suspect you are hesitant to make the arrests?" the Director asked.

"Personally, Sir, no, I've been treated like something dirty under their feet and I'd relish seeing them all go down. However, that is a personal opinion and as a soldier, to express a personal opinion is a luxury not afforded to us, we take orders. I've come directly from a meeting at Number 10 to make the Prime Minister aware. He is concerned with the repercussions if I go ahead with the arrests and I respect his concern. He has asked if Unit T would consider an alternative. At this stage, that is possible. Mainly because we are not after the ones at the bottom, in it just for money, we want the men holding the purse strings. So providing we receive full confessions and names, we will be content with resignations and a lifetime ban on holding any public office in the future and nothing will be made public."

"I cannot see why I'm here, I've done nothing that in my opinion can be construed as a conspiracy," Carl commented.

"You think, Mr Wright? We have recordings, details of payments and matching bank records and photos of you with known criminals engaged in human trafficking. I wouldn't be over-confident you will walk out of this room unblemished, to continue your career, because you won't. So I advise you accept what's on offer, rather than take the legal route," Karen told him, then she looked at her watch. "I'm sorry, Sir, with having to see the Prime Minister, I'm now running very late. A Dark Angel unit is waiting outside and we have a target. I'll leave you all to discuss your responses with the Director General. If you accept my offer and believe it will be a soft ride, by telling me a lot of rubbish, think again. What you tell us needs to match the information we already hold, and believe me we have a great deal; we will know if you're lying."

With that Karen left.

"It would seem, gentlemen, you all underestimated Colonel Harris. It was a dangerous game to play with someone so powerful, and I might add knowledgeable, in the fight against human trafficking. I suggest you accept her offer and come clean. Take your pensions and be thankful the PM intervened on your behalf, because have no doubts, without him she would have crushed you all, leaving your families on the street, and I wouldn't blame her if such inane comments from you, Mr Hart, are what you think of her," the Director General told them.

Karen, along with Hardy, walked back to the reception, but she stopped him for a moment. "A word in your ear, Hardy," Karen said very softly. "The two policemen, Smart and Clifford were murdered by a man we know as Mongkol of the Sinaloa cartel." She handed him a small piece of paper. "That is where he's holed up along with another called Sokna. You will have difficulty proving it, unless he's stupid enough to still have the gun, but if you watch them closely, early next week, they are taking delivery of three tons of class A drugs, hidden inside the guts of fish. Not much compensation I agree, but they will do prison time if you play your cards right and perhaps save a great deal of lives if the drugs are prevented from getting on the street. You never heard it from me."

"I appreciate that, Karen. It never surprises me any more, just what you do know. Did the PM give you any inkling if Unit T will be still in the UK after we leave?"

"It was intimated and at the very least he still wants LBNF to remain here. I assured him LBNF wouldn't let the British people down and will be here for them."

***

"How did your meeting go, Karen?" Stanley asked, once Karen was in her vehicle and travelling.

"Hart still had a go at me, then Wright was convinced we had nothing on him, otherwise I held my own and left them with the ultimatum."

"Let's hope they are nervous enough not to call our bluff. We need the name of the leader in the financial loop, Karen. One of them could well know that name."

"I think when the Director General reminds them about losing their fat pensions, they will see sense. What about a possible informer, are you any closer?"

"I'd like to say yes and I also have my suspicions, but nothing concrete."

"We'll get the person, they won't avoid us forever. What about any names we got from Amalia, have you found anything out about any of them?"

"Of them all, the one she called Madelhari has turned out to be of considerable interest."

"Why is that, I'd never heard the name and he's not on our database?"

"You're correct; in fact we couldn't find anything about him on any of the police international databases. It was Brad that gave us a breakthrough. He remembered he'd come across that name, or similar, in the list of directors at the bank where Julian works. It was such an odd name that it stuck in his memory. He was correct, the man's full name is Madelhari Richter and he lives in Dubai, but comes to London on a regular basis. It could also account for the fact that we never picked anything of interest up in Julian's telephone calls or the places he visited. But Richter has been in London for the last month, so they could well have talked inside the bank. Is it possible we're looking at the financial leader in that man, Karen?"

"If not the leader, certainly very high up. Then if the reports can be believed, Dubai is fast becoming one of the world's worst dirty money hotspots, from Nigerian kleptocrats and Mexican narco traffickers, to a variety of criminals, corrupt politicians and money launderers, who now call Dubai home or operate from inside its glistening towers. So the ingredients are all there. This is a new ball game, Stanley. A game I'm not qualified enough to participate in. We need people who can chase the money, delve into bank records with the enthusiasm and the ability to see the tiniest of clues that can take us forward."

"What are you saying, Karen?"

"I've spent fifteen years fighting in the underbelly of society. Many have died, even my family along with friends. What have I achieved - nothing, when with everyone I bring down, more take their place? To smash the cartels, we need to get at the money men and I believe everything else will fall. It's time I stood aside and allowed a new breed of investigators to take over. They will need Unit T of course, when it comes to raiding a location. But me, Jasmin and what we represent, I don't think so. We are from the past and what we do, how we operate, is not the way forward."

"But a few days back you were all fired up to take on the money men. What has changed?"

"Time, Stanley. I've lived a life where I go from operation to operation, pitting my wits against some of the most dangerous criminals in the world. All I can see now is weeks, months and maybe years of meticulous data gathering. That isn't me; I'm the all-action girl, not a pen-pusher."

Deep down Stanley knew what she was saying was true. There was no longer the need for someone like her at the helm. She was too much of a risk-taker; extremely dangerous if cornered and at times wouldn't listen to reason. Even so, if Karen walked away, who would take her place? In the short term, no one. They wouldn't have the contacts, or her depth of knowledge, proved as valuable so often when she could turn to her extensive resources and find a child, where everyone else had failed. Now she was about to pick up Ryan, who everyone had given up on, but Karen had located. Who else could have done that? He could think of no one, because there wasn't anyone.

"We should sit down and talk, Karen. I believe there'll always be a role for you. Maybe not as high profile, but you cannot just walk away. There are too many children, like Chinwe, who believe in you, because they have no one else. You can't let them down."

"Five minutes, Commander," her lieutenant's voice came over the walkie-talkie attached to her belt.

"I have to go, Stanley, we're only minutes out."

"Very well, Karen. Good luck in finding Ryan, then take him home."

"We can only do what we can do. But fingers crossed, he's still alive," she replied, at the same time cutting the call.

She sat for moment, the day hadn't started well. A man's body found floating in a canal turned out to be Charlie. The meeting with the PM had in reality forced her into agreeing to let Hart, Sutton and Wright effectively walk away with a slap on the wrist and the Knight's prosecution to be conducted behind closed doors. This was the price for his backing in Unit T remaining operational in the UK. Deep down Karen knew this had to happen, if she wanted the money men that is. Particularly if like was suspected, they were moving funds through the UK money markets, because without such access, her investigation would grind to a halt. Then her thoughts drifted back to the meeting with Julian. Ryan's location was part of the deal along with the Knight's and their conspirators. It would seem, according to Julian, Ryan had not been sold to the paedophiles, but working on a farm, producing cannabis. Now the harvest was over, the farm shutting down and moving to the continent. Ryan's future was at serious risk. The people who ran the farm were not taking him with them, although Julian couldn't tell her what his fate would be. Even so Karen couldn't make a move immediately, while Ryan had been made part of the deal, she only received his exact location on a text from Julian when she was in with the PM. Now with a location, that was where they were heading.

Karen removed her handgun from its secure cabinet, checked it before slipping the gun into the holster on her belt. Pulling a balaclava over her head, followed by the helmet Karen switched on its communications. Finally she took off the removable labels on her combat clothing that identified who she was. Just how many times had she done this over the years, she could no longer remember, except once again it was time to do what she did best, face the human traffickers head on.

Have you enjoyed Chinwe? Did you know this book is one of eighteen titles that follow Karen Harris from the age of seventeen to taking command of Unit T?

Has Chinwe's story interested you to want to know more about Karen? How and why she formed the charity LBNF? Where the money she has came from? What happened that made her sister Sophie so bitter towards her? Maybe you are interested in how Karen first met Sherry, or how Karen become involved with the contract killer Jasmin? And what happened that brought the Knights into her life?

While the first two titles are a must-read in understanding Karen, all the other titles are stand-alone, yet follow Karen on the journey to where she is now. Listed below are the key titles in the series where her friends and sometimes her enemies become part of her life.

The start of Karen's journey.............. The People Traders

Why Unit T was formed ....The People Trafficker

How Karen financed LBNF .... Unit T - Special Forces

Karen meets Sherry Malloy .... Goin Goin Sold

The loss of Karen's parents .... Nigerian Connection

Karen looks for her sister Sophie ...... Russian Connection

Karen becomes Lady Harris............... The Royal Grandchild

Karen and the contract killer Jasmin... Circulo

Karen meets Midnight .... Covert Operator

Karen's worth £500,000,000 .... Jasmin - Contract Killer

Karen meets Sir Richard Knight .... Contracted to Kill

Books by the Same Author

International Crime featuring Karen Harris

The People Trader
The People Trafficker
Unit T Special Forces
Goin Goin Sold
The Royal Grandchild
Nigerian Connection
Russian Connection
Italian Connection
Romanian Connection
English Connection
Irish Connection
Spanish Connection
German Connection
Circulo
Jasmin Contract Killer
Covert Operator
Contracted to Kill
Chinwe

Crime

Girl in a Web
Corrupt Money

Romance

Catwalk Supermodel
Gemma's WhiteCliff

Fantasy

Plagarma
Timeless Chamber
Tall Ship Magic

Fairies

Sparkle and the Insect Collector
Sparkle and the Hole in the Ground
Sparkle and the Whirlwind

Audio

Nigerian Connection.......... 15 Hours
Russian Connection............ 9 Hours
Italian Connection............... 11.5 Hours
Corrupt Money.................... 7.58 Hours

Read the first few chapters of all the above books free at http:// www.keithhoare.com

www.ingramcontent.com/pod-product-compliance
Lightning Source LLC
Chambersburg PA
CBHW010406310726
48979CB00012B/2143/J
* 9 7 8 1 9 0 8 0 9 0 6 6 9 *